WILDSEED WITCH
Charmed Life

MARTI DUMAS

AMULET BOOKS · NEW YORK

Cataloging-in-Publication Data has been applied for and may be obtained from the Library of Congress.

ISBN 978-1-4197-5563-7

Text © 2023 Marti Dumas
Book design by Deena Micah Fleming

Printed and bound in U.S.A.

10 9 8 7 6 5 4 3 2 1

Amulet Books are available at special discounts when purchased in quantity for premiums and promotions as well as fundraising or educational use. Special editions can also be created to specification. For details, contact specialsales@abramsbooks.com or the address below.

ABRAMS The Art of Books
195 Broadway, New York, NY 10007
abramsbooks.com

To my father, who may or may not find himself in the pages of this book

CHAPTER ONE

SHADOW AND GLOSS

I may be a witch, but the center of my heart isn't magic. It's a checklist.

Don't look at me like that! Checklists are dope. They help you out, they keep you organized, and they stay exactly where you put them. I mean, when was the last time you ended up accidentally surrounded by checklists? Never, right? Well, I can't say the same for magic. It seemed like magic was everywhere, including all over my room. My kitten, Othello. The wall of morning glories for my YouTube backdrop that sparkled with dew and stayed open all day and night. The janky little intention I wove to keep the palmetto bugs out. Even the herbal tea left in my thermos. Magic was all over the place, even the places I didn't want it to be. So especially after spending half the summer in a supersecret training camp for hoity-toity witches—hoity-toity witches who kept reminding me that I was not hoity or toity—you better believe I was happy to put magic on the side for a minute.

It felt good to be back in my room with my math books, my giant whiteboard, and a dry-erase marker ready to check the next thing off my to-do list. Knocking stuff off that list gave me joy in a way magic never could. My YouTube channel, MakeuponXtheCheapCheap, had gone from 18 subscribers to 779,442 in less than two months and, believe it or not, was still growing. No magic required. I started it all with a checklist, and that's how I planned to keep it going.

Items one through three were easy. I thought number four would be, too. I mean, how long could it take to edit a new seven-second intro? Forty minutes?

Correct answer: four hours.

I'm pretty good at drawing, but apparently animation is some next-level stuff, especially when you're trying to make it look like morning glories are growing out of your channel name. Totally worth it, though. My animation didn't look professional or anything, but it was cute, and the roughness actually added to the vibe—kind of like me—so I decided to stick with it.

When I finally put my laptop down, popped the cap off my dry-erase marker, and checked number four off the list, the checkmark made such a perfect swoosh sound that I almost did a little dance. Okay. I did do a little dance. Don't judge me. That was a lot of work!

People have no idea what it takes to keep a YouTube channel going. Every time I checked something off that list, I felt a little tingle. Not magic—better than magic. Pride. Like I said, magic is cool and all, but mine is wild sometimes. Real wild. That's the one good part about the fancy witch camp I went to. Les Belles Demoiselles: Pensionnat des Sorcières was basically the most sought-after, exclusive finishing school for witches in the world. You'd never know that hidden in a sugarcane field in Vacherie, Louisiana, is the training ground for witches who pull strings all over the world. I wasn't exactly their cup of tea, but since I managed not to get kicked out, I got an official Belles Demoiselles charm: a silver fleur-de-lis. I wore it along with the dolphin charm I got from the Vacherie witches. My dolphin charm mostly turns up the volume on the magic that passes through it, but the Belles Demoiselles fleur-de-lis soaks magic up the same way my kitten, Othello, does. Except, unlike Othello, the Belles Demoiselles charm went everywhere I did.

I'm not gonna lie. That fleur-de-lis charm was a lifesaver. Without it I would have been spilling magic and growing flowers left and right. But just because I had a Belles Demoiselles charm didn't mean I was suddenly living some kind of charmed life. Yes, my YouTube channel was growing like crazy, but I was basically working on it all the time, and we're not even going to mention my family. I don't have any brothers or sisters, but my parents were more than enough drama to make up for it. My family isn't rich. I'm not related to any-body important, unless you count my second cousin going to school with some kid who claimed to be Beyoncé's nephew. And, unlike every other belle demoiselle, I hadn't been watching people do magic my whole life. Those other girls were charmed. Me, I was just making it, but, for real, I wasn't even mad about it. I didn't need to be one of the charmed girls with a giant house and a mom who could teach me magic. It just meant I had to work a little harder. That's all. And if there's one thing I knew how to do, it was work harder. That included item five on my list: brainstorm new makeup looks for my channel.

My brainstorm list was up to nineteen entries, including a mini-series of low-key lip gloss looks that will work with any school dress code. My school didn't have any rules against makeup, thank good-ness, but apparently my friend Angelique's old school did. Tragic—but I had a few ideas for those suffering under the thumb of tyranny. The thought of using Vaseline and lip stain to help people fight the patriarchy made my heart sing.

Creating ideas for looks is fun, but keeping them all under ten dollars is not easy, especially if you want to keep it fresh. Plus makeup companies were asking to send me so many freebies that my mom legit opened a post office box. According to her, it was less work for her to say yes than keep telling them no, and she was going to open a post office box anyway for her new herbal tea business. So every few

days my mom walked in with a new pile of makeup palettes and glam kits that I could never afford and my mom would never have agreed to pay for. Of course I opened them. I'm still human. But there's no way I was going to use them, at least not on a video. That would basically be betraying my followers—selling out. I even ignored my best friend, Luz, every time she hinted that I should monetize.

Hinted? Who am I kidding? Luz never hinted at anything a day in her life, and that was part of the reason I loved her so much. That and the fact that she was literally THE COOLEST. Luz and her little brother, Miguel, had basically been a part of my cheering section since the second day of second grade, and I couldn't imagine life any other way. What would I do without Luz busting into my room at basically all times of day or night, or Miguel literally jumping up to cheer for me every time I scored a point at a Mathletes tournament? For reference, those tournaments are quiet. Or at least they used to be before Miguel started going. I think it was an accident the first time. Miguel is supershy around most people and, since I scored the first point, I think he didn't know that he'd be the only one clapping. But when he saw the smile on my face, he kept going and hasn't stopped since.

It's a good thing Luz was so cool about Angelique and Dee. Luz isn't a witch, but I think she could sense our connection. Our literal connection. Angelique, Dee, and I had formed a coven, so the three of us are now and forever linked by magic. We see and feel each other's magic better than if we were blood relatives. Better than if we were wearing a pair of fancy rose-colored glasses from Belles Demoiselles. Even with all that, Dee and Angelique could never take Luz's place in my heart. Which is why I knew it was weird that I still hadn't found the right time to tell Luz about being a witch.

That sounds bad, but hear me out. I kind of couldn't. The whole finding-out-I'm-a-witch thing happened so fast. Luz was on a road trip, and by the time I really realized what was going on, I was basically under a gag order because of Belles Demoiselles. The Belles Demoiselles campus may be all sunshine and roses, but those witches are no joke. The punishment for revealing the existence of Belles Demoiselles is being banished from the Internet. And from what I've seen of them mixing magic and tech, believe me. They can do it.

So whenever I actually told Luz about being a witch—and I was definitely going to tell Luz about being a witch—I had to figure out a way to do it that wouldn't mention Belles Demoiselles or out Dee and Angelique in the process. I just needed time to think. Besides, Angelique, Dee, and I agreed that eighth grade would be a magic-free zone. Dee was already used to having to keep her magic in check at school. Back in Vacherie, her school was filled with cousins who would have seen her magic and ratted her out to her mom in a hot second. And Angelique was so good at using charm that she hardly ever used magic, anyway. It was perfect.

If I finished enough things on my channel checklist, I could spend the last week of summer chilling with my bestie and my linked sisters without worrying about leaving my subscribers hanging or tanking my channel stats. That was the real magic.

My whiteboard gleamed in front of me, making the to-do list sparkle. I could have started working on recording stuff for the new videos I was planning. That was gonna be fun. But number six kept staring at me: Check comments.

Problem: Nothing good ever happens in the comments.

But instead of tackling my own comment section, I went to Annie's channel to check hers instead. AnyaDoOdle was my favorite YouTuber, but I was _AnnieOaky_'s number one fan. No joke. _AnnieOaky_, aka Anne Johnson, was this supertalented kid in the grade below us who made wooden dolls on her YouTube channel. Her videos were supercool and the dolls she made were straight-up works of art, but it seemed like nobody else could see that. That was my fault. My wild magic was just trying to protect me, but all it really did was send Annie the hate that should have been coming my way. The bullying got so bad that she ran away. That's why Dee, Angelique, and I finally formed a coven. It took all three of us putting our magic together to dig out the bad magic so we could find her. Ever since then, I had been trying to fix it. I did a collab with Annie and everything, thinking that a bunch of my followers would flock to her channel, but weeks after that collab and removing the unfortunate side effects of my magic from her channel, Annie was still only up to 11 subscribers, and that included me, Dee, Angelique, Luz, and Miguel.

I had only seen Annie once since then, and that was for a few minutes during the craziness of my dad and Sandy's wedding. I mean, I get it. If people had bullied me so badly that I ran away, my parents would have tried to keep me in a bubble, too. My mom said we needed to give Annie and her mom some time to work through what happened, and that I shouldn't be surprised if Annie wasn't ready to go back to school right away, but none of that mattered. We promised Annie's mom that she'd have a group of friends when she was ready, and that was a promise I intended to keep. That meant checking Annie's comments for bullies and boosting her channel wherever I could. That's what friends are for, right?

Annie hadn't posted any new videos since the last time I'd checked, but she still had one video I hadn't commented on yet. I figured I'd just leave a comment there and, you know, support her channel the normal, non-magic way. But when I pulled the video up, someone else had already beat me to it. I knew the commenter. SilverbellsandCockleShells was Thuy, a girl I had sort of made friends with at Belles Demoiselles, but that didn't stop me from squealing. Othello gave me a look and jumped off my lap. He

wasn't used to me shrieking randomly, but he'd get over it. This was a big deal. So what if it was just Thuy? A new commenter was a new commenter and Annie needed all the support I could get her. And if Thuy was joining in all the way from California without any of us telling her to, that meant word about Annie's channel was already spreading pretty fast.

Instead of making a new comment, I replied to Thuy's comment with a heart. That way it'd look like Thuy and I were having a conversation, and according to my research, the YouTube algorithm loves it when people have conversations. I kind of wish it didn't love when people talked back and forth, because then maybe people would chill out in my comments.

No such luck. While I was on Annie's page, the number on the little red dot over my username kept climbing. I couldn't ignore it anymore. If I was going to keep my channel, I had to mod the comment section the old-fashioned way—one comment at a time. According to Angelique and Dee, most witches used bitbots. Bitbots are magic-infused code, emphasis on the code. Supposedly bitbots are self-contained and never go further than their coding allows, but I wasn't taking any chances after what had happened the last time I let my magic loose on YouTube's algorithm.

I took a deep breath, reminded myself of who I was, and dove in.

Y'all, it was bad.

Who knew my stance on purple and orange eye shadow would be so controversial? Not me. Sure, that combo might not be everybody's thing, but some people got big mad about it. Then other people got big mad that those people got big mad in the first place. The whole thing was a mess. Six hours after I uploaded my last video, it already had 722 comments and the count kept climbing. I could practically hear Dee's voice in my head telling me to close them, right after I heard Luz's voice saying I should monetize and hire an assistant to take care of them. I couldn't do either. I didn't know how my channel was still growing after I pulled my magic out of YouTube's algorithm, but MakeuponteheCheapCheap was my responsibility.

I know I can't literally be friends with every person who subscribes to my YouTube channel, but the comment section on a channel is like a community. It would be one thing if people were in there just arguing about makeup, but some of the comments were turning personal. After everything that happened with Annie this summer, I could not let that happen. Every time I saw the subscriber count go up, I thought of a person. Were they in middle school like me? Did they have friends? Did they have good enough friends to hold them up when people put them down? Or were they like _AnnieOaky_?

That's why instead of getting ready for eighth-grade orientation, getting a jump start on Geometry, or figuring out how I was going to

stunt on everybody with my new waist-length coils, I was slogging through comments most of the night. Blocking people. By hand.

You're not even a girl. Why are you here?

Delete. Block.

Give up. Not even makeup can fix you.

Delete. Block.

My channel. My responsibility.

But seriously? Why are people like this?

I'm not gonna lie. I was tempted to use magic, and I wouldn't have even needed a bitbot. My magic had a mind of its own. If I let it, magic would have flowed and fixed everything so that no one could leave a mean comment and everything on my page would just be love and light and happiness. That sounds cool, but every time I thought about it, I got sick to my stomach. Blocking the bad stuff from my videos didn't make the bad stuff disappear. It just got redirected to someone else. Someone who might not be able to block it. That's not what good witches do.

There's no way that stuff came from the Dollar Tree. That ain't nothing but Fenty. The box is in the background.

Rihanna's makeup company did send me a promo pack, but I would never use it on my channel and try to pass it off as the cheap stuff. And no way did a stray promo box end up in one of my videos.

11

Delete. Block.

Othello crawled between me and my laptop to snuggle next to me while I worked. He knew what was up. I petted him whenever I felt magic moving toward my fingertips, and while I was in the stupid comment section, it welled up like every three seconds. Othello would have soaked my magic up all day every day if I let him, and I usually did, even though Angelique kept reminding me that cats can get magic-spoiled. So I split the job between Othello and my fleur-de-lis charm, channeling most of the magic into the charm and letting Othello catch whatever drips the charm couldn't. That kept my magic in check and stopped any witchiness from changing the algorithm while I deleted comment after stupid comment. I didn't think it could get any worse. Then I hit a comment that wasn't a reply or part of any thread. It was just one word by itself.

Fake.

Who knew one word could hit you like that? I gasped. The Fenty comment had nothing on this one. That one accused me of doing something shady, but that one word all by itself was way bigger. Like, they didn't even have time to go into the reasons why. Just all of me was fake. All of me. And one thing I know for sure is that I am as real as they come.

Othello looked up at me and I stroked the back of his little head and I calmed down enough to dive back into the threads around it.

There was no way that comment was meant for me. It was probably a reply posted by accident as a new comment. But I couldn't find anything that made that make sense. Was somebody actually calling me fake?

I sat for a minute, petting Othello and waiting for the cavalry to come in and put this TMunnie2020 person in their place. New comments came in, but nobody came to my rescue. But, duh. I was the cavalry. I didn't need anybody to come to my rescue. I could rescue myself and all it took was: Delete. Block.

CHAPTER TWO

TWOS AND FOURS

My mom appeared right at that second, bringing the scent of rose and honey and sunlight with her. Plus actual sunlight when she opened the door. Honestly, it was not the best timing. Moms worry. And between the horrified look on my face and the bags under my eyes, I looked like somebody to worry about.

It was 7 A.M. on eighth-grade orientation day. My mom had come in smiling, holding a cup of her newest tea blend like she was bringing me a birthday surprise, but one look at me and her smile slipped right off.

"What's wrong?" she asked.

"Nothing," I said. I threw a weak smile her way, hoping she'd smile back. It's weird how quickly I'd gotten used to seeing my mom smile again. Things had been a little rough for her for a while. Some of it was my fault. But now, two weeks after my dad got remarried, my

mom was already living her best life, concocting herbal tea blends and dreaming up a new business. She may not have been a witch, but my mom made not being a witch look good. Maybe she couldn't do magic on command, but her kismet made her so lucky that every one of her new tea combinations tasted better than magic.

She shoved the tray of tea and honey onto my bedside table and sat down next to me, putting a hand on my forehead.

"No fever," she said.

Told you. Moms worry.

"You look like you were up all night. Were you practicing for the Mathletes tryouts again? I told you, when you're already prepared, sleep is the best thing you can do for yourself, and trust me, baby, you are prepared. There's no way you won't make the team." My mom pulled my new laptop from between us onto the bed. Othello didn't budge from his spot next to my chest. "You're doing math on the computer now? I thought Ms. Coulon made y'all use pencil and paper."

"She does." Ms. Coulon was my sixth- and seventh-grade Math teacher. The one who ruled the Mathletes with numbered scratch paper and perfectly sharpened pencils. "I wasn't doing math. There were so many stupid comments on my video"—*don't say anything about the ones about you*—"that I needed to stay on it at least until the comment section died down, and that didn't happen until literally just now."

"Just now? Did you stay up all night over your YouTube channel?"

I looked away, but not before I caught another look from my mom, and not a good one. Based on how big the crinkle on her forehead was, I thought she would say something about what happened with Annie not being my fault. Or that I should let the comments go. Or let my channel go. Or something else I didn't want to hear. But my mom didn't say any of that. She said something worse.

"Hasani," she said, smoothing my hair back with one hand. I could smell the tea on my dresser. The sunshine was satsuma. But there was something else with the rose and honey. Maybe cinnamon? "I know how important your channel is to you, and I'm proud of you for wanting to do the work on your own, but this isn't sustainable, especially not once school starts. There must be a better way."

"I'm not gonna use magic," I said.

"I know," she said. "But what about Sandy?"

"What about her?"

Sure, my dad's new wife was a witch, but she wasn't even good enough to get into Belles Demoiselles. If I wanted to use magic to solve my problem, Sandy was the last person I'd turn to. Her or the "circle of friends" she was always trying to introduce me to. Ever since I agreed to go to their wedding, Sandy had been texting about the two of us hanging out like we were suddenly best friends or something. If

she and my dad wanted to be married, that was cool for them, but as far as I was concerned, the less Sandy, the better.

"Hasani, Sandy makes a living on social media. Don't you think you should ask her how she'd handle this? Maybe there's something that would stop you from stuffing that cat full of magic all night. Didn't Angelique tell you not to do that?"

"Othello's fine, Mom." I grabbed the mug of tea and took a sip. Satsuma and cinnamon were exactly what I needed, and the honey made it go down so smooth that the smile I gave my mom was really real. "Angelique is just more strict than I am. You know me. I'm more about going with the flow."

My mom looked at my whiteboard and raised an eyebrow.

"That is a chill checklist," I said, waggling my eyebrows right back at her. She laughed.

"I got this," I said.

My mom sighed and shook her head, but she let it go.

I know it looked bad. But she really didn't need to worry. I didn't need Sandy or magic or an assistant or anyone else to clean up for me. I could do it. All I needed was, like, a minute to rest and be normal again. What I needed was school.

17

"We decided on orange, right?"

Luz was FaceTiming me. My screen wasn't that big, but it was big enough for me to see how cute she was, rocking an orange T-shirt with orange earrings and a jean skirt.

I was still in pajamas with my hair tied up, cradling the last little bit of that cup of tea. Not exactly screen-ready, but it didn't matter. It was just Luz. And after dealing with the comment section on my channel all night, this was so normal and perfect and real that I could have hugged her.

Leave it to my bestie to swoop in and give me exactly what I needed.

"My bad!" I said, jumping up to look for a shirt like the one she was wearing.

We both knew we hadn't decided on anything, and we both knew it was my fault. Luz had asked me about our Orientation Day 'fits right after I got back from "camp," i.e., secret witch school, but stuff just kept getting in the way. First it was my video collab with AnyaDo0dle, then my parents, then the whole thing with Annie, then my discovery that I had basically been accidentally using magic to mess with my mom's emotions for years, then my dad got married, and now I had to make a bunch of videos to get ahead on content for my channel before school started. Twenty-nine videos to be exact.

That would be enough to get me through the rest of the daily uploads I had promised to do all summer, plus the first quarter of school when I could finally switch to twice-weekly uploads.

Banking that many videos was . . . ambitious . . . but it'd all be worth it when I could chill with Luz during our last week off without thinking about how much work I had left to do for my channel. I hadn't even so much as cracked a math book since the summer started, and if you know me, you know that's *not* me. But I shook all that aside and focused on finding that orange shirt. Come hurricane or high water, nothing was going to stop me from twinning with my bestie on Orientation Day.

"The struggle is real over there, huh?" Luz laughed.

I didn't blame her. At that point I was throwing clothes behind me every which way like I was the main character in some Disney Channel show, not a person whose mother was gonna come in any minute and make her fold all those clothes.

I laughed, but I kept looking for the shirt. Luz switched to catching me up on something happening on IG. She knew I was never on Instagram. She thought it was so I could avoid Sandy's new account. I had followed it in a moment of weakness right after the wedding, but that wasn't the reason I wasn't on Instagram. I really just didn't have time.

". . . and Jenny tagged you in a post, too. She was doing your freckle look."

I was only half listening. I kept thinking about the first time Luz and I twinned. We barely knew each other before then, but somehow we both showed up on the second day of second grade wearing the exact same outfit, down to the ribbons tied at the tops of each of our two ponytails.

She said, "Hey, twin!"

I said, "Hey, twin!" back. And that was that. We'd been besties ever since, and we'd never let the twin thing go. We didn't do it every day. Just the special ones: the first day of school, the last day before vacations, and, once we got old enough for orientation to be its own thing, on Orientation Day, too.

I knew I had the orange shirt Luz was wearing. We'd ordered them at the same time. Luckily, I found it clean and folded in the bottom of a drawer.

"That's the one!" Luz said.

I waved it around like a matador to make Luz laugh before I went digging for the jean skirt. I had the same one, but it wasn't in any of my drawers. The next step would be digging through the dirty clothes. If it was dirty that would be bad, but it would be even worse if I had left it at my dad's. I couldn't remember. For the past two weeks, my parents had been trying to convince me to split time between them. Sunday night to Thursday morning at me and my mom's house, Thursday afternoon to Sunday afternoon at my dad's. Sandy called it "The Sunny Summer Split." She used a sun emoji every time she typed it, which was annoying, but even more annoying was the fact that Sandy insisted it was my dad's idea when we both knew it wasn't.

To be fair, there was only one week of summer left. But even one week of the Sunny Summer Split was enough to make dealing with my comment section seem like fun.

Sandy's all right. She's not mean or anything. But there's only so many times you can hear "Hey, girl, hey!" before you start to cringe. Ever since the wedding she had been trying to bond with me about witch stuff. Yet another reason school couldn't start fast enough.

"You looking for this?" Luz asked, holding up my jean skirt. It looked clean, too.

"Yep!" I said. "Thank goodness. I thought I might have to go all Sobby."

Luz and I both rolled our eyes. Sobby was our couple name for Sandy and my dad, who had recently changed his name from Hassan back to Robert—"Bobby" when Sandy was around.

"Nah. No need to sob. You left it over here. My dad washed it. I ironed it, though." Luz flicked her hair back to emphasize that

I should give her props. "I'm gonna send Miguel to bring it to you while I clean my shoes."

"Oh! I don't have those earrings, though. I'll just wear my hoops."

Luz held up a pair of dangly orange earrings identical to the ones she was wearing.

"I got you, boo. I also got everything in purple in case you wanted us to rep MakeupontheCheapCheap."

I shook my head. "Orange is perfect. You are the best."

She was, and it was hitting me how much I missed her. Between trying to get ahead on content and keep an eye on the community tab for my channel, we hadn't hung out in days. Thank goodness she FaceTimed me.

Correction.

FaceTimed us.

Angelique's square popped onto the screen.

"Did we decide to go with purple or orange?" Angelique asked.

She looked gorgeous, but Angelique always looked gorgeous. I'd say she was doing it by magic, but since we were in the same coven, I could see when she was doing magic. She wasn't. She was just that beautiful. The definition of a charmed girl living a charmed life. I'm not hating or anything—I'm congratulating. Angelique's hair was in perfect coils as usual, and she was wearing basically the same outfit

as Luz, except with a light purple top. That shade of purple was one of the colors in my backdrop, but somehow it looked even better in Angelique's room. To be fair, Angelique's room was all white with little gold accents that made everything look like an advertisement on some lifestyle influencer's Instagram feed.

"Orange," Luz said, just as Dee popped in. Dee looked great, too, with fresh lines cut in on one side of her fade.

"Orange? Bet." Dee's square went black for a few seconds before she reappeared in an orange bow tie and suspenders the exact shade of the shirts we were wearing. She had the earrings, too. One of them was in one of the holes in her ear and the other one was pinned to her shirt. She looked dope.

Everybody looked dope.

Well . . . I didn't look dope.

My was hair tied up, I hadn't washed my face yet, and it was possible there was a tea stain on my pajamas. I didn't care. A few weeks ago, if Angelique had popped in basically looking like a goddess while I was the crustiest of scrubs, I would have turned my camera off so fast that none of them would have even known I was there. But this summer had changed a lot. I didn't have to do all that. Crusty as I was, I was with my peeps, and it felt good.

"Y'all put all this together? Y'all are the best," I said.

I could hear Miguel's voice in the next room at my house. My mom must have let him in to drop off the skirt and earrings.

"Nah," Dee said, "this is all Luz. I'm just over here following directions."

"Same," Angelique chimed in. "And since this is my first year not wearing a uniform, I'm just glad Luz has really good taste."

"It's not a big deal," Luz said, acting shy for once. "I just figured if we're all gonna be together, we might as well start the year off right. Right?"

The excitement washed over me all over again. After everything that happened over the summer, Angelique's mom pulled some strings to get Angelique and Dee into school with Luz and me. It was only for one year, but I was planning to make the most of it. In ninth grade, Dee would be at NOCCA, the artist high school, Luz would probably be at Ben Franklin, the proud-to-be-a-nerd high school, and Angelique was literally already choosing between a boarding school in France and one in Connecticut. After six years of Riverbend Elementary and three years of Riverbend Middle, I was staying at Riverbend High. There's no place like home.

"Meet y'all out front, right?" Dee asked. "Outside the gate?"

"Right." Angelique nodded. "Nine fifty-five."

They both closed out their screens, Dee giving a "wassup" nod to Miguel, who poked his head into the frame behind Luz—he must've

left my house already and run home. Baby brother delivery service is one of the many benefits of having your best friend live two doors down, especially in outfit emergencies.

Miguel nodded back at Dee, but straight-up disappeared when I waved at him.

"Wow," I said. "I'm offended. He didn't come say hi when he dropped off my skirt, either."

"Don't worry about it," Luz said. Then added, loudly, "Miguel is being weird because Miguel wants to be on your YouTube channel but Miguel is too shy to say it."

Why she had to loud cap him, though? Every time she said his name, she got a little bit louder.

I laughed.

"Tell Miguel I said, 'Anytime.'"

Luz waved me off, but I suspected that was more for Miguel than me.

"Meet you out front?"

I nodded.

For Dee and Angelique, "out front" meant the front of the school. Between me and Luz, it meant in front of my house. We lived on the same block, but my house was closer to the corner and pretty much everywhere we wanted to go, so we always met on my front steps.

"Nine thirty?"

"Yeah. You gon' be ready?" Luz raised an eyebrow at me.

"Yeah."

Luz's eyebrow went up even higher. "That's in like twenty minutes. You sure?"

"Yes! Trust me. I have a plan."

CHAPTER THREE

GOATS AND OAKS

Nineteen minutes and two cups of tea later, I was standing on my front steps looking and feeling like a million bucks. Plus, I had recorded a Get Ready With Me, which knocked one video off my list. Score!

My mom wasn't the only one who had been dabbling with tea blends. After I got off with Luz, I dashed to the kitchen to grab a blend of my own. Mint and orange peel added to my mom's normal black tea was perfect for feeling like myself again, even if I hadn't gotten any sleep. Some witches might consider that tea a potion, so they would also say I was squeezing my magic, but I wasn't. Squeezing your magic makes it wilder and harder to handle. My mint-orange tea blend only made me feel awake and normal. Feeling awake and normal helped me keep my magic in check, so if anything, my mint-orange tea was the opposite of squeezing. So, technically, all good.

If I were a kismet like my mom, I'd have it easy. A kismet's magic basically just shows up as good luck. They may not have had very much, but at least kismets don't have to fight to keep their magic in. That was not my life. Luz had said the struggle was real when I was looking for my shirt, but she had no idea how right she was. The struggle *was* real. My magic was like a slippery kitten, constantly on the move, coursing through me like the blood in my veins. I couldn't stop it. I couldn't make it disappear. I just had to contain it, which was exactly what I had learned to do at Belles Demoiselles. Miss LaRose, one of the teachers, who also happens to be Dee's mom—long story—literally drilled me until holding magic in while it circulated through my body was almost automatic. Almost. I still had to think about it, but thanks to Miss LaRose, at least the path my magic traveled on had guardrails. So instead of letting it spurt out, growing flowers and randomly changing Internet algorithms, I looped it through my dolphin charm and into my Belles Demoiselles fleur-de-lis, where it was stored safely for future use.

Ever since I realized what I had been doing to my mom, every single drop of magic either went into Othello or the fleur-de-lis. It had been two weeks since I used magic on purpose. A tiny bit of it was brightening my smile, but that was charm, not magic. Besides the flowers in my backdrop and the barrier I'd set up around our house to stop the flying roaches from coming in, I was basically magic-free.

And since I had anchored the magic in the trees the way Miss Lafleur taught me, I barely even needed to maintain it.

I waggled my fingers at Luz as she walked up, flashing her a huge smile. Thanks to the rainbow nail polish series, I already had my nails done. Only two of them were orange, but it legit looked like I had planned it that way. My makeup was simple. Just a faux-freckle look with eyeliner, mascara, and a little loose powder to help blend the freckles in. The first time I did that look it took me an hour, but thanks to having to record the video seven times to keep the magic out of it and the YouTube algorithm, I now could find the perfect spots for freckles in five minutes flat. A little lip gloss and BAM! Face done. I think I literally said that in my GRWM right before I did my outro: "I hope your day is magic." I knew mine would be. My hair looked good, too. It was hot as anything and already sticking to the back of my neck, but it had only taken me two minutes to untie my scarf and pull all the twists apart, and now, thanks to the humidity, my hair was fluffy and perfectly coiled on the ends, thanks to Angelique's twistout technique. Maybe mine wasn't goddess level like Angelique's, but demigod was good enough for me.

"Hey, twin!" Luz shouted when she saw me.

"Hey, twin!" I shouted back.

We hugged. One of the best things about school starting again was being able to see your friends pretty much every day no matter what. That and Mathletes. Even rusty, I couldn't wait to crush the qualifying test.

"What kind of magic is this?" Luz said.

Magic?

I froze.

Luz laughed. "There's no way you could have gotten ready that fast. I've seen you take an hour when all you had to do was put your shoes on. I thought for sure your mom was going to have to let me in to wait for you."

"And I recorded a Get Ready With Me." I laughed, relieved. "I told you I had a plan."

"Does your plan involve witchcraft? If so, hook me up. Those freckles are on point. I seriously would have thought they were real. Jenny is gonna freak."

Laughing, Luz grabbed me by the arm to walk down our block.

She was joking about the whole witchcraft thing, but I hoped she couldn't feel how tense I was. It was scary how close to the truth she was. Besides my mom, the only people who knew about me being a witch were witches, too, including Sandy. I hadn't even told my dad. There was a day after the wedding when I almost told him, but then he acted like he didn't know what I was talking about when I pointed out he'd left me hanging multiple times when he was sup-

posed to come pick me up, and I decided not to. He could live his life. I'd live mine.

The difference between my dad and Luz, though, was I really did want Luz to know.

It's not like I didn't trust her. But once Luz knew about the magic thing, she'd find out the whole story about what happened with Annie. I didn't even want to think about how she'd look at me if she knew how much of that was my fault. I felt bad enough as it was.

"What's going on with you?"

Luz knew something was up. She only said that when she thought I was upset.

"Nothing!" I said. That wasn't a lie. It was just me getting myself to look at the bright side real quick. All I had to do was think about how grateful I was that me and Luz had survived adding two new members to our crew and—boom—I smiled for real. "Thanks for pulling together the orange and the purple and the earrings and everything. You're the GOAT. You know that, right?"

"Everybody helped." Luz smiled.

I raised my eyebrows at her.

"Okay. I got everybody's sizes and ordered everything and dropped it all off, but Dee is cool. And Angelique is prissy, but she's all right. I couldn't just leave them out."

"You could have," I said, "but you didn't. That's why you're the GOAT."

Luz squeezed my arm, but I could tell she was getting uncomfortable being showered with compliments, so I changed the subject.

"Where's Miguel?" I asked.

Miguel was only going into sixth grade. The sixth graders had a separate orientation day, but I was used to Miguel tagging along with us when their dad had to work.

"He was supposed to come, but he was being so weird about it that my dad just took the day off from work. I swear, Miguel thinks you're some kind of celebrity now. It's like he's afraid to talk to you."

"Oh, no! Who's going to cheer me on while I try out for Mathletes? Who's gonna be my good-luck charm? Miguel's never missed one of my Mathlete tryouts."

"First of all, do you really need somebody to cheer for you while you sit there and take a test?" Luz teased. "Second of all, nobody is afraid that you won't get into Mathletes, least of all Miguel. This is your third year. You're gonna be the captain."

"No! Tell Miguel I need my good-luck charm."

Luz pulled out her phone. "Tell him yourself."

We video chatted with Miguel the rest of the way up St. Charles Avenue. That is harder to do than it sounds. First of all, St. Charles

Avenue doesn't go straight. It twists and bends, following the Mississippi River until it's forced to take a sharp turn and become Carrollton Avenue. If that's not bad enough, the oak trees are so old and tough that they lift up the concrete at weird angles. It looks more like an abandoned skate park than a sidewalk, so if you're not careful you will definitely land on your face.

Riverbend Middle School was in an old courthouse in The Riverbend, right where St. Charles took a sharp turn and became Carrollton Avenue. The school took over the building in the 1990s, but the courthouse was built back in the 1800s, and you could tell. Everything about it, from the worn marble steps to the columns out front, screamed "old." Everything except the thousands of plastic beads hanging from the two biggest oak trees just inside the gate. Every year, the kindergarteners from Riverbend Elementary came to show off their shoebox floats and throw beads to the "big kids" the day before Mardi Gras break. And, every year, as soon as the kindergarteners had adorably paraded their way back to the lower school, we threw the beads they'd tossed us right up into those trees. They were nothing compared to the stuff on the Belles Demoiselles campus, but when the sun was shining just right or the wind was rustling through, those "bead oaks" had a magic of their own.

We hung up with Miguel, and I was in the middle of telling Luz about somebody having the audacity to call me fake, as the first bead oak came into view and two streetcars rumbled past. I didn't know it, but I swear it must have been an incantation. All I did was say the word "fake" and, out of nowhere, the patron saint of fake appeared: LaToya.

CHAPTER FOUR

LOCKS AND LOCKS

Luz said something, but I couldn't hear her over the streetcars and the kaleidoscope of colors in the tree. My heart beat faster. The magic that I had been looping straight into my fleur-de-lis threatened to jump the guardrail like the river overtopping the levee. Angelique and Dee were waiting for us outside the gates. I barely saw them. All I saw was LaToya smirking twenty feet behind them in a private school uniform.

My skin buzzed like I was holding fifty phones on vibrate. At the beginning of the summer, that buzz was a sign that half the world was about to be covered in morning glories. No way was I going to let that happen right across the street from my school, the one place I had left to be normal. I closed my eyes and took a deep breath, pulling the flow away from the prickling in my skin and forcing it into the fleur-de-lis charm where it belonged.

By that time, Dee and Angelique had already crossed the street-car tracks and were standing right next to us.

Dee put her hand on my shoulder. "You all right?" she asked. I could feel some of the magic draining off me. Linked sisters could do that, thank goodness. It helped.

Angelique touched my elbow. "Public school isn't that bad, is it?" She was making a joke to play it off, but Angelique was helping me, too. "I mean, I know it's scary, but if *you're* nervous, maybe we should all rethink this. It's not too late for us to go to McGehee. They haven't even had orientation yet."

Before I took my next breath, the magic was back in check. I opened my eyes, bracing myself to see LaToya's face again, but when I did, she was gone. Or maybe she had never been there in the first place.

"I'm fine," I said. "I thought I saw LaToya. That's all. But it wasn't her. That girl had locks, and LaToya's mother would never let her lock her hair."

Angelique and Dee looked back, confused, but Luz was not having it.

"Who cares about LaToya? She doesn't even go here," Luz said.

"You know LaToya?" Angelique asked.

"Not really," I cut in. "LaToya hung out with us a few times after camp."

I said the word "camp" extra hard. Like, reminder: Luz does not know any of us are witches.

Angelique got the hint. I don't think Luz noticed.

"Yeah, I know LaToya," Luz said. "I know she's stuck-up and she thinks she's better than everybody and she can keep her prissy self right over at Academy of the whatever-whatever where she belongs."

"Dag," Dee said, laughing. "Now you're dissing the girl's school, too. How do you even know she goes there?"

Luz laughed, too. "She only mentioned her fancy private school every five seconds like clockwork. But who cares? I don't. Especially not when there is an actual emergency in progress. They opened the gate early! They're letting people line up. Look!"

Sure enough, the gates were open and a bunch of other eighth graders were already lining up at the table just inside the door.

"The locks!" Luz shouted. "I'm gonna go hold our spots."

Luz was already sprinting across the street, her long black ponytail streaking out behind her.

Dee raised her eyebrows like, *Should we follow her?*

I nodded and the three of us took off running. Luz was right. The locks were a really big deal. They were the only real reason to come to Orientation Day. Sure, you could meet your teachers and buy new P.E. uniforms. And there were tryouts for Mathletes and soccer and the debate team. But all of those had makeup days. You could get a lock on the first day of school, but nothing could make up for picking a locker on Orientation Day. Nothing.

Sixth graders are assigned lockers in homeroom on the first day of school. The homeroom teacher does a whole lesson on how to use the locks, then passes out locks and combinations for everybody to practice before they're allowed to put them on their assigned lockers.

There are no assigned places in seventh and eighth grades. Seventh and eighth graders get to choose their own. In theory, that's a good thing. In reality, in seventh grade Luz and I had only managed to find two lockers together because they were bottom lockers in front of the smelly bathroom next to the old gym, which, in addition to being rank, was basically in Timbuktu. It was horrible. But that was last year in the seventh grade. Eighth grade was our time to shine . . . if we could get a good place in line.

Luz made it to the line before the rest of us finished crossing the street. That was good. My coven had agreed to make Riverbend Middle a magic-free zone, but that didn't mean there wasn't any magic. There was something special about the bead trees, and I didn't want Angelique and Dee to miss it.

"Look. See that one?" I said, pointing at the aqua bead I always looked for on my way in. "That's the first bead I ever got to stick."

"Cool," Dee said.

Angelique nodded.

They were probably being polite, but that was okay. They'd get hype about it before too long. I was about to tell them so when a girl I had P.E. with in sixth grade said, "MakeupontheCheapCheap! I love your channel!" while gesturing at her layered glitter eye shadow.

"Thanks, Jenny," I said. It was weird that she called me MakeupontheCheapCheap when she knew that my name was Hasani, but okay.

Jenny was staring at me like I was supposed to say something more, so I added, "It looks good on you."

It did. But instead of saying "Cool" or "Thanks" or something normal, Jenny squealed. Then, I kid you not, she said, "I hope your day is magic." Double two-finger kiss heart. *She did my whole outro.* And I'm pretty sure she wasn't messing with me, because afterward she gave me a thumbs-up.

I don't even know why I did it back. It was awkward. When we finally broke eye contact, Dee put her hand on my shoulder again.

"Fan?" she asked, barely holding back a smile.

"No!" I said. "Jenny isn't a fan. We were partners in square dancing."

Dee shrugged, but when we made it over to the line, Luz was way less chill. She had apparently seen the whole thing.

"I told you you were famous," she grinned, playfully bumping me with her shoulder.

"I'm not."

Besides _AnnieOaky_, I'd never met anybody IRL who liked my videos. I mean, Luz liked them, but Luz was basically my sister, so that didn't count. My other friends liked them, too, but the thing with Jenny felt different. Like she was a fan. It was weird.

"She just liked the faux freckles," I said, hoping Luz would let it go. She didn't.

"Don't get shy now, Miss YouTuber," Luz laughed. "You are giving serious queen bee vibes."

I laughed. "I'll settle for captain of the Mathletes."

"You're gonna be like Beyoncé. No! Like Lizzo. 'If you're shining everybody gonna shine,'" Luz sang. Then, just as fast, she got serious. "But your stardom is not going to help us get lockers. Four together is a big order. We need a strategy. Library or snack room? Ooh! Or cafeteria? Those are pretty good when it's not french-fry day."

"It only takes one," I said. "After that, all our books will smell like old grease no matter what we do."

Dee laughed, but Luz nodded, serious.

"Judging by the number of people ahead of us, the lockers by the library and snack room will be long gone. I guess we should shoot for the third-floor hallway?"

The third-floor hallway was far from any amenities, but the Math

and History classes were both on that hall, meaning less distance we'd have to lug those ginormous textbooks.

I smiled. The more we talked locker strategy, the better I felt.

Luz tried to convince Angelique that we needed to run, but once we got our locks and entered the building, Angelique did not quicken her goddess pace.

"Every school has a no-running policy. I'm not going to get a demerit on the first day."

"This isn't private school. We don't have demerits."

Angelique looked unconvinced.

"Well, can you at least not walk all delicate? We need to hustle. The way you're walking, the seventh graders are gonna start coming in before we even get started. I'm telling you, the good ones—"

"Are these free?" Angelique said, strolling up to four open top lockers. They looked brand-new. Not only that, they were right across from the library and three feet down from a brand-new snack machine and water bottle–filling station. As Mary Berry would say: Sheer perfection!

"That'll work," Dee said, pulling the assignment tag off the first locker and sliding her lock into place.

"Wow," Luz exclaimed, pulling the tag off the one next to Dee. "Y'all must be good luck."

"Something like that," Angelique smiled. "It's not luck, it's—"

"You're right," I cut in. No way was I letting Angelique finish that sentence. "It's not luck. Last year, we were seventh graders. Seventh graders get the leftovers. We're eighth graders now."

Angelique smiled politely. "I was going to say that when my mom toured the building, she felt like the facilities should match the quality of the academics. Riverbend Middle is nationally ranked. A school like this should at least have matching lockers and vending machines that dispense actual food. So she made it happen. No luck required."

"Nice." Dee nodded, spinning the dial on her lock. "Smooth."

Luz threw her arm around Angelique's shoulder. "I knew I liked you," she said. "Now, what does your mom say about the debate team uniforms? Right now we just wear T-shirts, but I'm thinking blazers and straight ties. What do you think?"

I wanted to smile, but I was too busy trying to push the magic building in my fingertips back onto the track where it belonged. I was getting the hang of it, though. Every time it felt like it would burst out, it just . . . didn't. Even when the thought of LaToya and her little crew popped into my head out of nowhere.

Cool kids!

I shivered. The memory made my skin prickle. I shook it away.

LaToya had played me. Pretended to be my friend, then left me hanging when she thought I needed her the most. It wasn't even me

42

she hurt, though. It was _AnnieOaky_. And the worst part was that LaToya knew it.

"Hasani?"

Luz, Angelique, and Dee were all looking at me. Dang. I guess I was in my feelings. My skin was buzzing like crazy but . . . no flowers. I called that a win.

"I'm just trying to figure out if my locker number is prime," I said, trying to play it off. "Got to warm up for Mathletes."

"Well?" Angelique raised an eyebrow.

I hadn't even looked at the number. "Thirteen twenty-one. Prime. Now, should we go get ID pictures or head straight to the auditorium to get a good spot for assembly?"

"ID pictures," Luz said. "If we're sitting down in the auditorium, how are people going to see our group ensemble?"

Dee adjusted her bow tie. "I mean, we do look good."

"Here come the cool kids!" I said.

I don't know why I said it. It just came out. Luckily, Dee didn't seem to catch it, and even better, it was my cue to pull myself together. This wasn't Belles Demoiselles. This was Riverbend Middle. And at Riverbend Middle, I knew all the rules.

CHAPTER FIVE

BUZZES AND BURNS

The rest of the morning couldn't have gone any better if I had written it myself. My ID pic came out amazing, the line for schedules was supershort, and Luz and I were in the same P.E. class.

It was a little weird at first, when people were coming up to me saying they liked my YouTube channel, especially once the seventh graders joined the mix, but I flipped that awkward into awesome by using it as a chance to introduce Angelique and Dee. It went kind of like:

Them: Hasani! I love your channel!

Me: Thanks! Have you met my friend Angelique?

Them: Hasani, your blush-layering demo was mad aesthetic.

Me: Thanks! Speaking of aesthetic, have you met my friend Dee? Her art skills are off the charts. She codes, too.

Okay. Maybe not the smoothest since I didn't throw any charm into it, but Riverbend Middle was a magic-free zone and I. Was. Loving it! By the time we all had our schedules and IDs, Angelique was already talking to some people who were going to be in her homeroom and Dee had dapped up at least three people she knew from her dad's neighborhood. They hadn't been in the building for an hour, and they already seemed like they belonged.

Homerooms were alphabetical by last name, and so were the lines to pick up the official copies of our schedules. Dee and Luz were in the same line, but Angelique and I both had to wait alone. I literally squealed when I saw Ms. Coulon's name in the last slot on my schedule. Room 313. If there was anyone in the school I would love to charm, it was Ms. Coulon, but getting into her seventh-period Geometry class was better than magic. You can only get in by getting a perfect score on the placement test. Apparently, I did. And I did it before I had ever even heard of magic, so you know I was on point. It was paper and pencil, anyway. Ms. Coulon was old-school like that. She always insisted you show and number your work, even the scratch paper—which she counted! Getting a perfect score was nothing short of a miracle, and since every captain in the history of the Mathletes has been in Ms. Coulon's seventh-period Geometry class, the only thing between me and being captain was Ms. Coulon herself.

That wasn't exactly a good thing. Ms. Coulon didn't like me. I'm pretty sure she didn't hate me, either, but she definitely didn't like me. I had her for Pre-Algebra in sixth grade and again for Algebra in seventh, and at no time in either of those years did Ms. Coulon ever smile at me. She'd maybe nod if I was right or something, but she never smiled. All that was about to change. Riverbend Middle was a magic-free zone, but ninety percent of what I learned at Belles Demoiselles had nothing to do with magic, and for once that actually felt like a good thing. I was about to make a magic-free good impression. Ms. Coulon wouldn't know what hit her.

"Seventh-period Geometry!" I blurted out when Luz, Dee, and Angelique were getting close.

"I told you!" Luz said. "This is your year! I have Ms. Fontenot seventh period. Her room is right across from there. We can walk together."

"Nice!" I said. "Where's your seventh period, Angelique?"

"It's Geometry with Ms. Coulon in room 313."

I didn't know how Angelique landed in that class when she wasn't there to take the placement test. I assumed her mother pulled some strings, but I was so hype at that point that finding out Angelique was in that class with me only made it better. I couldn't wait.

"Maybe we'll all be on the third floor, then," I said.

"I'ma be at Tulane," Dee said.

We all looked at Dee.

"Tulane University?" Luz sounded impressed. "I thought they only did that for the high school kids. You some kind of math super-genius like Hasani?"

If Dee was taking college math while I was in Geometry, that would have made *her* the math genius, not me, but I didn't point that out.

"Nah. It's a coding class."

"So, a coding super-genius," Luz said. "I should have guessed. I mean, I knew you were good, but I didn't know it was like that."

Luz was gearing up her hype machine. I could tell.

Dee shook her head a little, but that didn't stop Luz from grinning.

"I did this li'l program after camp, that's all."

Dee was being chill even for Dee, but now I knew why. The "li'l program after camp" was the Belles Demoiselles protégé program. Some of the teachers work one-on-one with girls who have earned their charms. Miss Lafleur chose me, so I learned more about influencing animals. Angelique was Miss LeBrun's protégé, using magic to correct the record of history, whatever that meant. But Dee's time with Miss Villere upped her game so much that she was about to get college credit in the eighth grade. Sweet!

By the time we were done comparing schedules and stuff, people had stopped randomly mentioning MakeupontheCheapCheap, and everything felt totally normal, like we'd all been together for years. It was perfect. No—it was better than perfect. For the first time in a long time I could focus on what was really important: Mathletes.

Step 1: Make a good impression on Ms. Coulon.

"I know we're supposed to meet the teachers in order, but let's pop in to introduce you to Ms. Coulon right after assembly," I said.

"Great! I love introductions," Angelique said.

I thought for a second Angelique was making a Belles Demoiselles joke. We did have an entire class called Introductions, not to be confused with Greetings, an entirely different class, but from the look in her eyes she was dead serious.

That was why I loved Angelique. When it came to math, she did not play.

The auditorium was already half-full when the four of us got to Assembly, but there were four empty seats in a row waiting for us. It wasn't magic or luck, though. It was _AnnieOaky_, aka Anne Johnson.

"Annie!!!!" I shrieked, running over to her. "You're here! I didn't know you'd be here!"

"Doesn't she go here?" Dee asked quietly.

Annie smiled, looking a little shy or embarrassed or maybe both. People were looking at us, but who cared? I was happy to see her. We all were.

"I saved you seats?" She said it like a question, pulling three books and a bag off the chairs. "I hope you don't mind. I saw Luz's Instagram update."

"Of course we don't mind. Thank you!" I said, sitting down in the seat next to Annie's.

"Y'all look really cute. Did you already post a pic?" she asked, pulling out her phone.

"Nah," Dee said.

"Dee doesn't like putting her picture online," I said.

"Oh! You should. Y'all look perfect. You're even wearing the same earrings. Do you mind if I take a picture? I won't post it."

Dee nodded her approval, so we all huddled up and let Annie take a pic.

"I love it," she said. "You match, but you've all got your own style. Like Dee's suspenders and Luz skipping the charms. If you were all exactly the same it wouldn't be as cool."

Luz didn't say anything, but she did look at the three of us, her eyebrows squished together like she was trying to figure out what Annie was talking about.

Dee's charms were hard to find. She wore her fleur-de-lis in the top hole on her left ear and the dolphin in a ring on her right. But Angelique's were both front and center on a thin chain she wore around her neck. Same as mine, but it was mine Luz stared at before she looked away.

Fleur-de-lis stuff is extra regular in New Orleans. Flags. T-shirts. Footballs. Shoes. They're everywhere, so it's really easy to forget about them. The dolphin, not so much. The dolphin was a red flag. I tried to think of something to say, something so it wouldn't be a big deal. I didn't get a chance.

"Yeah, don't worry about that little charm," a tiny voice said. I cringed. I would have known that voice anywhere, especially with the fake British accent. "It's a camp thing. All the cool kids got them."

Cool kids!

LaToya sat down on the other side of Annie. The private school uniform should have looked strange at Riverbend Middle, but that and her locks—faux locks, knowing her—just made LaToya look like some kind of cool anime girl. Besides that she was exactly the same. Unfortunately.

"It's okay, right? I know I'm supposed to sit with the seventh graders, but LaToya says y'all know each other from camp, so I thought we could all sit together?" Annie asked, looking around at us.

My fingers were buzzing like I was wired on five cups of coffee. Why was LaToya bringing up "camp" to a girl she didn't even know? And not just any girl. A girl she'd refused to help when she had the chance.

"Yeah," I said. "She can sit with us." Before I thought about it, I let loose a little charm to brighten my smile. An incantation reminding myself who I am would have been better, but I was honestly not chill enough for all of that. The charm didn't work anyway. I was already too heated. The best I could do was try to calm myself down by saying, "Charm, not magic. Charm, not magic," over and over in my head like a loop track of Miss LaRose's greatest hits.

"Great!" Annie said. "Because LaToya and I are going to make WeBops at my house this afternoon. Do you want to come?"

LaToya and Annie? Was this a joke? Dee and Angelique were pointedly not looking in our direction, staring up at the stage like there was already somebody on it. I wish I could have done the same. I wish I could have let it go. But there was no way I heard what I thought I heard.

"You made a WeBop account? The one where everybody does the same li'l dances?" I don't know why, but I was genuinely confused.

"Yeah." Annie suddenly sounded nervous. "But I just started it. I might not keep it, though."

I didn't know much about WeBop, but I did know the videos were silly and funny. Basically the opposite of LaToya.

"You should keep it if you want it. I'm just surprised that LaToya's doing it," I said before glaring in LaToya's direction. "You're going to make WeBops with Anne? You know she's _AnnieOaky_, right?"

As in, *The girl you refused to help when she needed us the most just to get back at me when I hadn't done anything to you in the first place?*

"Yep." LaToya flashed double peace signs and a smile.

Annie nervously joined in. "Why? Is there some kind of law against making friends here? Or just the wrong kind of friends?"

I looked at Annie and couldn't read her face. Confused? Disgusted? I didn't know her well enough to know.

"Don't worry about her." LaToya was talking to Annie, but loud enough for everyone to hear. "She was fake at camp, too. The charmed girls are always stuck up."

Seriously? *Seriously?* LaToya was calling me a charmed girl? Me?

LaToya took a dramatic swig from her water bottle and slipped it into her backpack. Of course the water bottle perfectly matched the stitching in her blazer and of course she had another one in her bag just like it. It would have been cute if LaToya weren't so annoying. "You're one of the cool kids now."

"Oh, I'm not cool," Annie said. That time she definitely sounded nervous. "I couldn't be cool if I tried."

"And that's exactly what makes you so cool," LaToya said. "You're just being the real you, and the real you is a vibe."

. . . says the girl with faux locks and a fake nose ring . . .

Annie looked like she wanted to say something, but it wouldn't come out.

My fleur-de-lis burned against my chest, but it couldn't swallow the flow of magic building up inside me.

"She's right," I said. "You are cool, Annie."

And LaToya definitely was not. If LaToya kept pushing me, I might not have been able to stop myself from doing what I was itching to do with the roaches I knew must have been in the ceiling and were definitely in the trees outside. New Orleans is tropical. As beautiful as it is, there are always roaches nearby, and they fly. I started to get up and leave, but then I realized I didn't need to. Magic pounded against my skin, but not a bit of it leaked out. Not one drop. That's that coven for you, boy. Angelique and Dee were holding me down. The looks on their faces didn't change, but just the fact that they were helping me made me feel better.

That's when I actually took a deep breath and remembered who I was. If LaToya wanted to play dress-up and do her impersonation of a public school kid, let her. She was not about to get me riled up. I was better than that. But that didn't mean I couldn't have the last word.

"My bad!" I said, so brightly that she'd know I didn't mean it. "I didn't know you were transferring to Riverbend Middle. The uniform threw me off. What happened? Did Mummy and Daddy decide sending you to the Academy was a waste of money?"

"Burn," Luz coughed.

LaToya's eyes narrowed before she fixed her face. I'd struck a nerve and I was kind of loving it.

"Whatever," LaToya huffed, shoving her water bottle in her backpack. "You don't know my life." She turned to face the front just as our principal stepped onstage.

Good, I thought. Maybe she'd be upset enough to go back where she came from and leave us all alone, especially _AnnieOaky_. Annie had no way of knowing how awful LaToya was. I had spent all day every day with her at Belles Demoiselles, and it took me weeks to find out.

Time must have passed.

Our principal, Ms. Reid, isn't exactly short-winded. But the next thing I knew, Ms. Reid was saying, "And what's the number one rule?"

"Be kind!" We all chanted in unison, the exact same way we did in kindergarten.

I had kept my eyes forward during Assembly, but once it was over, I turned to see what LaToya was up to. She was gone. Annie was still there, though. Thank goodness.

Annie just kind of sat there as everyone else started getting up, like she was waiting for someone. Friends, maybe. Then I remembered that maybe she didn't have any.

"Um . . ." Annie looked down. I thought she was going to ask if she could stay with us, so I was already ready to say, "Great!"

"I deleted it," she said.

I blinked. Good thing I didn't auto-respond.

"What?" I asked.

"_AnnieOaky_. My old channel? I deleted it. I know it was kind of embarrassing and I didn't want you to think I'd embarrass you or anything, so I just wanted you to know it's gone."

"When?" I was literally just on there.

"During Assembly," Annie said matter-of-factly. Like she didn't delete hundreds of hours of work while the principal was talking about the new salad bar. I didn't have to turn around to know what Luz's face looked like. It was that cross of puppy-dog eyes and who-did-it-'cause-I'm-gonna-set-them-straight she always got when somebody was hurt.

I didn't know what to say. Thank goodness I had Dee.

"You gotta do what's best for you," Dee said. "But, for what it's worth, I liked your channel. Those dolls were dope."

"We ALL liked your channel," I added. Luz and Angelique both nodded. "You could never embarrass me, period, but especially not in front of LaToya. She may go here now, but I promise she will never follow the number one rule."

"Be kind!" Dee and Angelique chanted in unison. They were kind of making fun of us, but it was still funny.

The bells chimed. A regular, ordinary three pulses in a row that they used to mean everything from "It's time to eat" to "Leave this place." This time it meant "Start meeting your teachers before they go home." It was glorious.

"Are you gonna hang with us?" I asked. "We're going to do a quick run of everybody's schedule. That way we'll already know the best places to meet in the hall between classes and who'll get to the cafeteria first to hold us a table at lunch. You in?"

Annie looked between us like she wasn't sure she was welcome.

Luz took care of that. "Of course she's in! Here. You can wear these," Luz said, pulling another pair of orange earrings out of her pocket. "I got them in case you came."

For a second, I thought Annie was going to cry. But then she smiled and took the earrings from Luz's hands. "I don't have pierced ears, but thank you! I really appreciate it." Then she pinned one of the earrings to her dress. It didn't look as cool as it did on Dee, but that didn't matter. Annie's smile was golden.

The five of us did a crazy zigzag across the building. Upstairs. Downstairs. Through the hidden hallway at the back of the library and down the custodian's stairway straight to the gym. Between Annie, Luz, and me, we mapped out the perfect route through everybody's schedule and kept Annie giggling and laughing all the way until the next bell. That was the one that meant "If you're trying out for something, head to that, but the rest of the teachers are going home."

"My mom's waiting for me," Annie said.

"Well, would your mom let you stay any longer? Luz is about to go kick butt at the debate team tryout and I'm going to the Mathletes—"

"So am I," Angelique cut in.

I blinked, but not slow enough for anyone to notice. Of course Angelique was going out for Mathletes. I just hadn't thought of it. Once I did, though, there was no doubt she'd be good for the team. If she made the team, we were going to the state championships for sure.

"I'm gonna go see wassup with the graphic design club," Dee added.

"Is there anything you want to check out?"

"Not really," Annie said. Her smile started to fade.

I put my hand on her shoulder, trying to look so serious that she'd for sure know I was joking.

"Any interest in being my cheering section?" I nodded my head toward Luz. "After years of friendship and camaraderie, her little brother, Miguel, has abandoned me. Any chance you'll step in? When we're all done, maybe your mom will let you come hang out with us at my house? You said you wanted to record WeBops, right?"

For a second I thought Annie was going to say something about LaToya, and I honestly don't know what I would have said if she had. How do you say, *Girl, you need friends, and trust me, LaToya is not friend material,* but in a nice way?

Luckily, Annie's grin slid back into place.

"Okay," she said. "Just let me call my mom."

I hadn't cleared it with my mom, but I was sure she'd be okay, and for the moment there were bigger fish to fry. Angelique and I hadn't popped in to see Ms. Coulon at the start of the block, and by the time we got there at the end, her room was empty and dark. It wasn't that big a deal. I knew she'd be in the gym with all the other clubs and try-outs. We just needed a chance to throw a little charm her way.

Unfortunately, we were not the ones who got to her first.

CHAPTER SIX

PLUSES AND MINUSES

The gym smelled amazing. That should have been my first clue. It was mint and lemon and something else I couldn't catch.

Gyms are supposed to smell like sweat and tennis shoes and MAYBE wax if the custodians tried to make it fresh for the start of school. In no world is a gym supposed to smell like one of my mom's good cups of tea. Something was up.

Annie was saying something about chairs or bleachers, but I was barely paying attention because my eyes were scanning the room to see if I would see what I thought I'd see. And I did.

There was LaToya. She had marched her private school uniform–wearing self into the gym and was talking and grinning at Ms. Coulon. I couldn't hear what she was saying, but I knew what she was doing. LaToya's voice was always high-pitched, but when she clasped her hands and tipped her head to the side, that was her "sweet" voice.

The sweet voice was an extra-high, extra-annoying, borderline baby voice that adults always seemed to fall for. Under normal circumstances, Ms. Coulon was immune to foolishness like that, but from where I was standing, it looked like Ms. Coulon was smiling back.

Ms. Coulon? Smiling? On Mathletes tryout day? That was clue number two. I knew LaToya was up to something, I just didn't know what. It was pretty obvious that she was trying to work Ms. Coulon, but influence was not her thing. She could barely even keep her kitten off the dining-room tables at Belles Demoiselles. She definitely wasn't good enough to influence a human. Not that she was above it. She was the one who suggested I influence my dad to stop him from marrying Sandy. If she could have done it, I'm sure she would have, but animal affinities weren't LaToya's specialty. Potions and incantations were more her thing. The Art of Fragrance was basically complicated potions, but airborne.

Duh.

That's when I started to put it together. I knew it was weird for a gym to smell like lemon and mint. LaToya was using magic to influence Ms. Coulon, but the fragrance wasn't just by Ms. Coulon. It was getting everywhere.

"Do you want me to stick close?" Annie asked hopefully.

"The bleachers are good. Behind Ms. Coulon."

As far as the Mathletes were concerned, it didn't matter where Annie sat. Ms. Coulon always set up enough desks and chairs with tennis balls on the feet for like fifty people when max ten would show up. If Miguel were there, he would have sat on the floor like ten feet away from us. Under normal circumstances I would have told Annie to pull a chair from the back row and sit close, but fragrance was not my specialty. We all learned the basics, but LaToya was advanced. I had no idea what her citrus-mint fragrance would do. Annie was safer in the bleachers, away from the smell.

"Okay," Annie said. Her voice was always so small. I wanted to make it bigger.

"Or you could wait outside," I said. That was even safer. "The bleachers have a good view, though. Wish me good luck?"

Annie smiled, gave me a thumbs-up, and headed for the bleachers.

When she got out of earshot, I let out a literal sigh of relief. Annie out of LaToya's line of fire was one less thing to worry about.

Angelique was already moving toward Ms. Coulon. I grabbed her sleeve.

"Wait. Notice anything?" I asked.

Angelique looked around, but I know she knew what I was talking about.

"Yes," she said, pushing her long, coily hair back over one shoulder. "It looks like LaToya's interested in math. Good for her."

"Good for her?" I hissed. "She's up to something. This is public school. I promise you the gym never smells this good. LaToya is using a fragrance."

It was Angelique's turn to sigh, but at the end of hers she looked almost regal.

"Well, then I guess we've waited long enough to make our introductions," she said.

Angelique had this way of walking that, even if you didn't know she was the first daughter of a first daughter in a long line of witches, you knew she was legit. She didn't have to stomp or mean mug. She just walked like the world belonged to her and no one who saw her doubted that it did. Including me.

"Accidental witch whose mom is a kismet" wasn't on the same level, but I followed Angelique across the gym to the Mathletes tryout area and tried to catch up without looking like I was trying too hard. It helped to put a little "first daughter of a first daughter" in my walk, too. We got there just in time to hear LaToya saying, "I'm not officially enrolled yet, but math has always been a passion of mine. I would hate to miss out on the opportunity to participate in such an esteemed organization and represent my new school at competitions."

I put my hand out down low. Angelique caught the motion in her peripheral vision and stopped a few feet away. I could not wait to hear Ms. Coulon shut LaToya down.

I applaud your efforts, Ms. Coulon would say without so much as cracking a smile, *but the tryouts are for Riverbend Middle students only. You're welcome to attend the makeup session once you're enrolled.*

But y'all, not only did Ms. Coulon not say that, but before she said what she did say, she smiled AGAIN. I'm talking a squinting-eyes, I-didn't-even-know-Ms.-Coulon's-forehead-wrinkled kind of smile.

"I'm intrigued," Ms. Coulon said. "Have a seat. We'll begin in five minutes."

My heart was shouting, *Whaaaaaaat??? She doesn't even go here!!!*

I didn't say that, though. I walked up to Ms. Coulon with Angelique, trying to make sure my outrage didn't show on my face, not even when LaToya tossed us a look of triumph on her way to the tables and plunked her fancy water bottle down on the first one.

Whining wouldn't have done anything except make me look scared of competition, so I focused on remembering the rules of etiquette.

"Ms. Coulon," I said, addressing the older, higher-ranking person first. "This is Angelique Hebert. She's a newly *enrolled*"—unlike LaToya—"eighth grader who loves math and is interested in joining our team."

"The introduction was not necessary, but welcome, Angelique." There was no repeat in Ms. Coulon's smile. Her forehead was smooth as silk. Angelique didn't wilt, though.

63

"Thank you, Hasani," Angelique said. "I enjoyed Geometry and Algebra II, and the possibility of joining the Mathletes is one of the main reasons my family and I decided I should finish middle school at Riverbend Middle."

Angelique smiled. No teeth, but there was a little sparkle in her eyes. Enthusiastic, but definitely not desperate. It impressed me.

Ms. Coulon, not so much. She nodded. "Please have a seat, Angelique. We'll begin momentarily."

Angelique nodded and found a spot. I was the one who looked back at Ms. Coulon. Not long. I just wanted to see if Ms. Coulon's expression changed when she thought we weren't paying attention. I mean, Angelique basically already looked like she was on the cover of *Teen Vogue* for leading us to victory at Nationals. If Ms. Coulon wasn't smiling at her, there was nothing natural on this earth that could have made her smile. Nothing but magic, that is.

Ms. Coulon was not paying either of us the slightest bit of attention. Weird. Whatever LaToya mixed in with her citrus-mint concoction was already working to get Ms. Coulon on her side.

That's when I got heated. I wasn't worried about doing well on the test. Not everybody had played Mathletes before, so the test was just straight math, mostly arithmetic and stuff you'd learn in Algebra I. I could do that test in my sleep, and if dreams count, I had. Unless something crazy happened, I knew I'd get a hundred. Ninety-five if

there was like an eclipse or something and I managed to leave one blank. The same was true for my old teammates Amritha and Jason, and probably Angelique, too. The top five scores made the team, and on paper, the person with the top score was named captain. The thing is, there was always a tie, and Ms. Coulon was the tiebreaker. A tiebreaker who was apparently being influenced by the smell of citrus and mint.

It took everything in me to keep a smile on my face. I couldn't believe that LaToya had walked into my school and, within five minutes, given herself a shot at being captain—with magic. SHE WASN'T EVEN A STUDENT. Like, why? Seriously? It made no sense. She'd been going to the Academy ever since kindergarten. Riverbend Middle is a great school, but on snooty factor alone it could not hold a candle to the Academy. And LaToya and her family lived for that snooty stuff. So why come to Riverbend Middle, where you have no friends and the only thing that could really happen is you would have to spend more time around a girl you hate?

Answer: LaToya wasn't done getting back at me. Apparently refusing to help when I needed her to help us rescue Annie wasn't enough punishment. Now she needed to ruin Riverbend for me, too, starting with Mathletes. For the first time in my life I understood why people say "I was so mad I could spit."

"Hasani!"

You know how upset I was about LaToya? Yeah, well, take the absolute value of that, double it, and raise it to the tenth power. That's how glad I was to see Miguel.

Miguel burst into the gym like a literal ray of sunshine, waved, then plopped down on the floor a few feet from us like he'd done twice before. Ms. Coulon didn't bat an eye.

I gave Miguel a thumbs-up and looked around for Mr. Jose, Luz and Miguel's dad. He was a few steps behind. I gestured for Mr. Jose to bring Miguel up to the bleachers. He nodded and hustled Miguel off, but just seeing them was enough to make me feel calmer. The magic that had been buzzing at my fingertips died back, and no joke, I actually felt sorry for LaToya.

Everybody else in the testing zone looked chill. She was the only one who looked nervous, adjusting in her seat, sipping her water bottle, trying to figure out where to put those fake locks. That's when it hit me: LaToya wasn't good at math. I'd never once heard LaToya mention anything about math or math competitions. Judging by how much she was squirming, maybe she had this grand plan to ruin my year but didn't have the skills to pull it off. Because no matter what LaToya brewed and distilled to charm Ms. Coulon of all people, there was no charming this test. Paper and pencil was not something you could influence, not with potions, not with anything. Especially when you had to show your work.

Ms. Coulon walked along the rows placing thick packets on each desk facedown, then placing two perfectly sharpened pencils on top. When she was done, she put her glasses on, held up a stopwatch, and said, "Begin."

Speed didn't count for points, but Ms. Coulon marked the time you were done on the top of your paper. It may not have been worth points, but you better believe you didn't want to be last. After the first few problems, my pencil sang across the page. I worked each problem on the scratch paper, wrote my work out neatly and in number order on the scratch paper, then carefully transferred my answers to the answer sheet, double-checking as I went. All of it counted, and when I put my hand up, I knew I had every point. Angelique's hand went up only a second after mine. First and second. Not bad. I gave Miguel a wink. He double-thumbs-upped me, and all that was left was for me to sit back and watch the magic happen.

Be careful what you wish for.

LaToya took a sip of her water, licked her pencil tip, and kept writing. Weird, but okay. If she wants to eat graphite, that's on her. I was just watching her to see if she was any good. You can tell a lot by how much people erase or scratch out. She wasn't doing either, just moving steadily through, nervously sipping and licking between every problem. She wasn't fast, but she didn't have to be fast. She had to be accurate.

One by one, kids put their hands up and Ms. Coulon went to mark the time and collect their papers. We were all stuck in our places. Everybody competing for a Mathletes spot had to remain seated until the last person was done. Before long, there were only two people with papers left—LaToya and a kid I'd never seen before who must have been a sixth grader. The sixth grader put his hand up, LaToya made a weird sound, and the next thing I knew, termites were crawling and flying into the gym from every direction.

CHAPTER SEVEN

DANCES AND DODGES

Termites are no joke. I know because I see them all the time. We all do. They look like ants with wings. Giant, clear wings. I don't mean to make New Orleans sound like a horror movie, but there's at least a week every year when your parents keep all the lights off and the curtains closed and they dare you to even use a flashlight under the covers to read because any little bit of light brings the termite swarms inside. But that's at night in the spring, when school is about to let out, not the middle of the day in summer, when school is about to start.

And termite swarms in the daytime are even freakier than they are at night. We were all watching LaToya, waiting for her to finish her test so we could move on to Part 2: Try Not to Tear Out Your Hair Waiting for Ms. Coulon to Score the Tests and Announce the Rankings. Ms. Coulon always does it right there where everyone can see her, and the only thing between us and that horrible, barbaric, but weirdly fair practice was LaToya. We weren't looking at her for too long, though, because once the termites started coming, they did not stop. What started as a few of them flying around like moths was hundreds of them a few seconds later. No, thousands. Maybe *millions*.

Ms. Coulon was cool, picking up her purse and the stack of tests, then using her teacher voice to direct kids out the nearest exit.

LaToya jumped up and left with the rest of us at first, but I kid you not, she went back for her water bottle. There is no water bottle in the world cute enough to make walking through a swarm of termites worth it. I didn't see her again until she came outside and put her test on the top of the stack Ms. Coulon was still holding. I wasn't so much keeping an eye on LaToya as I was looking out for Annie. Annie had gotten separated in the crowd leaving the gym. I had to wave her down to join our little circle, and I did it just in time to stop LaToya from making a beeline in Annie's direction. So far it was me, Annie, Angelique, Miguel, and Mr. Jose. Luz and Dee found us before too long, and so did Annie's mom. She looked a nervous wreck.

"Baby, are you okay?"

Annie looked a little embarrassed. "I'm fine, Mom," she said.

"Do you want to go?"

"You said I could go to Hasani's house."

"With all this chaos, maybe Hasani isn't up for having people over anymore."

Annie and her mom both looked at me.

"I am!" I said.

"And it's okay if Annie tags along?"

"She's not tagging along," Luz said. "We invited her!"

Angelique and Dee both nodded. Annie's mom looked relieved.

I kept an eye out for LaToya, but thankfully, she had disappeared.

Annie's mom insisted on driving her to my house, but the rest of us walked. Miguel wanted to walk with us, too, but after a quick puppy-dog face from Luz, Mr. Jose insisted Miguel ride in the truck with him. Of course we talked about the termites the whole way back.

"Do you think the school has been infested this whole time?" Luz asked.

"Possibly," Angelique said. "Most buildings in the city have at least a few. It's just a question of whether or not it's bad enough to justify the damage of treating it." Angelique sounded like Miss LeBrun, the Art and Architecture teacher at Belles Demoiselles. But that made sense since Angelique was her protégé. Miss LeBrun had already invited Angelique to do an internship in Senegal over winter break. My teacher, Miss Lafleur, hadn't invited me to do anything extra. Not that I wanted to. I'd had enough magic lessons for one summer. Othello's cat-stagram was all the Animal Affinities I needed.

A message chimed on everyone's phones at the same time. All of us except Dee paused to read it.

"The building is experiencing a sudden and severe infestation," I read out loud. "We will send more information as the source and damage are assessed."

"The source? You think they're gonna be digging around like vampire hunters looking for some giant termite nest?" Luz shivered. "To think I used to love that place."

"I don't think they came from inside the building," I said. "That many termites would have already eaten the school to the ground. Something weird drew them in."

Dee gave me a look.

It wasn't me!! I tried to scream with my eyebrows.

Dee shrugged.

"Like what?" Luz asked. "A disturbance in the force?"

We all laughed.

"Does LaToya count?" I asked.

Luz raised an eyebrow. "Did they run out of caviar at the Academy or something? What was she doing at Riverbend Middle, anyway?"

"Besides bringing bad vibes and being fake friends with Annie?" I said.

"LOL, Hasani. You think she has enough bad vibes to draw a whole swarm of termites?" Luz laughed.

"She probably jinxed us," I said, hoping Dee and Angelique would catch my meaning. Our coven may have agreed that River-bend Middle was a magic-free zone, but LaToya didn't, and neither did her coven. The thirteen of them combined could definitely do something big.

"How you know they're fake friends?" Dee asked.

"Who?" I asked.

"LaToya and Annie."

Luz didn't miss a beat. "What other kind of friends could they be when one of them is LaToya?"

That's what I love about Luz. She's never afraid to say what all of us are thinking, and at that point I was laughing so hard it took me a whole block to recover.

That whole block Luz came up with ways to undo LaToya's "jinx," and every time she said something new I burst out laughing all over again. When I finally caught my breath, I said, "I don't know if any of those will work, but I bet we can come up with something."

Dee shook her head. "Don't fight fire with fire," she said.

Except you can totally fight fire with fire. People do it all the time.

By the time we hit my block, Annie and her mom were already parked across the street from my house. Annie hopped out of the car and ran over to us. Her mom didn't get out, but we all waved at her anyway as we went inside. My mom was surprised to see us all there. I had forgotten to text her. But she was chill about it and just offered to make iced tea.

"Thank you, Miss Nailah," Angelique said. Her parent skills were on point. "Do you need any help?"

"No, I'm fine. I'll just set it up on the dining-room table and y'all can get it whenever you're ready."

My room was not in the best shape. I mean, it wasn't horrible, but I definitely had clothes on the floor, blush samples in random places, and my lists all over the walls. Annie thought all of it was cool. Even the constant ding of channel notifications.

"Two oh nine!" Annie exclaimed. "I didn't even know the number went up that high. I think the most I ever had was two, and they always came from you guys."

"That's not true!" I exclaimed. "Thuy left you a comment today. Your channel was starting to gain traction."

Annie looked confused for a second. Maybe she hadn't checked the notifications before she deleted her channel?

"Oh," she said. "I get it. SilverbellsandCockleShells is your friend."

74

The look on Annie's face said it all. All this time I had been trying to steer people to Annie's YouTube channel, but what Annie really wanted was organic growth.

"I didn't ask Thuy to do that. She did it on her own because your content is good. Besides, Thuy's more LaToya's friend than mine. We're not tight or anything."

Annie didn't exactly look convinced.

"I bet Thuy was just the beginning," I said.

"It's okay. You don't have to try to make me feel better. I like WeBop better anyway. OMG, are these SILK?" Annie ran her hand across the morning glories in my backdrop.

"Something like that. But don't touch them too much," I said. "They're delicate."

And I don't want you to start asking me questions about how I keep them alive, but no biggie.

"Oh. Sorry. Is it okay if we use it as a backdrop for WeBops? Or, if it's just for your channel, that's okay, too. I understand. I was just—"

"Yes, girl," Luz cut her off. "We use this thing as a backdrop all the time. Right, Hasani?"

We did, but I'm not gonna lie. That was the moment it hit me: Those flowers were absolutely drenched with magic through and through. Not only were they grown from my magic, I had also sprinkled them with a potion and incantation to make the sparkles stick. The last thing I wanted was my magic oozing into Annie's WeBop, messing up her life. Again.

"We definitely can!" I said. "But the light's so good outside. We shouldn't waste it."

I mean, the light *was* good outside. It was hotter than anything, but the light was good. My phone kept dinging. Mostly texts from Sandy. She was really good at keeping up a text thread even when I only responded to like every fifth one. If it wasn't pics of cats that reminded her of Othello, it was showing me all the "cool girls' night in" stuff she got for when I slept over at my dad's. I don't think she meant any harm, I just didn't have time to be besties with my dad's new wife. The bigger problem was that every time a text came through, my phone also helpfully showed me how many notifications I had on my YouTube channel. Spoiler: It was a lot more than 209.

Once we got the dance down, Luz insisted on getting our wardrobes coordinated. The rest of us were already matching, so really she was just talking about Annie. In the end, she wore one of my white T-shirts and jean shorts, and since Dee was being our camera person even though she had learned the dance, Luz capped off the look with Dee's suspenders. The next thing I knew, Luz was rummaging through my jewelry box, disappointed. The only things in there were a cool Mardi Gras bead and a rosary my grandmother had given me for the first Communion I never had.

"Those charms didn't come in a pack?" Luz asked.

"What charms?" I asked. For a second I was actually as clueless as I sounded.

"The fleur-de-lis or the little dolphins y'all are wearing. Did those come in a pack or what?"

Dee and Angelique were both looking at very important things on the floor and ceiling in my room. I was on my own.

"They gave them out at camp," I said.

"What kind of chichi summer camp gives out jewelry?" Luz rolled her eyes. But then she smiled. And then she laughed. "That's all right. Me and Annie will just be rocking these earrings, with all due respect." Luz flipped her ponytail.

Annie looked at the floor, but I could tell she was smiling. We all could.

"We gon' do this?" Dee asked. "We're about to lose the light for real."

Leave it to Dee to pull a real camera and tripod out of her back-pack. She had it set up in no time, and because she's Dee, she also attached a mount to hold Annie's phone and connected it to her camera by some kind of magic Bluetooth connection in less than a minute.

"Camera has better resolution. Whenever y'all ready."

The music was hard to hear outside, and halfway through I noticed that Annie's mom was still sitting in the car in the exact same place she had been parked before, but the light was great and the WeBop came out supercute, especially when Dee was done working her magic. All witches can mix magic and tech. The way Dee explains it, magic is superlogical and so is tech, so the two of them just match. Like ginger and rose or peanut butter and jelly. Some witches have to try to get their magic to mix up with technology, but Dee made it look like an art form. She only put a little in. I saw her working it in as she edited. It was cool. Dee had been working magic her whole life. She didn't have to worry about ruining stuff like I did.

When the video was done, Dee transferred it from her camera to Annie's phone. As far as I could tell, there wasn't a trace of magic left in it.

"Thank you!" Annie said. "Y'all are the coolest."

"Nah. You good," Dee said, running her hand across one side of her head. "Watch it before you decide it's cool."

"Okay. I will. But I already know I'll love it. Thank you!"

"No problem," Dee said.

"I can't wait to show LaToya," Annie said. "Maybe she can be in it, too, next time."

Record scratch.

Everybody was looking at me like I was the only one who had beef with LaToya. What was I supposed to say? No? She can't come?

"LaToya's really smart," I said. That was something I learned at Belles Demoiselles. Always start with a good thing. "And we used to hang out a lot, but . . . just kind of keep your eye out. Sometimes LaToya isn't as nice as she seems."

"See you at school."

On cue, our phones chimed.

Families,

We regret to inform you that, while we have not yet located the source of the termite infestation, the school will need to be fully tented, fumigated, and cleaned. This will delay the start of school. We recognize that this will cause hardship for some families. The office phone will be routed to the district office during the closure, so feel free to call for resources.

"Oh, no!" Angelique exclaimed. I'm glad I wasn't the only one looking forward to school. "My mother is not going to like this. She totally rearranged a bunch of stuff so I wouldn't miss the first day at Riverbend. I was supposed be in Switzerland with her right now."

I had no idea what Angelique's mom did, but I knew it was some rich-people job that had her traveling all over the world. They had a driver and everything, and I'm not talking about Angelique's dad.

"Hopefully it won't take too long," I said. I seriously did not want to wait weeks to get back to school, especially not if it was LaToya's fault, and there was no way it wasn't LaToya's fault. I just needed to get Angelique and Dee by themselves so I could tell them what was up.

"Hopefully," Angelique said, her eyebrows looking a little worried. "Before my mom left, she mentioned that they were still holding my spot at McGehee in case I 'changed my mind.'"

Angelique's mom, who insisted we all call her Mrs. Hebert, wasn't just a witch, she was an old-school belle demoiselle. I didn't know what her specialty was, but I bet if she wanted to change someone's mind, she could, even if that someone was a witch.

"Maybe there's something we can do to help fix it. You know. Before your mom gets back," I added, hoping my coven would catch my drift and stick around.

"What? Are you an exterminator now?" Luz laughed so hard she was cackling. "Remember that time that roach flew down from Mr. Batiste's tree? Yeah. I don't think you want that life."

"I've grown," I said. Luckily neither Angelique nor Dee looked my way. Not that they would have been able to accidentally tell Luz all about how good I got with bugs at Belles Demoiselles by just glancing at me, but still. "It wouldn't go down like that now."

"Yeah, right." Luz laughed again. "We'll see."

Annie's phone dinged. "It's my mom," she said. "I gotta go. But thanks for having me."

Annie's mom texting her when we could all see her sitting across the street was a little weird, but parents are weird sometimes. Maybe Annie's mom thought it was cooler to text than to get out of the car. Who knows? Anyway, it was good to hang out with Annie for a bit, but honestly, it was also good that she was going home. Our school clearly had no idea what caused the termite problem, which meant they also had no idea how to make it go away.

Maybe we needed a little magic at Riverbend Middle after all. Not much. Just enough to get rid of a jinx.

CHAPTER EIGHT

TENTS AND INTENTIONS

Whenever I have a party or a recital or anything, Luz is the first friend there and the last friend to leave. Since she's my favorite person on the planet, I wouldn't have it any other way—except this one time. Because even though my bestie is my favorite person on the planet, my bestie is not a witch.

After some awkward standing around outside in the heat, Angelique called her driver to come get her and offered to drop Dee off on her way home, but not before I dripped a little magic on the ground. It was the end of the day, so the morning glory that appeared was closed up and raggedy looking, but I hoped they'd notice. In the meantime, Luz and I ended up sitting at my dining room table drinking tea. We'd been so caught up making the WeBop that I totally forgot my mom said she was putting stuff out for us. My mom hadn't just put the snacks out on the table. This was a Belles Demoiselles,

Instagram-ready spread. My mom isn't a food pusher or anything, but we couldn't let it go to waste. There were flowers and cookies and everything. Sugar. Not honey or agave or whatever extrahealthy almost sweetener she was on that week. It was practically a miracle.

"Your mom is a genius," Luz said. "I thought the whole thing was going to taste like air freshener or somebody's grandma's house, but the tea and the cookies together are amazing."

"My mom's pretty cool." I smiled, taking another bite of cookie. They were good, but for the first time ever I was starting to wonder how much longer Luz was going to hang out.

"That thing with Annie's mom is weird, right?" Luz said. "Do you think she sat in the car the whole time?"

"Nah," I said. "She probably left and came back and just parked in the same spot."

"And sat there while we recorded and never got out of the car?"

"Yeah, I guess. I mean, there's no reason for her to stay. Annie seems okay."

"Are you serious? She hardly talked at all. Annie used to talk a lot before."

I'm sure Luz was right. The truth was, I couldn't remember. Even though we had gone to the same school for six or seven years, a few weeks before I had barely recognized Annie's face.

I nodded and changed the subject.

"Do you want to bring some tea and cookies and stuff to Miguel?"

"He'd love this peach tea. Do you think your mom will mind?"

"Of course not!" I said, relieved to have a real reason to send Luz home.

"Cool. Let's bring him some," she said.

Let's? Uh-oh.

"You go," I said. "I still need to edit the video I recorded this morning, and you know that comment section is probably stupid again."

"Assistant," Luz sang. "You think AnyaDo0dle hit a million subscribers without a team?"

I gave Luz a look.

"Just saying . . ." she sang again. "At some point you're going to break down and hire somebody. Me, for example." She batted her eyes and put both hands under her chin. I laughed.

"What?" she said. "I'm great at socials."

Luz *was* great at social media, but there was no way I was letting my bestie wade through that comment section. If it was too gross for me, it was definitely too gross for her.

Two old kombucha bottles and one snap-top container later, Luz was loaded up with cookies and tea and headed home.

She was barely out the door when I dialed Angelique.

I felt a little bad, but I did plan to do some YouTube stuff . . . after the coven meeting.

84

"Did you make it home?" I asked as soon as she answered.

"No. We're at Dee's house. Well, technically, we're sitting in the car parked outside of Dee's house waiting for you to call. Do you want us to come back and get you?"

"Yeah," I said, breathing a literal sigh of relief. Dee's dad's house in Hollygrove was only two neighborhoods over. "You got my message?"

"Do you mean the flower you dropped on the ground practically in plain sight of everyone? Yes. We saw it. We're on our way. Oh! Yes. Dee says bring some of the tea your mom made if there's any left. It looked good."

I stood by the door with a Whole Foods bag of iced tea and cookies in one hand, scrolling through my YouTube comments with the other. Working on my channel made me feel a little bit better about having told Luz I would, but it also helped to knock a few items off my to-do list. The comments were mostly okay. I think I only deleted one before I saw one that stopped me in my tracks. I screenshotted it just as Angelique pulled up.

Angelique's car didn't look like a limo from the outside, but it did on the inside. There were two seats facing each other and a glass divider between the back seat and the driver's area and everything.

I say Angelique's car, but really it was her mom's. It's just that when Mrs. Hebert was out of town, Ms. Nancy drove Angelique around instead. It was like having a permanent, personal Lyft who'd pretty much take you anywhere. Yet another reason I was so glad to be friends with Angelique.

My mom said it was cool for me to take a ride as long as I was back by seven, so I hopped into the car and flashed the screenshot to Dee and Angelique.

"Am I tripping?" I said.

Neither of them really paid attention. Dee gave me the wassup nod and dug right into the paper bag to pull out the tea, but Angelique was busy weaving a curtain of intentions.

Once I realized what Angelique was doing, I had to stop and watch. The curtain was already filling most of the car like a tent, with the flap left open for me to climb through. I would have known Angelique's handiwork even if I hadn't seen her doing it. The weaving was rough and uneven, nothing like the sheer perfection that surrounded Belles Demoiselles, but at least eighty steps up from the floppy mesh I made to keep the palmetto bugs out of my house. My weaving worked, and so did Angelique's. Hers was making us silent and almost invisible to anyone on the outside, and on top of that it was low-key beautiful. Next to hers, the thing around my house

looked like old cobwebs. I was impressed. I had no idea how to weave an intention tight enough for it to work on people.

"Did Miss LeBrun teach you that?" I asked.

Angelique was Miss LeBrun's protégé at Belles Demoiselles, but I thought Miss LeBrun just did art and history. If I had known she could weave intentions, I might have agreed to be her protégé when she asked me. Nah. Who am I kidding. Miss Lafleur was my girl, even though I hadn't heard from her since we left campus.

Dee gave me a look like *Let her concentrate*, but Angelique answered me anyway.

"I learned it from Miss Lavande," Angelique said.

"I must have missed that class," I muttered.

"It wasn't a class," Angelique said. "When I turned down Miss Lavande's protégé offer, she agreed to show me the basics. I've been practicing."

Figured. Angelique had gotten a protégé offer from every single teacher at Belles Demoiselles. I guess that's what comes from "generations of proper education," or whatever it was Miss Villere had said. There was no denying it. The girl was good.

The protection inside Angelique's curtain of intentions was so strong that I could feel it the second she stitched it closed.

Judging by Dee's nod, she could feel it, too.

"My mom probably wove something longer-lasting into the glass, but I figured if you were dripping magic in the street like that, whatever you're upset about must be a big deal. So I thought we could use a little extra protection. What's going on?"

"The termites?" I said. "That's all LaToya."

Angelique didn't roll her eyes, but she may as well have. She looked so disappointed.

"For real, bruh?" Dee said, slumping back in the seat. "You were dripping magic in the street over LaToya? I thought you were trying to call a meeting about Luz."

"Luz?" I asked. "Why would I be calling a meeting about Luz?"

Angelique and Dee looked at each other.

"We thought you might be telling us that you're ready to tell her about being a witch, and for the record, Dee and I would fully support that decision."

"What? No!" I said. "Do you know how weird that would be? 'Oh, hey, Luz. Yeah. Magic is real, I have it and have been destroying lives with it all summer. Just thought you should know.'"

I laughed. Dee and Angelique both looked at me like they didn't get the joke. "I'm not just going to dump it on her. That would not be cool. I'm gonna tell her. I just need to figure out how."

"Hasani, it's not going to get any easier. Dee and I both think that she's starting to feel left out."

"No way!" I said. Then I thought about it. "Well . . . maybe, but not because of what you're saying. Maybe we should get matching charms for all four of us? I know! A crawfish because we all go to Riverbend Middle now. Go Mudbugs!"

Neither of them seemed impressed by my cheerleader arms, but I kept going. "And we're not even going to have a school if nobody checks LaToya. I'm telling you. She is up to something."

"Fine," Dee said, shaking her head. "What do you got?"

I laid out the whole thing:

- Her mysterious arrival in a school uniform
- The gym smell
- The fact that she was trying out for Mathletes at a school she doesn't go to
- The weird way she kept licking her pencil
- Ms. Coulon SMILING. Ms. Coulon never smiled.
- Ridiculous numbers of termites

"Most of that stuff is extraregular."

I gave Dee a look.

"I gotta give you the termite thing, though. That is wild," Dee admitted. "But that doesn't mean it's LaToya. She's not even that good at influence. Didn't you have to help her train her cat?"

True dat. LaToya's kitten, Laveau, was buck wild before I showed LaToya what to do.

"LaToya couldn't handle a cat, but you think she could call termites like that? Nah. Influence is your thing, not hers."

"First of all, it wasn't me," I said.

"I know it wasn't you," Dee said. "We would have seen it. I'm just saying, how would LaToya pull a megaswarm of termites when she couldn't even get her kitten to follow her around campus?"

"Don't underestimate LaToya," I said. "Smart and petty is nothing to play with. And she might not be good with animals, but don't you remember? From Fragrance?" Yes, at Belles Demoiselles we had a whole class about fragrance. "The thing Miss LaFleur said about permeating?"

Angelique and Dee did a synchronized eye roll.

"I'm serious. Miss LaFleur said witches who abuse any kind of potion, including fragrances, start to smell like lemons all the time."

"*Eventually* start to smell like lemons all the time," Angelique corrected. "I think all of us are too young for that. But even if that were happening to LaToya, how would she have made the whole gym smell weird? Miss LaFleur made it seem more like body odor."

"I don't know. Maybe it was coming out of her pores or something and just floated everywhere she walked. That's basically how air freshener works, right? You spray a little and it fills the whole room. Or, actually, LaToya is good with potions. Maybe she made one that influences people and turned it into lemon air freshener. And she was Miss Lavande's protégé! Who knows what Miss Lavande taught her."

More synchronized faces from Angelique and Dee, complete with raised eyebrow and head tilt.

"Okay. Probably Miss Lavande didn't teach her that, but I wouldn't put it past LaToya to put it together. That girl is determined."

"LaToya is determined," Angelique admitted, "but even if she could have come up with a potion that would squeeze her magic that much, what would be the point? Get back at you for going to a gathering of witches without her? That's a lot, especially since every other belle demoiselle from our year is in her coven. Why would she still care? No one is that petty."

Dee and I looked at each other.

"I don't know," Dee said after a few seconds. "LaToya is mad petty."

"You mean Grand Master Petty?"

Angelique cocked her head to one side.

"Fine," I said, holding out my phone again. "Look at this."

Dee and Angelique leaned in, but they both leaned back just as fast.

"Did you screenshot the wrong comment?" Angelique asked. "That just says, 'Another eye shadow tutorial. How charming.'"

"I mean, you do post a lot of eye shadow tutorials," Dee joked. "Maybe you should branch out?"

"No!" I said. Wait. *Did* I post a lot of eye shadow tutorials? "I'm talking about 'How charming.'"

Angelique and Dee looked at me blankly.

"Charming?" I repeated.

Still nothing.

"It's obviously LaToya," I said. "And somebody left a comment earlier calling me fake."

Dee chuckled. "Maaaan, if you gon' fall out every time somebody leaves a comment that rubs you the wrong way, you need a bitbot for real."

"I don't need a bitbot. I need LaToya to stop messing with my stuff. Charmed? *Charmed*? Who even says that? Wait. I know who. LaToya, when she was trying to make me look bad to Annie in the auditorium today."

"I think you were the one making her look bad, but okay. Let's say it was her. What do you think we should do?"

Dee said "we." That's what I love about Dee. For Dee, we were a "we." That meant she was all in.

Dee held her hand up to stop me from gushing. "Before you ask, no. I am not asking my mama. She wouldn't help, anyway. She'd just

make me go back to Vacherie. And I'm not taking any potions, either, especially not for no petty witch war."

Correction: Dee was sort of in. They needed more convincing. Luckily, Dee had just given me more ammo.

"Okay," I said. "Hear me out. What if it WAS her? Wouldn't it be too late? Wouldn't we already be in the middle of a petty witch war?"

"Not if we don't strike back," Angelique said. "By definition, a petty witch war would require two or more factions."

"Wait a minute. Petty witch war is really a thing?"

"Yes!" they both said.

"Oh. I thought Dee just made that up. Anyway, we don't actually have to do anything. But bullies are always worse when they think you won't strike back. We just need to come up with something to scare LaToya off."

"Scare? LaToya?" Dee had both her eyebrows up. "I can't think of anything that wouldn't be breaking a bunch of rules."

"A smart person once said, 'Students follow rules. Belles demoiselles make them.'"

"Who was that?" Dee asked.

"LaToya," I said.

Dee shook her head, but she looked at Angelique. I did, too.

Angelique smoothed out her skirt and sat up straighter.

"Is that look meant to ask me if I'll help you form a revenge plot against LaToya?"

"Not a revenge plot. More of a revenge plan. If everything goes back to normal, we wouldn't even need it."

"You think my mom would let me be involved with something that will probably end in some petty witch war? At a public school? Not a chance. I'm a Hebert. We're supposed to rise above," Angelique said, her chin raised just slightly. "But I am also a member of this coven, so whatever we do, we can't get caught."

CHAPTER NINE

BITS AND TRACES

*C*oven on board? Check.

That was a relief, because if there was one thing I learned this summer it's that I cannot do this witch stuff alone. And even though she showed up to Riverbend Middle by herself, LaToya was definitely not alone. She had a coven, too. A coven with thirteen members—every single member of our Belles Demoiselles class except me, Dee, and Angelique. She may not have been an influencer, but the girl had influence.

Angelique's phone chimed. It was a message from Ms. Nancy saying we had to stop wasting gas, so we went to Angelique's house for a little while. I always forget how nice that place is. And one of the nicest parts was Angelique's dad. He was in the kitchen making marinara sauce from scratch with tomatoes and herbs from their garden. Apparently it took three days to make, not counting the time you left it in the fridge for the "flavor to develop," but it was all worth it because Angelique's mom loved it so much.

"That's really sweet," I said as we headed up to Angelique's room.

"Yeah. My dad's sweet," Angelique said, like having the kind of dad who loved your mom enough to spend three days making sauce for her was no big deal. I guess for Angelique, it wasn't.

Angelique and Dee both said they were in, but I knew neither of them would really be in-in unless they were convinced that LaToya was trying to hurt one of us. I mean, fair. Maybe it was just a huge coincidence that LaToya, the termites, and those comments about me all appeared on the same day. I was pretty sure it was her, but I like proof as much as the next person. Then Angelique had a different idea.

"So how should we get rid of the termites?" Angelique asked. The way she said it was like that's what we had all decided we were going to do, and she was just reminding us of the one and only item on our agenda.

"What about LaToya?" I asked.

"What about her? You said you think we should show whoever did this that we're not easy targets, and I agree. No matter who is responsible, getting rid of the termites would be the best way to let them know that whatever they do can and will be undone with minimal fuss. They'll get bored. They'll go away. Case closed."

"You think that'll work?"

"Once, at camp—actual camp, not Belles Demoiselles—two people I did not care for very much moved a girl's nameplate into the shower. I mean, it was true that the girl never showered, but if you're not good enough friends to be able to tell her that without being a jerk, then you also aren't around her enough for her body odor to be a problem for you. Anyway, I moved the doorplate back where it belonged. They were ticked, but after that they left the girl alone. If we just put it back to normal, whoever did it will know they don't have the power to make us run. And that'll be it."

I refrained from saying Angelique had basically done the same thing to me at "camp" as those kids had done at actual camp, but I let it go. That was before we were friends. I guess she did have a point, but clearly neither of them knew LaToya. She was petty, but she was not a quitter.

"And that way we don't risk starting something with somebody who might not have done anything in the first place," Dee added. "I'm with Angelique."

Great.

"Fine," I said. "Let's just get rid of the termites. So how do we do it? Some spell?"

"Don't look at me," Dee said. "You need potions for spells, and my mama does not mess with potions. She wouldn't even drink Grandmé Annette's lemonade once she found out what it was."

"That was a potion?!" I squeaked.

"Duh," Dee and Angelique said at the same time.

That was some delicious potion.

"Witches are mad secret about their spellbooks, anyway. If my mama has one, she wouldn't tell me."

Angelique gave a little shrug. "Same. My mother is totally against witches squeezing magic. She says it's beneath us. I mean, she dabbles in incantations, of course. Who doesn't? But combining potions and incantations to make full-blown spells is strictly off-limits. Even if she had one, and I doubt it, she wouldn't show it to me. Our magic isn't even compatible. It'd be too dangerous."

"Witches keep their spells on lock like that?" I sounded shocked, but it made sense. KFC never would have gotten on the map if everybody knew all eleven herbs and spices. "But LaToya had her spellbook right out in the open in her room. She wasn't being slick at all."

"Frontin'," Dee said, like that explained everything.

It kind of did.

"So you don't think the spellbook was real?" I rolled my eyes. LaToya was so . . . LaToya. "She said she'd been eavesdropping on her grandmother and stuff and writing everything down."

Dee gave me the side-eye.

"I know," I sighed. "LaToya says a lot of stuff."

Dee threw her hands up like, *Exactly*.

"It doesn't matter if what you saw in LaToya's room was a spell-book or not. We just need something that will get rid of the termites. What about Miss Lafleur, Hasani? Can you just call her?"

Awkward. I was Miss Lafleur's protégé, so, yes, in theory, I should have been able to call her. And since Animal Affinities was her specialty, I was pretty sure she could have at least given us a hint about how to get rid of an unexpected swarm of termites. The thing is that, after the program ends, teachers have to reach out and make an offer to continue teaching you, and Miss Lafleur never reached out.

I shook my head. "I guess she didn't want to offer me an apprenticeship," I said. "So what do we do?"

It wasn't so much a question as a way to keep Dee and Angelique talking. Even though they were mad different, they were both from long lines of witches and had watched people do magic their whole lives. Between the two of them, they knew pretty much everything about being a witch. That's why I was so stunned by their silence.

Dee, at least, shrugged. Angelique just sat looking off into the distance. Regally, but still. Clearly the next step was going to be up to me. Too bad the only thing I could think of was "What if I do it?"

They both looked at me.

"Bruh. You good with animals, but if a potion brought those termites in, you might not be strong enough to get them out."

"Not just me. WE."

"Go in the gym with termites?" Dee sounded skeptical. She was great with coding, but influencing animals wasn't Dee's thing.

"You're scared of termites?" I teased.

"That many termites? Yes," Dee said flatly.

One of the many things I loved about Dee was that there was never any shame in her game.

"They're just like mosquitoes. They'll never get near you," I said, knowing Dee and every other belle demoiselle at least knew how to keep those suckers away.

Dee sucked her teeth and threw me another side-eye. Angelique and I *were* the best ones at Animal Affinities, but Dee wasn't bad. She could have held her own, but I didn't mind protecting her. That's what friends are for, right? I'd be Gandalf and the swarm of termites would be the Balrog.

But instead of shouting "They shall not pass!" like any halfway decent *Lord of the Rings* fan would, I said, "Fine. I'll make sure they don't come anywhere near any of us."

As soon as I said it, I felt sick to my stomach. Not like get-out-of-the-way-'cause-I'm-gonna-hurl-right-now sick, but sick. Keeping a few roaches out of our house was one thing, but that was a lot of termites. Angelique and Dee both stared at me.

It didn't help that I suddenly remembered what happened to Gandalf. I tried not to let the feeling show.

"I'm an influencer," I said. "It's not cool to do on people, but I can at least get the bugs to go away. I'm pretty sure I know what to do. If I draw them all close enough together, I don't have to influence all of them. If I get some of them to go, the rest will follow. Kind of like the heart swans. Getting one swan to do it is hard, but getting two or three to follow is not that much harder if they're close enough." Everything I was saying was true, but my stomach was doing some serious gymnastics.

"Shoooo . . ." Dee made a face. "You're good, but those termites were all the way in the computer lab."

"Dee's right. You are naturally gifted with influence, but no offense? When was the last time you did magic? Are you, like, practicing on your own?"

No. I hadn't done a single thing since we found Annie. Since I found out how much my magic had messed up my mom. But I didn't feel like going there.

"That's why I need my coven," I said, reaching out to squeeze them both. "I might not be strong enough on my own, but with the power of three . . ."

"Now you trying to make 'power of three' happen?" Dee laughed. "What happened to 'best friend squad'?"

I threw on a grin. With extra cheese. "I could bring it back if you like that one better. Or how about 'Wonder Twins, Plus One'?"

"Nah. You good."

I *was* good.

Hopefully my magic wasn't too rusty.

ngelique dropped me off and we all agreed to meet back at my house at sunrise. That gave me a little while to choke down some dinner—my mom was on an asparagus kick, which was still fine on night three but could only be called torture on night eight—organize some video clips, and settle down with Othello and the comment section.

It had been hours since I checked the comments. I expected them to be awful. They weren't. There was only one gross comment, but somebody replied to it with "Femme bois for the win!" and after that everything kind of settled down. People were still leaving comments, but they were all about makeup, not other people. Refreshing.

I pressed CTRL+U to view the code, just like Dee had taught me. Sure enough, that section of the code glistened like it was sprinkled with water or dusted with glitter. Magic. Magic so tightly folded into the code that I could barely see it. There were probably lots of witches who could do something like that, but only one whose magic I could see without rose-colored glasses. Dee.

It wasn't Dee's username or anything. Dee didn't have a username. She barely even used the Internet. When I needed her to make a comment on YouTube one time, she literally had to make an account, which she promptly deleted. But I didn't need a Dee-style username to recognize Dee on the Internet. I guess it could have been Angelique, but as good as Angelique was at everything, nobody could wrap magic in code as perfectly as Dee. This magic was so tight it barely shimmered. Leave it to Dee to quietly post a bitbot on my channel and keep it pushing.

I know Dee was just trying to help, but I didn't want that kind of help. My channel, my responsibility. And here was this bitbot doing all the work for me. I didn't know what the code part actually did, but I knew what the bitbot was doing. "Femme bois for the win" had almost a thousand likes and dislikes, and all the comments after it were normal. The comments weren't all good. I mean, somebody did kick off a thread that a bunch of people jumped into about how bad throwaway dollar store products are for the environment—but nobody was calling anybody names or hating on anybody just because of who they were or what they liked. It's crazy how often that usually happened, but after Dee's comment, it stopped.

It would have been a good thing if I didn't already know that hate like that doesn't just disappear. It goes somewhere. That's why, no matter how much Dee was trying to help, the first thing Othello and

I did once we found that bitbot was delete it, then scan for traces of Dee's magic left in the page's code. There wasn't any that I could see. It all flushed away when I deleted Dee's comment.

I felt a little bad about it once the bitbot was gone. Not like I should have kept it or anything. More like, I didn't want Dee to think I was mad at her or being ungrateful or anything. Dee had literally been there for me since day one when she rescued me from a bunch of mean girls my first night at Belles Demoiselles. She was my people. I just couldn't take chances with magic in my YouTube channel.

I started to call and tell her that, but . . .

1. Dee doesn't hardly answer her phone.
2. I was going to see her in the morning, anyway. I'd tell her then.

CHAPTER TEN

POTIONS AND AROMATICS

*O*thello circled my legs a thousand times while I was trying to get ready. I ended up dripping a full trail of magic around the room to keep him occupied. I was only pulling on jeans and tying my hair into a puff, but thanks to his adorableness it still took me like ten minutes to get ready, and even then I basically went outside still wiping crust out of my eyes. Don't judge me. It was early and I spent the time editing and posting a GRWM instead of taking a shower. We were going somewhere bug-infested, anyway. I'd shower when I got back. Plus, who was going to see me besides Angelique and Dee? And my mom, who was in the living room either meditating or doing extraslow yoga. She stopped when she saw me.

"You're up early," my mom said.

I tried to keep it casual. "I was gonna walk to school and see if they've made any progress."

True, but not exactly the kind of thing that would usually put my mom at ease. Luckily, she supplied the perfect cover herself.

"And take early-morning pictures of the school for Luz's Instagram."

I stood there with my mouth half-open, not knowing if I should smile and agree or what.

"What? I know about golden hour." My mom grinned. "I follow Luz's Instagram, too. Those pictures will be perfect for her 'aesthetic.'"

My mom put air quotes around "aesthetic" like it was slang even though I'm pretty sure it wasn't and I'm a hundred percent sure my mom was an art major in school—but at least she used it right?

She laughed, probably thinking it was a joke between us. I didn't, because my mom was right. Luz's Instagram was all about school. School people. School events. School gossip. School parties. Her feed was basically Riverbend Middle up and down, and right now, when it was light but the sun hadn't actually risen in the sky, was a perfect time to take pictures, especially of giant things like our school building right after something major-event-like had happened. My mom was right . . . only I couldn't invite Luz.

"Thanks, Mom," I said awkwardly.

"Remember you promised to go with me to the French Market today, so be home by ten," my mom said, moving back into what may have been tai chi and not yoga at all.

Angelique's car was waiting outside. I thought we'd all be wearing sweatpants or pajamas. Well, I didn't really think Angelique would. I couldn't even imagine her casual, but I thought at least Dee would be down for some early-morning solidarity. Nope. Wing tips, pastel suspenders, and a camera with a matching camera strap.

"I might catch a few shots," Dee said when she saw me staring. "I've been messing around with a filter that might break magic into light haze. Like a tinted blur. It kinda works on mine."

"Like rose-colored glasses?"

"Nah. I wish. Miss Villere keeps that formula on lock. This is just me messing around."

"Oh, yeah? Let me see. I bet it's great."

"You know I didn't keep them."

True dat. Dee barely kept pictures of her face, let alone her magic.

"It's not for us. I figured I'll take a li'l video of the gym. If magic brought the termites, we might be able to see it."

And if nothing showed up on the video, maybe I'd stop blaming LaToya. I didn't say that part, but I swear, sometimes it was hard to know whose side Dee was on.

Angelique, on the other hand, seemed down for the cause. "Hasani, I realized after I dropped y'all off that I wasn't really taking the LaToya thing seriously. But I thought about it and you're right. Everything she's done so far has been supersketchy. Why *was* she at the school and trying out for a team if she isn't even enrolled? I should have done a better job hearing you out. I'm not going to, like, sneak into her room and steal her spellbook or anything, but . . . peace offering?"

Angelique held out a purple paisley square.

"A . . . sandwich bag?" I didn't try to stop the confusion from filling my face.

Angelique pulled it a little so that the accordion sides showed.

"Air sampler," she said. "It's meant for collecting fragrance samples, but you kept saying the gym smelled strange, so I figured it wouldn't hurt for us to get a sample."

I could have hugged her.

"Trust me. Citrus in the gym is NOT normal."

The car pulled up in front of the school just as we finalized our plan. But I didn't expect Riverbend Middle to already be covered in a giant tent, especially not one that clashed with the bead trees so badly. Luz's Instagram was not missing out on anything aesthetic.

"That was quick," Angelique said. "Do you still want to go inside? They may have already started fumigating."

"They haven't. Look. They're not done yet," I said, pointing at people unloading more tent stuff from a truck that said Billiot's Pest Control.

Angelique unstitched her magic curtain and asked Ms. Nancy to let us out on the Hampson Street side. There weren't as many workers on that side, but the tent around the building looked even worse from that angle.

"Oh. I told Ms. Nancy that we were coming to take pictures for your Instagram, Hasani," Angelique said after Dee shut the car door.

"My Instagram? Why mine? I barely use it."

"She follows mine and Dee doesn't have one. Do you have a better idea?"

It wasn't really a question, and that was good because I didn't really have an answer. So Angelique and I paused and took an ussie with the tented building in the background just to keep it convincing, but as soon as Ms. Nancy drove away I started trying gates until we found an open one on the Maple Street side.

The gate was creaky, but it was easy enough to slip inside. Our school wasn't built as a school and there were lots of temporary classroom trailers set up in the yard, which was annoying on rainy days when you forgot your umbrella and needed to make it to the last portable, but right then I was grateful. All the trailers and trees made it easier to stay hidden until we got to the back door of the gym.

You could open that gym door even when it was locked—something I found out in sixth grade when I left my backpack at P.E.

The knob was stiff, but if you yanked it anyway because, say, the study guide you'd been working on for over a week was in there and Ms. Coulon was about to give you a zero, it gave.

The closer we got to the gym, the more nervous I got. I really was out of practice doing magic—not that I was very good in the first place. There was a reason everybody at Belles Demoiselles whispered about me being a wildseed behind my back. There was a reason I was the last one to get my fleur-de-lis charm. I barely remembered what life was like before I had one. I just knew I never wanted to go back to being that kind of out of control. I tried to tell myself this was just one little thing. Like heart swans or that insect barrier at my house. One little thing and we could go home and laugh and hang out and school would start on Monday. I just needed to make sure Riverbend Middle stayed a magic-free zone. I could do that. I might throw up, but we'd cross that bridge when we came to it.

Getting to the gym was taking longer than I thought. There were workers all over the grounds. I don't know what I thought exterminators did. Maybe walk around in Ghostbusters jumpsuits spraying poison? But, nah. These people looked more like they were setting up a janky circus, and you could barely go five seconds without one of them walking by. I couldn't imagine us charming our way through it if one of them stopped us. Like, maybe they wouldn't yell at us, but they'd definitely make us leave. Luckily, we had a plan.

I was still nervous, though. For real, a lot of times being a witch is more trouble than it's worth. Magic is *magic*. I get it. And sometimes magic makes things easy that should be hard. Cool. But just as often, magic makes things hard that should be easy.

But the closer we got, the more I thought about the fact that, for once, I could use my influence for something good. Something better than making swans tell time. For once, I could actually help. I was Jedi mind-tricking myself, but it was working. And if in the process we found something that could put LaToya in her place . . . let's just call it lagniappe. Who doesn't like getting a little something extra?

I was excellent at keeping flying cockroaches and mosquitoes out of the house, but a school is way bigger than a house, and that was a whole lot of termites. Good thing I wasn't alone. All I had to do was shape the influence. Once Dee and Angelique intertwined their magic with mine, it would get way bigger. The whole thing would be finished before anyone knew we were there. Yes, there might be termites flying out of the school in the daytime, and yes, that might attract attention, maybe even the news again. But if people were going wild about the termites flying away, that would make it even easier to slip out without anyone paying attention to us.

So as I yanked the door of the gym open and motioned Dee and Angelique in, I was legit feeling good. Not magic tingling good. Control good. Charm good. Belle demoiselle good.

111

The first thing I noticed when I stepped in: the smell. It wasn't right, and it wasn't the same as yesterday. Instead of being all lemon-lime-orange, it was mostly mint. I knew we shouldn't have waited until morning. Maybe Angelique was right and the exterminators had already started spraying chemicals in there, but minty chemicals? That couldn't have been it. I started trying to go through my head, sorting out all the magical properties of mint.

I didn't get very far. It's hard to keep thinking about herbs when you realize there is a panther in your school gym.

Okay. Maybe panther is an exaggeration, but it was a legit huge cat. As soon as the door swung shut, it dropped from the bleachers and stared us down with scary blue eyes. I promise you, it was something straight out of a horror movie. Magic built up, stinging my fingertips, making my fleur-de-lis run hot, but none of it would come out. Not a drop. That's when I panicked. We all did. Dee gripped her camera, wide-eyed. Angelique was in some kind of fight stance, accordion bag spread wide. Me? I took one look at that lynx and ran, busting out of the gym door like Chucky was after me, magic pulsing in my ears like a bass drum. The next thing I knew, all three of us were running through soggy grass back behind the trailers, the massive cat on our heels. We were headed for the gate. Instead, we ran straight into Ms. Coulon.

Magic buzzed against my skin. We were trapped. Ms. Coulon was staring right at us, and at the same time, the cat had stopped behind us, blocking our way back, making everything about me freeze—including my magic.

Of course, I couldn't explain any of this to Ms. Coulon, who had launched into teacher interrogation mode.

"Why are you girls here? What were you doing in the gym?"

I started talking so fast. My school. My plan. No way was I letting Angelique and Dee get in trouble. "It's my fault, Ms. Coulon. We—"

Ms. Coulon put a hand up, her eyes suddenly bored behind her glasses.

"Never mind. Whatever it is, you can tell it to the principal."

Dee sighed and ran a hand across her head.

Angelique's shoulders fell back, her face exuding a subtle charm.

Me? My mouth fell open. The principal, Ms. Reid, was coming our way, but she wasn't alone. Miss Lafleur was walking with her.

CHAPTER ELEVEN

PARTICLES AND

PARTICULARS

"You found her!" Miss Lafleur exclaimed, clasping her hands together under a huge smile.

Miss Lafleur was the one who told me I was a witch and brought my invitation to Belles Demoiselles. She had come to my house and talked to my mom. I'd spent some part of every day at Belles Demoiselles with her, which was especially true after she chose me as her protégé. It was also true that she had taught me almost everything I knew about animals, which means in a way I had to give her props for Othello being so great. Even with all that, it was still stoopid weird to see Miss Lafleur standing outside of Riverbend Middle. Miss Lafleur was a witch. Witches belonged in Vacherie, not Riverbend Middle.

And before you say anything, no. My coven didn't count.

"Thank you so much!" Miss Lafleur continued brightly. "Lynx usually stays close, but I guess that's why I have one of these." She reached into the pocket of her khaki Billiot's Pest Control overalls and pulled out a leather leash.

"Lynx!" she called, then clicked her tongue twice. The monster cat from the gym walked straight to her and sat like a trained dog until Miss Lafleur clipped the leash onto a harness. As scary as that cat was, it still looked dope.

New goal: Teach Othello to walk on a leash.

"What an unusual cat," Ms. Reid chuckled nervously. "Has it been here on campus all this time?"

"Of course! No matter where I am, Lynx is always nearby. She's a rescue. We think she may be part Maine coon, but of course we can't be certain."

"Oh, I think you can be," Ms. Reid said, her eyes still firmly on Lynx.

"Well, in any case, Lynx is a huge help. She helps us ferret out the source of some infestations naturally, but she usually does a better job of sticking close to me. Don't you, Lynx?" Miss Lafleur scratched the top of Lynx's head. She didn't have to reach far. The cat's head was basically at her waist. Lynx leaned into that scratch, too, like she was petting Miss Lafleur back. I knew that move. Othello did it every time he expected bigger drips of magic than he was getting.

"These young people passing by saw my distress and offered to help me look for her, which I very much appreciate. You're students here, yes?"

"Yes."

"Yes, miss."

"Yes, ma'am."

That Belles Demoiselles training clicked right into place.

"All three of you? Excellent. Where did you find her?"

"In the gym," I said. Dee and Angelique nodded.

"Of course! No wonder she couldn't hear me when I called her. Did you find anything else in the gym?"

We all stared at her.

"That's okay. I'll go have a closer look myself before we enter Phase II of the abatement."

Miss Lafleur smiled her real smile as she pulled three business cards out of the pocket on the bib of her overalls and pressed one into each of our hands.

"It was a pleasure to meet you. Thank you for all your help. If any of you are ever interested in the pest-control business, we're always looking for bright, young apprentices. Give us a call."

Did Miss Lafleur just say "apprentice"? I almost got hype. Then I realized she handed the cards to all three of us and my hype-meter dropped to zero. It was just a part of the act for Ms. Coulon and Ms. Reid. The cards were cool, though. They were pink with crisp writing the exact shade of brown as Miss Lafleur's skin. With all the embossed moths and butterflies in the background, the card had more of an "I love bugs" vibe than an "I kill bugs" vibe, but I'm not judging. Exterminator Miss Lafleur was bailing us out of a whole lot of trouble. If she weren't pretending not to know me, I would have hugged her.

"What a generous offer," Ms. Reid said. She was still keeping an eye on the enormous cat, but her voice was less jittery.

"Oh, it's not generous at all. We really are always looking for talent, and our apprenticeships are quite rigorous. We take pest control very seriously."

All the adults stood there looking at us. Ms. Reid and Miss Lafleur were smiling, but none of them were saying anything. Angelique got the hint.

"We were happy to help, but we should get going."

"Yes," I chimed in. "We just came to check for the Mathletes list. We couldn't find it, but it was worth a shot."

"Oh! Is one of you hoping to be team captain?" Ms. Reid looked relieved. "A little birdie told me that there is going to be some exciting news."

Ms. Coulon was stone-faced, but Ms. Coulon was always stone-faced, at least when LaToya wasn't squeezing her magic to influence her. But it didn't matter, because when Ms. Reid said the part about "exciting news" she was looking right at me. I didn't need Ms. Coulon to smile and I didn't need whatever LaToya's stupid potion was, either. Mathletes captain was in the bag.

"Dag. You lie easy," Dee said.

We were walking down Maple Street. Ms. Nancy was going to pick us up at a coffee shop there. I said I could walk home, but Angelique insisted.

"Excuse me?" I said, clutching imaginary pearls. "That lie was NOT easy. But it worked, right?"

We all laughed.

"I mean, the way Ms. Coulon was looking at us like we were up to no good, I had to say something, right?"

Ms. Nancy pulled up, the three of us got in, and Angelique wove her little tent of intentions closed. The stitches were smoother and tighter than the last time.

"I'm going to be sad to pull this apart," Angelique said.

"Do you have to take it down so your mom won't see it?" I asked.

"My mom won't see it," Angelique said.

I blinked, then remembered something about Angelique's magic not coming from her mother's side.

"Then why do you have to take it down?"

"Waste not, want not. Anyway, look what I got!" Angelique held her little accordion bag in front of us.

"Sweeeet," Dee said. "You did good. Once that cat popped out of nowhere, I was NOT thinking about this camera."

"Right? Is Miss Lafleur really walking around the city with a full-grown mountain lion?" I asked.

"You keep dripping magic to Othello like you do and he'll be a mountain lion before too long."

"For real?" I'm not gon' lie. Lynx was a little scary, but a giant Othello sounded awesome.

"For real. Miss Lafleur's cat is overfed. I haven't seen a cat that big—"

"Ever," Angelique finished. "Lynx was impressive. Not purebred Maine coon, definitely overfed, but impressive. Maine coons are normally very large. Nose-to-tail lengths of forty inches or more are not uncommon."

Dee tipped her head to the side and stared at Angelique like, *Seriously?* "Dag. How many Maine coons have you seen?"

"They're very popular at cat shows. My father takes me to four or five every year. I'm a card-carrying member of the Cat Fanci-ers' Association."

Before Dee or I could react to that piece of information, Angelique kept talking.

"Anyway, I don't want to seem melodramatic, but Lynx isn't what made that whole thing scary."

"It isn't?" I asked. I mean, again, the cat was pretty scary.

"No. Couldn't you tell? Something was stoppering our magic."

All I could do for like a minute solid was blink and shake my head. "What?"

Angelique shook her head. "I keep forgetting that you're green. Okay, so, witches only have so much magic. Once you've used it up, it's gone. That's why they're so big on charm at Belles Demoiselles. They don't want us to burn all our magic off. Stoppering is different. I'm sorry I didn't believe you before, but I do now. I thought I felt some-thing strange when we walked onto the school grounds yesterday, but since we were trying not to use any charm or anything, I wasn't sure. Not using magic was really easy. By the time we got to the gym for the tryouts I thought I had just gotten used to it, but that wasn't it. I didn't have to try to hold my magic in because something else was holding it in for me. Something on campus is stoppering our magic."

I had to let that soak in. Obviously, burning your magic off is not cool, but at least if you do you only have yourself to blame. But the idea that something could just stop us from using magic? Randomly? Against our will? At school of all places? That was just scary.

I let a little bit of magic ooze out and form a flower in my hand. It was a waste, but Othello wasn't there to lap it up, and I just needed to feel it. Make sure it was still there.

Then I felt stupid. At least, I did until I realized Angelique and Dee had basically done the same thing. I couldn't tell exactly what they had done, but I could see little traces of their magic hanging in the air.

"Stoppering our magic?" I repeated, still shaking my head. The flower in my hand wasn't enough. I needed to pull something. Influence something. Just to be sure I still could. A butterfly. Anything.

I went to click the button to roll down my window, but stopped when I saw the weave in Angelique's tent of intentions getting thicker and more intricate. At least I knew where her magic was going.

"Can I . . . ?"

Angelique was two steps ahead of me. She rolled the window down a crack and made a tiny slit in her intentions. It was just wide enough for me to pull something small through. The magic felt like it wanted to leap out of me, but I didn't let it. *Charm, not magic*, I told myself. I took a deep breath in, held on to the feeling of who I was, and reached out for something beautiful. Within seconds a Gulf fritillary fluttered into the window like it had floated there on the wind.

Angelique sealed her intentions, the butterfly landed on the morning glory in my hand, and I breathed a sigh of relief. I think we all did.

"How?" I asked, focusing on the butterfly's wings. The orange was a perfect contrast for the pale purple morning glory winding around my hand. Part of my brain was planning another eye shadow video, but the rest of it needed answers.

"How what?" Dee asked. She was obviously totally chill again, all traces of her magic gone from the air.

"How is stoppering magic a thing and nobody ever mentioned it?"

"Well, it's more of a working theory than an actual thing at this point. Kind of like the Bermuda Triangle."

"Wait. Is THAT a thing?"

"Yes," Angelique said.

"No," Dee said.

Dee and Angelique looked at each other and shrugged. "Maybe," Dee admitted.

"That's the point," Angelique said. "There isn't proof, but sometimes you get a feeling like someone has put a cork in your magic."

"Yeah," Dee added. "It's dark. You're supposed to say 'grigrishá' and touch both your shoulders when that happens."

"What does that do?" I asked.

Dee shrugged. "I don't know. That's just what people say. Ask them. I'm not superstitious."

"So it's like one second: magic. The next second: gone?"

"No," Angelique said. "More like a stopper in a bathtub. Whatever water is in it stays in, but no matter what you do, it can't flow out."

"In theory," Dee added.

"In theory," Angelique agreed.

"Well, that didn't feel like a theory to me. At least it explains why I was so freaked out by Miss Lafleur's cat," I said. "I love cats."

Dee shook her head. "Nah. You were freaked out 'cause that cat is freaky."

I was confused. "But what does the cat have to do with people stealing our magic?"

"Not stealing," Angelique said, pulling first daughter of a first daughter back onto her face. "Stoppering. And it's just a theory, or at least I thought it was, but we all felt it most in the gym, right?"

Dee and I both nodded.

"Well, normally, no one does anything. People just explain it away. They say the witch was scared. We weren't scared."

"Speak for yourself," Dee mumbled.

"Well, if we were scared it was only because we couldn't use our magic. I could have kept that cat away from us, and if I could have, I know Hasani could, too. Something was forcing us to hold our magic in."

"You're right," I said. Running into Ms. Coulon and Miss Lafleur and *the principal* had made the whole thing extra, but thinking back on it, Lynx really wasn't what scared me.

"Okay?" Dee's eyebrows were all the way up. "Where are we going with this?"

"My guess is whoever flooded the school with termites is using whatever smelled so minty to cover their tracks."

"From what? The witch police?"

Angelique practically glared at me. "There's no such thing as the witch police."

"Police?" Dee scoffed. "Then what? Inquisitions? Witch trials? Nah. Nobody got time for that."

"We might not need anyone else to figure it out." Angelique pulled her paisley accordion thing to the front.

"Think about it this way. We don't need to try to get anyone in trouble. What's in this here is like when you erase the pencil lines after you trace over the parts you want with ink. Or deleting the sketch layer on your drawing app when the art is done to make it less messy in the end."

"Oh, I get it," I said. "So if we undo the undo, we'll be able to see what they did in the first place. Then maybe we can undo it for real. If we find out what was in the minty aromatics, we can figure out what they were trying to erase. And once we know that, we'll know how to

counter it. Every ingredient has a counter." I sounded all knowledge-able, but ironically, I learned that stuff from LaToya.

"Exactly!"

"So . . . how do we figure out what's in it?" I asked.

Dee shrugged like, *Don't ask me.*

"We just need somebody who can analyze aromatics. Maybe I could ask Miss Lavande?" Angelique offered.

All of us were silent. Maybe Miss Lavande liked Angelique, but LaToya was still Miss Lavande's protégé.

"Miss Lafleur!" I said. "She literally just gave us all her card and she teaches Fragrance. She probably knows what's up and wants to help. Should we call her?"

"Worth a try," Dee said.

We all pulled our cards out, but they'd changed since she handed them to us. The insects and flowers had shifted, changing and blocking the phone number. Dee's literally said 010-011-0101. Angelique's at least started with 504, but she called and it was the actual main number for Billiot's Pest Control. Since she didn't want to schedule an extermination for her home, she made an excuse about having the wrong number and hung up. Mine wasn't a number at all. There were so many bugs and flowers so close together that it basically all looked like chicken scratch. So much for that.

"Now what do we do?" I asked.

"Well, it's not like any of us know any stopper counter-spells. And without knowing who did it—"

I didn't mean to, but I must have glared.

"Without knowing *for sure* who did it," Angelique repeated, "or exactly what's in the aromatic, we'd need an actual spell to reverse it. Something strong. Maybe a freedom spell, but it's not like we can find spells that would totally free up a space like that by searching on the Internet. None of you have access to the Interweb, right?"

Dee shook her head.

I flushed. Half because even I'm not dorky enough to call the Internet "the Interwebs," half because of a memory that flashed through my head. It was from around my dad's wedding.

I shook my head. "We don't need the Internet, y'all. I think we just need to check under my bed."

CHAPTER TWELVE

ABUNDANCE AND CAUTION

Going back to my house was more eventful than I thought it would be. I didn't think about what would happen if Angelique, Dee, and I rolled up to my house early in the morning with me basically still in my pajamas. I didn't think about it until Luz said it from two doors down.

"Did y'all have a sleepover?"

The words rang out like church bells, or the drama music in a telenovela.

It looked bad. I panicked.

"No!" I said, hustling toward her. "We were just coming to knock on your door. Can you come over?"

Luz shook her head. "Knock on my door? C'mon. I have a phone," she said. Then she laughed. "All right. Give me a minute. It's my turn to make breakfast."

I gave her a hug.

"You might want to run through the shower," she laughed. "I'm smelling less flower and more dirt."

I poked her. "It's like that?"

"Yeah. It's like that."

"Fine." I smiled. "Give me twenty minutes and I'll run through the shower."

"I'll give you thirty so you can walk. If I give you an hour, can you stand still and shower like a normal person?"

"Ha, ha, ha," I said. "We'll see you in thirty. Bring biscuits, please!"

"There won't be any left," she said. "You know how Miguel eats."

I sure did. As skinny as he was, I once saw Miguel eat twelve drop biscuits with butter and jam in one sitting. And then he asked for more!

"I'll save some for y'all," Luz said. Then she grabbed the newspaper and went back inside.

Dee was staring at me like, *Daaaaang, son!*

I ignored her and Angelique's looks and brought us all inside. The spellbook Sandy gave me was exactly where I had shoved it under my bed. I pulled it out and handed it to Dee.

"Check this while I go take a quick shower," I said. "Sandy gave it to me after the wedding. I think I remember her saying something about freedom being her thing. There might be something in there."

Dee flipped the banana-leaf book open and—no lie—she and Angelique gasped in unison, like all of us were in some Disney Channel show.

Angelique shook her head and blinked her eyes faster than I've ever seen. "Sandy . . . GAVE you this?"

"Yeah," I said.

"No. I mean, like, she handed it to you of her own volition and said out loud and in words that you could have it?"

The blink was still going hyperspeed.

"Yes," I said.

"Daaaaag," Dee said. "She must really like you."

"She was trying to buy me off. I guess she thought I'd be impressed or touched or whatever. It's cool, but you don't have to go overboard."

Angelique was still blinking. "And you've been keeping it like this? Shoved under a bed?"

"Stone-cold soldier." Dee whistled. "If you don't want it, I'll take it."

"I thought you weren't into spells and potions and stuff."

"I'm not. But I'm not gon' look a gift spellbook in the mouth, either."

"Fine. My bad. It's a big deal," I said. "Can you check it before Luz gets here so I can take a shower?"

I know it's kind of weird, but I kind of didn't want to be the one to look. Getting stuff from Sandy still felt kind of like a betrayal, no matter how cool my mom was being. Maybe I would have felt differ-ent if my dad had given it to me, but Sandy and I weren't even related.

By the time I got out of the shower, Luz was there and the spell-book was out of sight. I had no idea if they had found something help-ful, not found anything at all, or if they had just been drooling about how cool it was that Sandy had given me a spellbook the whole time. From what I remembered from flipping through quickly, it barely even had any spells in it. Eventually, Dee gave me a slick thumbs-up, so I figured they found something. But when Angelique started wondering about where we could get really fresh figs and ginger, I knew they had.

Luz brought drop biscuits. Enough for everybody, of course, because she's Luz.

"These are just as good as your mom's," my mom said, grabbing Luz up in a hug after taking a huge bite slathered in butter. Definitely not vegan. Though, to be fair, Luz always made them like that. "She would be so proud of you."

Luz's mom died not long after we met, but her mom's family was from Edgar, which apparently is right next to Vacherie, and according to my mom, that practically made them cousins, no matter how long she knew her.

"Well"—my mom wiped biscuit crumbs off her hands, not say-ing a word about animal fat, sugar, or cholesterol—"Hasani and I are

about to go to the French Market to scope things out for a potential new business. Is everybody coming?"

"Dee and I need fresh ginger and figs for a recipe she's teaching me, but we wouldn't want to intrude, Miss Nailah," Angelique said.

"Aw! Too bad it's not June. Otherwise I could have given you figs off the tree by our back steps. I bet they have some at the French Market, though. And of course you're not intruding. I plan to put y'all to work. Programming. Website. Market research and messaging. Product design. Looks like a perfect business development team to me. This first time I'll pay in beignets, but after that we can talk cash. Deal?"

I don't know who in their right mind passes up beignets, even after a drop biscuit or two.

Somehow, we all ended up piling into my mom's little electric car, Lucy, instead of Angelique's magic limo, but it was cool. My mom may be weird and a little overprotective, but she makes an excellent playlist. The one playing on the way there was "Girls with Guitars." Phoebe Snow is on that one, and I don't care how old she is, Phoebe Snow is my jam. My mom and I both sang so loud that even Dee was laughing at us from the back seat. Car karaoke is good, but in this case it was even better because as long as we were singing, my mom wasn't saying anything that might remind Luz about being left out this morning. I'd tell her about it later, but for now I was hoping that we could just let it slide.

The French Market is right by the river. I mean, so are my house and my school, so I guess the river is pretty much everywhere in New Orleans, but down by the French Market the river has a different feel. Wide and deep and so old you could get lost in it, just like the market. Every time we walked up to it, my mom said the exact same thing.

"Did you know that this market has been here longer than this place has been America?"

Yes. And if I didn't know it by then, I couldn't imagine her telling me one more time would make a difference.

Dee and Angelique did a better job of looking interested, but Luz was all business.

"Is the spot you're looking at one of the stalls in the front or one of the tables in the back? I think the stalls would be better for a tea business. We'll get better pictures, and you could put stools on one side of the counter so people could sit and drink samples right there."

"I think it's a table, but I like the way you're thinking, Luz. Tell me more."

My mom and Luz started walking ahead, which gave me a chance to talk to Angelique and Dee. I could have been texting them, but that would have been really obvious inside my mom's tiny car.

I thought we'd be looking for the ginger and figs Angelique mentioned before we left. I was pretty sure we had ginger at my house already, but the French Market was a good place to look for figs. Instead, we stopped at a table of turquoise jewelry none of us could afford and pretended to shop.

My phone buzzed.

Hey girlie . . .

Sandy again. I stuck the phone in my pocket. I'd get back to her later.

"Well?" I said, trying to give them the eyebrow.

Dee gave a little nod. I had no idea what that meant.

Angelique started saying something that I thought was directed at me. I was wrong.

"How much is this one?" she asked, showing the seller a turquoise on silver ring that looked like it was made for her hand.

"Two hundred," the woman said calmly.

"I'll take it," Angelique said.

Correction. I guess only two of us were pretending to shop.

Dee and I didn't even try not to look at each other.

"What?" Angelique said as the vendor pulled out packing for the ring. "It's a welcome home present for my mom. We may not have the same blood type, but our ring fingers are exactly the same size."

A welcome home gift for your mom? Is that even a thing? I am definitely not Angelique enough to have ever thought of getting my mom a welcome home gift. Then again, my mom never went anywhere, so who knew?

While the vendor was distracted wrapping the ring, Angelique said, "One of the recipes looks perfect, but it calls for fresh ginger, fresh figs, and picture jasper."

"We have ginger," I said. I didn't even know what picture jasper was, but at least I could be a little bit helpful.

"The 'fresh' was underlined twice, so I think it needs to be really, really fresh."

"Fresh ingredients?" the vendor asked, tying a little blue ribbon on Angelique's package. "You're looking for Marie's stall. It's in the back on the left-hand side. She has all kinds of specialty ingredients. Always fresh. Perfect for bringing a little New Orleans spice back to wherever you're from."

"We're from here," I said, filling my smile with charm to cover how annoying it was to be mistaken for a tourist. "But thank you."

I hustled my friends away from the turquoise table. We wandered through the fruit and vegetable stalls. None of them had figs, and no one's ginger looked any fresher than what we already had. We kept following my mom and Luz. My mom was kind of tall, plus she had her hair tied up in a colorful scarf. She was easy to spot.

You know who else was easy to spot? Sandy.

Sandy-brown hair. Perfect beach waves that looked like they were literally made from the ocean breeze gently finger-combing her hair. A laugh that carried across the market even though it was filled with people. It was hard to miss her. That part I was used to. What I wasn't used to was my dad's new wife standing next to my mother, and my mother seeming cool with it. No—more than cool with it. Happy about it? I could see them being cool eventually. My mom was basically cool with everyone. But two weeks after the wedding? No. Too soon.

Then Sandy put her hand on my mom's shoulder, and I closed the distance between us in what felt like two steps. Sandy looked surprised to see me come out of nowhere, but no way was I letting Sandy put a hand on my mom. I'd bob and weave between them all day if I had to.

"Hasani!" Sandy smiled. "Your mom was just introducing me to your bestie. I mean, I saw her at the wedding, of course, but everything was so busy busy busy that I don't think we were properly introduced."

Sandy put a hand on Luz's shoulder and I cringed.

Suddenly, I was regretting not taking a closer look at Sandy's spellbook. She said her thing was "freedom," but who knows how she got there. She wasn't good enough to get into Belles

Demoiselles, but that did not mean she wasn't using influence. And what's the easiest way to influence someone? Touch. I should know. I probably did it a million times before I realized what was happening. My mom was only just recovering, just really seeming like herself again. Sandy could try that on me if she wanted to. I'm a witch. Her influence wouldn't get to me. But being a kismet didn't make my mother immune, which meant Luz definitely wasn't. I needed to keep Sandy off them both.

"Sandy!" I said, not even trying to match Sandy's enthusiasm. I mean, who could? "What are you doing here?"

I threw on a smile. I didn't want Sandy influencing my mom or Luz, but I didn't want to be rude.

"Your mom invited me!" Sandy grinned. "Isn't that great? I texted, but you must not have seen it."

I cringed a little inside. She must have seen I left her on read.

"Your mom was telling me about her tea business, and I got all excited about it. I mean, the city has tons of coffee shops, but it is DYING for a good tea shop, you know? I was telling your mom that I have connections with all kinds of markets around the city, and the next thing you know: boom! Here we are! Besides, I figured it would give us a chance to talk. I heard the school might stretch out your summer vacation. That's awesome, right? It'll give us time to do the Sunny Summer Split. Your dad is so excited."

I looked at my mom. She was giving the guilty-as-charged-but-we'll-talk-about-it-later-Hasani smile, nodding and agreeing with Sandy like they went to school together or something.

I could not.

Yes, that is a whole sentence.

I. Could. Not.

Unfortunately, Sandy always could. And with Sandy, that meant doing the most.

"Oh! You brought all of your friends. Hi! I'm Sandy. I recognize you from the wedding, but you might not recognize me without the white dress. I'm Hasani's stepm—"

"Dad's wife," I jumped in. It was instinct. I think my body knew that if I heard Sandy call herself anything that included "mom," "mum," "mother," or anything like it, I might have literally crawled out of my skin right then and there.

"Right," Sandy said, putting a clunky amount of charm into her smile. I mean, I couldn't see Sandy's magic or anything, but I didn't need to. It was obvious. "Well, no need to get bogged down in the particulars. Are you ready to check out the possibilities? This market only has tables available right now. I mean, they're not available-available, but they can come available if you're interested. And if none of these work, we can always start with the Tuesday market on Broadway and work our way up . . ."

Honestly, I kind of zoned out. I was too busy watching Sandy's hands and making sure she didn't lay them on my mom. At one point, it looked like Sandy was about to link their arms, and Dee literally put a hand on my elbow to stop me from running up on them. My mom did look happy, but honestly, that didn't mean anything. She looked happy before and she wasn't.

"They all right," Dee said.

"You all right?" Luz asked.

There was no point lying. She could see it on my face.

"Sandy," I said. "It's like, she just keeps trying to worm her way in. It's annoying."

Luz put her arm around my elbow. I flinched. Not because of Luz, because of me. For a millisecond, I could feel my magic moving to influence her. Luz. My friend. My best friend in the world. I went to pull away the moment I felt it, but before I did I remembered who I was. Being a wildseed didn't mean I was wild. It was my magic. Mine. I was in control. As quickly as it came, any little thought I had about influencing Luz, even just to undo any damage Sandy might have done, melted away. Charm, not magic.

I locked my arm in tight with Luz's and tried to give her a reassuring look. She smiled.

"Well, she won't worm her way into my heart. Not all of us fall

for Sandy's charms," she said, dramatically flipping her hair over her shoulder. She was trying to make me laugh. It worked.

"It's fine," I said. "My mom asked her to come. And I guess she's just trying to help."

"Well, let her. You know how hard it is to get a spot in here?"

I shook my head.

"Hard. Really hard. If Sandyandfree83 wants to use her connects to help your mom, just let it happen. You can hate on her afterward."

"I'm not hating on her!"

Luz cocked her head to the side.

"Okay. Maybe I'm hating on her. A little. Okay, never mind. You're right. If Sandy wants to help, she can help." And I'll keep an eye on her, but cool.

"I know I'm right," Luz said. "I'm always right. Just kidding. I'm right like ninety-nine-point-nine percent of the time. Nobody's perfect."

We both laughed, then started winding our way through table after table of everything from vegetables and feather boas to porcelain masks and potholders until something at one of the weirder tables caught Luz's eye.

I was mostly keeping an eye on my mom and Sandy, so I didn't see the table as much as I smelled the herbs and incense wafting up from it. The table was covered in tiny candles and bundles and jars and alligator heads in a bunch of different sizes, but Luz was looking at the silver.

"What's with y'all and the jewelry today?" I said. Then I realized what she was looking at: a silver fleur-de-lis charm that could easily have come from Belles Demoiselles. Honestly, I wasn't sure it *wasn't* from Belles Demoiselles.

"How much?" Luz asked.

The woman behind the table was giving off faking-the-funk-for-tourists Marie Laveau vibes. I mean, only the cheesiest of tourist baiters would fake being a superfamous, superdead voodoo priestess from the 1800s. Fake Marie Laveau looked from me to Luz slowly, like she was looking at us through a crystal ball, and when she talked, her voice was all high priestess. Definitely an act.

"The silver on that piece is infused with particles of power. Whoever is wearing it will always be grounded in their own strength."

"How much?" Luz repeated. This was not her first time at the French Market.

"Thirteen hundred dollars."

"Thirteen hundred dollars? For silver?" I asked.

Luz shook her head. "I don't need that much strength. I'll become one of the charmed girls another day. Let's go," she said, starting to walk away without even checking to see if I followed.

"Hasani," the woman said.

I froze for a second, trying to remember whether or not Luz had said my name.

"Here."

The woman laid a card on the table. It didn't look anything like the business cards Miss Lafleur had given us earlier, but I knew they were the same. This woman's card was carved into a thin piece of stained, polished wood. What it and Miss Lafleur's card had in common was that most of what was carved into the wood wasn't legible. Besides the MARIE carved into one corner, the rest was a mass of words or pictures or letters that weren't quite any of those things.

"Come to the Friday Market," she said. "My other stall is for people like you."

"People like me?"

She glanced at my fleur-de-lis. "Charming, talented people who would rather not spend . . . money. Scan it," she said, looking down at the wooden card.

I swear I'm not stupid enough to follow the directions of a random stranger, but I was stupid enough to take a picture. I thought I'd show the picture to Dee or Angelique. Maybe even Miss Lafleur if I could find her again. But of course the picture was not just a picture. I mean, it was for like half a second, but then my phone got taken over by witches. Again.

I promise you that every time your phone turns on you it is as surprising as the first time. First, the camera flipped from looking at the card to looking at my face. Then the phone took a picture of me. Up the nose. With flash. It could not have been flattering. I blinked, my brain not quite knowing what to do. My thumbs, on the other hand, went straight for the camera roll. The picture I took wasn't there. Neither was the up-the-nose picture of me. My thumb tapped the home button, and there it was. A new app blinking—3Thirteen.

I looked up at the woman, her yellow hair wrap and burnt-orange shawl rustling in the wind. Trust me, it was too hot for all that, even with the breeze from the river, but there's a painting of Marie Laveau where she's wearing an outfit exactly like that. I peeped the game. In the French Market with all the tourists, it was probably even working.

"Marie" smiled at me. "You're new," she said. It wasn't a question. "I'll expand your invitation. It's probably best you don't come alone. Bring a friend. Someone less green. And try not to be overwhelmed. None of the deals are ever as good as people say they are."

I nodded and walked away. The whole thing was so weird that my brain felt surrounded by a fog. I couldn't help thinking about the last time witches took over my phone. It was my invitation to Belles Demoiselles. Everything went so fast that it was basically only two

feet short of traumatic. I had no idea what I was doing, and it felt like it was all about to go that way again. Then my brain did me a favor and put two and two together. First of all, no one could make me click on an app on my phone. I could leave that thing there for- ever. The blinking might be hard to ignore, but I'd get used to it. And there was an upside. At least I'd figured out how to get in touch with Miss Lafleur.

Miss Lafleur had given all three of us business cards, but of the three, I was pretty sure only mine would work. To be fair, Angelique tried the number on her card, and Dee probably never would. Mine was the only one left.

The problem was that I had to sit through a whole morning of color schemes and test shots and Sandy talking to some poor dude who was selling kites at a table in a spot with "good energy" like she wasn't plotting to have him kicked out as soon as my mom was ready to open her place. Very uncool. I mean, uncool in my mom's favor, but still uncool.

My phone buzzed. It was a text, not a channel notification, but I checked my page anyway. The eighth-grade orientation GRWM that I posted that morning had 319 comments. I'd deal with whatever people were in their feelings about when I got home, hopefully soon. But in the meantime, the text had bad news.

The assessment of our middle school campus is complete. Out of an abundance of caution, we will be delaying the start of school by two weeks. We recognize the hardship that this represents for many families. Virtual school options are being explored.

Virtual school?

No lockers? No hallways? No Mathletes? No way.

Sandy came rushing over. "Your mom just showed me the good news! You can do virtual school from anywhere. How about the beach? I have a great house in Gulf Shores. You, me, and your dad can—"

"It's hurricane season," I said. "What if we have to evacuate?"

"But hurricane season is all summer," Sandy said.

Sandy was right. I had been to the beach during hurricane season plenty of times. That was just the first thing that popped into my head.

I know Dee and Angelique were hype about whatever they found in Sandy's spellbook, but if people were talking virtual school, things were truly getting out of hand. Whatever little make-people-love-me spells Sandy had come up with were not going to cut it. We needed real help.

Maybe I'd met fake Marie Laveau at exactly the right time.

CHAPTER THIRTEEN

UP AND UP

I texted Angelique.

> I know where to get the ingredients. Need an hour without Luz.

> On it.

Angelique didn't even have to make up a reason to hang out. Annie gave us one. The minute we had all buckled back into my mom's car with go-bags of beignets, all four of us got a video invite. Dee couldn't open the link on her un-smartphone, but Luz played hers for everybody.

It was, hands down, the most adorable six seconds of video I had seen in a long time, and this from a person obsessed with cat videos—specifically the "If I fits, I sits" ones. I did not think that it could get any cuter than a full-grown cat voluntarily curling up inside a pickle jar, but I was wrong.

First Annie shoulder-danced, bouncing the words "I bopped" around the screen.

Then there were clips of me, Angelique, and Luz synced to the new music, dancing with the phrase "You bopped." Then all of us were together, every foot stomp and elbow pop throwing out a new letter to spell "We bopped." Fade to black, then "WeBop?" popped up like it had just burst out of a bubble. It could have been a commercial. It was that good.

"Aw!" Luz said. "Annie wants us to come over this afternoon. Is everybody in?"

"I gotta make groceries," Dee said.

Groceries? Ah. *Ingredients.*

"I'll go," Angelique said, genuinely sounding excited. "It should be fun! We can take my car so we don't tire out Lucy." After a trip to the French Market, my mom's electric car definitely needed time to recharge.

"You coming, Hasani?" Luz asked.

"I need to respond to comments," I said.

"Sad face!" Luz shouted from the back seat.

"Sad face is right," my mom added. "Her last video has more than a thousand comments on it. That's too much for one person."

"I keep telling her that," Dee mumbled.

Small car. I heard it.

"It's not that bad," I said, opening the app on my phone. I thought I was going to show my mom that it was maybe eight hundred, max, but when I opened the app, the comment count on that eye shadow video was just over a thousand—1,011 to be exact.

"Mom, are you checking my YouTube channel? On an electronic device? On the Internet?"

My mom got the joke. I don't know if anybody else in the car did, but my mom burst out laughing.

"Yes, Hasani. I am a member of the twenty-first century. I made a profile and everything."

My mom was legit beaming. It was very cute. And maybe I should have been a little annoyed that she was maybe stacking data to try to force me to get a personal assistant, but mostly it just made me want to hug her. She was trying. I mean, I know I'm her kid and everything, but it still felt good. And from the look of my mom's smile, she hadn't seen any of the comments attacking me. Hopefully I could keep it that way.

"Fine," Luz said. "Well, until Hasani stops living in denial about the fact that she is a big-time YouTuber and obviously needs to hire a team, Angelique and I will have fun without her."

Luz stuck out her tongue. She was mostly kidding, but for real, I was glad they were going to have fun without me. Annie needed all the friends she could get.

It took some doing, but Ms. Nancy picked up Angelique and Luz, and my mom eventually decided to drop me and Dee off at our house while she picked up groceries and charged the car at Whole Foods.

"So, what's this hot tip you got about ingredients?" Dee asked when we finally got to my room.

"The Marie Laveau–looking lady at the French Market said we should go to the Friday Market."

"It's Tuesday."

"I know. I think that's the name of it." At least I hoped it was just the name of it. Friday was a long way away.

"All right. Lead the way."

I tapped the blinking app on my phone.

"Guest access activated," I read out loud to Dee. "Time to expiration, one hour. Would you like directions? Voice or visual."

"Visual," Dee said, then she looked at me sheepishly. "My bad. I should have asked which one you wanted. I just hate when they say the directions out loud."

I would have said voice, but cool. It pulled up a map with a route marked from my house to someplace near Carrollton and Claiborne.

"I know where that is," Dee said. "It's by a convenience store."

"Is it as far as it looks?" I asked.

"We'll make it," Dee laughed.

We started walking. It was hot, so when there wasn't enough shade on one side of the street, we crossed to the other. Mostly we were quiet, so I pulled out my phone and kept going through the comment section as we walked. If my mom was keeping tabs on me, I needed to check them first.

"If we get the ingredients, I'll do the spell," Dee said.

I looked up. "I thought we were all supposed to do it," I said.

"Nah. Technically, since it's your spellbook, you should be the one doing it. And since Sandy gave you the spell, you should be asking her to help you. But I'm guessing you don't want to do either of those things."

"What are you talking about? I don't want some creeper stoppering our magic for fun. Whatever that thing is at school, we have to fix it."

"Magic is really freaking you out, right? If I was as strong as you, I'd probably be scared, too. It's all right. I got you. I'll do it. Or here's a thought: We don't have to do it at all."

"Huh?"

"We don't have to do the spell. I'm just saying, it's your spellbook, so if you want to back out because you're scared, say so. I'll tell Angelique we don't want to do it and that'll be that."

I opened my mouth to argue, but I couldn't.

"How did you know?"

Dee shrugged. "You don't want the bitbot. You don't want us doing magic at school. You look like you're afraid for anybody to touch your mom, including you, and as far as your best friend is concerned, magic doesn't exist. Sounds pretty scared to me. Not that I blame you. If I got as much power as you did all of a sudden, I'd be scared, too."

"I am scared," I said, "but this spell is the only choice we have left, right? Freedom spell or bust?"

"Nah. There's other things we can do."

"Like what?"

"We can just let whatever happens happen. So what if school doesn't start on time? So what if Angelique has to go back to private school? So what if some witch stops us from doing magic at River-bend Middle? I mean, isn't that what you wanted in the first place?"

Dee was right, but there was one thing she didn't have on her list. And, honestly, until that very moment I didn't realize it was on mine, either. The comment section. I pulled up the comments on the GRWM and showed them to Dee. I didn't just show her screenshots of the worst ones. I just scrolled and let her see them as they were.

Fake.

Sellout.

Stuck up.

"Somebody even accused me of faking the mess in my room. I'm a messy person! The mess is real, y'all! These are the same jeans I wore yesterday!"

"It's really bothering you, huh?"

I nodded.

"I'm proud of you, bruh."

"Uh . . . why?"

"I thought for sure you were gon' say something about getting rid of LaToya, but look at you trying to do personal growth. I thought you were on personal suffering. But personal growth? That's some real witch stuff right there."

"I was never trying to make myself suffer."

Dee raised her eyebrows at me.

"I wasn't! What I did to my mom and Annie was awful. I'm just trying to remember the feeling. Isn't that the whole point of feeling bad when you hurt people? To stop you from hurting people again?"

"Yeah, but once you learn the lesson, you think you're just supposed to suffer forever?"

"No. Maybe? I don't know. Is that bad? I just don't want my mom to worry about me. She's been through enough. The comments aren't that bad, right? I can handle them."

"They're bad enough for you to not tell your mama," Dee said. True dat. "You keep acting like everybody else's struggles are real, Hasani, but your struggles are real, too."

"I'm a witch. I should be tougher. I shouldn't care, but I do, even though I really want to just laugh it off and be carefree." Like Sandy. "That's why I'm thinking we could test it on me."

Dee gave me a look.

"What? It can't be any worse than the chevelure potion."

"You did that one with the person who gave you the spell. You sure you don't want to call Sandy?"

"Sandy couldn't even get into Belles Demoiselles. How strong could one of her spells be?"

"Wait," Dee said. "Let me get this straight. You'd use a potion—a freedom potion—to stop those comments, but not a bitbot? Bruh, a bitbot is way less invasive."

I shook my head. "I don't want the comments to stop," I said. "Those comments are nothing compared to what people were saying to Annie. I want to not care. I want to be free."

Sure enough, the map led us to a Circle K. If Dee hadn't been there I never would have found it. I would have gone inside and found ICEEs and CheeWees and absolutely no fresh food of any kind, let alone ginger and figs, and gone home.

"Inside is too obvious," she muttered to herself. Then she made a beeline for an old photo booth outside the store. The kind that prints paper pictures for you while you wait. She pushed back the curtain and revealed . . . an old photo booth that smelled even dirtier than it looked.

Dee slid the curtain closed again.

"Thank goodness," I said. "I did not want to go in there."

"Nah, that's it," Dee said. "It's not really dirty. You were the one invited, so you have to go first."

I slid the curtain open again. "Still looks gross."

"Put your face in."

Great.

I leaned forward just a little. There was a flash, a camera click, and everything changed.

"Told you," Dee said. "Hurry up. The app said we only have an hour."

I'd obviously seen plenty of magic at that point, but the sudden change in the booth was hard to believe. The seat was clean and smooth, and while not brand new–looking, at least without any suggestion of already-chewed gum. Dee slid in next to me, closed the curtain, and a timer appeared on the screen in front of us.

Seventeen minutes, eight seconds. Seven seconds. Six seconds.

"Wait. I thought the app said we had an hour?"

"The hour must have included walking over here. I guess we should have walked faster. My bad."

I waved Dee off. We didn't have time to figure out the time.

"This is the Friday Market?" It was small. I expected . . . bigger.

"Nah. It's a vending machine. My cousin Dionne took me to one in Baton Rouge one time."

"What happened?"

"She got in trouble."

The screen roared to life with a prerecorded message.

"You have been invited to a limited preview with limitless possibilities," a pixel guy said. "No member detected. Do you wish to link one now?"

"What's a member?"

"Witch stores are like Costco. Who invited you?"

"Fake Marie Laveau?"

"Member not found. Do wish to link a member now?"

"If it's like Costco, we need an adult. What about your mom?" I said.

Dee looked at me like I was out of my mind. "Ha, ha. No."

I shrugged.

"What about Sandy?"

"Ha, ha. No."

Dee shrugged.

"Do you wish to proceed as a guest?"

"Yes," we both said. That countdown clock really makes you feel like you need to move fast, even when you don't know what you're moving to.

"Nonmember guests have limited access. Do you wish to continue your preview?"

"Yes."

"Please make your selection."

"How?" I asked.

The pixel person, who I desperately wanted to call Steve, answered me. Of course he did. "Guests can make selections by entering voice commands or the vendor or item ID."

"Fresh figs, fresh ginger, and picture jasper," Dee said.

Pixel Steve dimmed the lights until it was pitch-black in the booth. I could feel Dee next to me, but I couldn't see her at all. Then the pixel person was replaced by a million tiny ones.

"One thousand eighty-three results found. Display all?" Okay. Maybe a thousand. "Warning, displaying all will exceed allotted time."

Luckily, Dee seemed to know what she was doing.

"Local delivery," she said.

"Seventeen results found. Display all?"

The thousand tiny pixels grew into a bunch of videos. It was hard to make out what was happening, but at least I could tell they were people.

"Instant local delivery," Dee added.

"Four results found. Display all?"

"Yes."

Four of the videos stretched out to fill a normal four-screen split. In one, a woman was hustling up to the screen, holding up a potted fig tree a little smaller than the one my mom and I had by our back steps. The real difference was that her potted fig tree was full of perfectly ripe figs.

"Gw'on. Taste it." The lady held the pot toward me.

I was being goofy when I reached out to grab one. Like hardy-har-har, look at me picking a fig through a screen. The way I hollered when I actually did it, though? Even I was laughing at me. I popped it into my mouth. It smelled so good on the way in that I could basically already taste it, but the flavor was gone by the time I closed my mouth. Actually, the whole fig was gone. It reminded me of drinking LaCroix.

"Ghost food?" I asked.

"It's a simulator. It just gives you an idea. You can't really eat it."

Okay, duh. But I didn't know.

"Are those figs potion-grade?" Dee asked.

The lady looked sheepish. Dee shook her head and added a new search parameter before the lady could launch into a spiel about why her figs would work anyway.

"Potion-grade," Dee said, and the lady with the potted fig tree disappeared.

Unfortunately, so did the vendor with the dried figs and both people holding up giant stalks of ginger with the roots still attached.

"Aw. I wanted to taste the dried ones." Kind of taste the dried ones? Smell the dried ones? Whatever. I liked dried figs, even the LaCroix essence of dried figs.

"No point in buying what we don't need."

"Potion-grade fresh ginger and potion-grade fresh figs. Same-day local delivery."

Our options went back up to twelve, and Dee and I spent the next few minutes virtually smelling, squeezing, and sort of tasting figs and ginger until we found one of each that Dee thought would work. The picture jasper was easy. Dee pointed to a teardrop-shaped one that kind of reminded me of the pyramid at Giza.

"Why'd you pick that one?"

"It's pretty," Dee said, like there couldn't be any other reason. "Add to cart."

"Nonmembers are limited to instant local delivery. Do you wish to add a member?"

"Dag," Dee said.

"Wait. That's a bad thing? Don't we want them now?"

"Well, it wouldn't be bad if the ingredients we picked were available for instant delivery, but the stuff we picked is same-day."

"It's supposed to be ready in thirty minutes!"

"Yeah," Dee said. "And apparently that's not instant."

Dee shook her head, but I wasn't defeated. Not yet.

"Fake Marie Laveau," I said. "She can be our member."

I pulled my phone out of my pocket thinking maybe fake Marie Laveau's real name was on her card somewhere. But you know what was on my phone? Miss Lafleur's business card. It was wedged just along the edge where the phone case touches the phone screen, and I wasn't fast enough to pull it off before . . .

"Member recognized. Please hold while we contact your prospective member connection for verification."

CHAPTER FOURTEEN

GHOSTS AND MACHINES

"Uh . . . that's not good," Dee said.

"Undo. Stop. Decline!" I shouted at the screen.

"Transaction declined. Order canceled. Goodbye."

Whew.

"Wait. No. Order canceled? Did that thing just say 'order canceled'?"

"Yep," Dee said.

This was not good. "So we're not even getting the ingredients?! Do you think they called Miss Lafleur? Should I try to call her? I should try to call her, right? And explain?"

"Yeah. Call her." Dee's face looked as bad as my nerves felt.

"Oh, man! Dee! What if she tells your mom?"

"Aw! I did not think of that."

"My bad. I'm gonna call Miss Lafleur. I'm gonna call her right now."

At least I was gonna try. Thanks to fake Marie Laveau and this magic vending machine, I was pretty sure I knew how.

The card should have been wrinkled or dented or something, but it was just as crisp and beautiful as when Miss Lafleur handed it to me. I ignored the 3Thirteen icon still blinking on my phone's home screen and tapped the camera app. For a second, Miss Lafleur's card looked the same on the phone screen as it did in my hand, but before I had a chance to do anything but look, the phone was doing its own thing. The screen went dark, then a light pulsed along the edge of the screen. First it just appeared at the top, bottom, left, and right, like my phone was turning into a compass. But then the light started sliding around the edge, getting brighter and going faster until it looked like the whole perimeter of my phone was lit up. It was making my eyes hurt. I don't know why I didn't look away. I guess because I didn't think of it, but the second I did, it stopped, the screen went black again, and an electronic voice said, "Please state your name."

I leaned in. "Hasani Marie Schexnayder-Jones."

Another flash. Again, right up the nose.

"Voice key accepted. Your call is being connected."

Okay. I know I'm the one who pulled out the card and tried to scan it and everything, but the whole thing was going so fast I didn't have time to get my mind right before Miss Lafleur answered the phone.

"Hello, dear." Miss Lafleur's voice rang out like she was standing right next to me. "I'm so glad you called. What's this about trying to use my credit at a vending machine?"

Dee winced. Apparently just hearing us talk was stressing Dee out.

"Wait," I said. "How do I turn off speakerphone?"

There wasn't a keypad or anything. My screen was just black.

"Put the phone to your ear, dear," Miss Lafleur said.

Why didn't I think of that?

It worked. "Miss Lafleur?" I said.

"Yes. I can hear you just fine. I was hoping you'd call because you were ready to extend your studies, but do you need credit, dear? Are you in trouble?"

I blinked. I was not ready for that one.

"I apologize," I said.

Never say you're sorry. You're not sorry. But if you have offended or possibly caused an inconvenience, you may, at your discretion, apologize.

Dag. That Belles Demoiselles training popped up out of the blue sometimes.

"I didn't mean to scare you. The vending machine scanned your card by accident."

"No need to apologize. I must admit that I am disappointed to have been a butt dial, but I'm even happier to know you're safe. Enjoy the rest of your summer."

Disappointed? "Wait!" I said. "You really meant for me to call you about an apprenticeship? When you gave cards to all three of us, I thought you were just covering for us in front of Ms. Reid. Thanks for that, by the way."

"I would not have reached out if I hadn't meant it sincerely, and you will note, yours is the only card that works. You are an extraordinary talent, Hasani. It would be a shame to see it wasted."

Talent? Wasted? I was more confused than ever.

"Your school won't be back in session for a couple of weeks. Why don't I set up a meeting with your mother, and we can see how she feels about your spending a week or so in Vacherie. Your mother is welcome, of course. The guesthouse is open year-round."

"Miss Lafleur?" I could barely get a word in. "Just to be clear, are we talking about witch tutoring or witch grad school? I mean, are you inviting me or telling me?"

"Oh, no. I'm not saying you have to come back. As always, that choice is up to you. I am inviting you to expand your learning in ways we could never do here in the city. Lynx quite enjoys the occasional trip to the city, but there are so many other creatures who would never make the trip. However, I must admit that now I am the one who is confused. When I saw you at Riverbend Middle, I thought for certain you had been signaling me with this burst of unseasonal termite activity and that I was the one who should be apologizing because at the end of the session I didn't give you another way to get in contact with me."

"The termite thing wasn't me."

I could practically feel Miss Lafleur's disappointment. I mean, you'd think attracting millions of termites to possibly destroy a historic building and delay the start of school, thereby putting hundreds of kids' educational futures at risk, would be a bad thing. But Miss Lafleur was acting like whoever did this had sent up a clever Bat-Signal.

"It was LaToya," I said.

Miss Lafleur sat silent. Too silent.

"Allegedly," I added. "I don't know for sure. But yeah. If it's about the termites, you probably want LaToya, not me. Allegedly."

"I was offering you an apprenticeship, but I'm afraid I have to stop for a moment to consider the seriousness of what you just said."

"It's all right. You can take it back. I get it."

"I'm not considering whether or not you're talented enough. That matter of fact is not in question. What I need to think more carefully about is taking on an apprentice who seems so casual about engaging in a petty witch war."

Miss Lafleur insisted on coming to my house. The first time that happened, I was asleep when she got there. By the time I woke up, she and my mom were already on their second cup of tea. This time I greeted her at the door. Dee had gone back to her dad's house. She did not want to see Miss Lafleur after our vending machine debacle, but even if I was going to get in trouble, I was looking forward to another glimpse of Lynx. No such luck. Miss Lafleur came in alone, and as soon as she sat down, my mom sent me to get the tea.

I came back with three cups and a teapot balanced perfectly on a tray. I was in the process of elegantly placing it on the coffee table when Miss Lafleur hit me with this:

"Your mother tells me you're afraid to use your magic."

Dag. Why was everybody on this today? Was I wearing a sign? I promise you that if the spirit of Miss LaRose were not right next to me daring me to so much as rattle a cup, I would have dropped the whole thing.

My mom sat there, looking sheepish and busted. She probably didn't expect Miss Lafleur to just come right out and say it, but now that she had, I couldn't ignore it.

164

"It's not that I'm afraid," I said, carefully offering Miss Lafleur a cup. She took it. My mom had to reach up and get hers off the tray. "It's that it isn't necessary. Charm, not magic, right?"

I threw a look in my mother's direction.

"Yes, of course. But in the proper circumstances, witches should not be afraid of their power."

"In the proper circumstances," I repeated. That wasn't really an answer, but she took it, thank goodness.

"Hasani, I was telling your mother that you and I spoke briefly. I'd like you to tell us both what is happening, but before you do, I strongly caution you against naming names, particularly since it seems that you may be making some substantial allegations against a person who quite possibly has already spent time in your home. You're a belle demoiselle and therefore of age and free to do as you choose. However, being free to do as one chooses is also being free to accept the consequences of one's choices."

I think it was obvious to both me and my mom that Miss Lafleur was looking at both of us, but she was talking to me.

I get it. Witches don't out other witches, and belles demoiselles especially don't out other belles demoiselles. But once you earn your charm, there's supposedly only one rule: Don't do anything that would reveal the existence of Belles Demoiselles. Nobody was stupid enough to do that. Even Dee didn't want to be deleted from the Internet, and Dee was barely even on the Internet. But LaToya was a different story. She may have been a belle demoiselle, but she was also a bully. A sneaky bully. The worst kind. And one thing I know for sure is that bullies only have as much power as you give them.

"Why does it matter if I say the person's name? My mom won't say anything," I said. "She's met a bunch of belles demoiselles. We've had a bunch of them over. She probably knows that L—"

Miss Lafleur held up her hand. I don't think it was magic, but I stopped talking instantly.

"Names have power, Hasani. For instance, if I slip these on"—Miss Lafleur reached into the canvas bag at her feet and pulled out a pair of rose-colored glasses—"I have no doubt that your home would be covered in the afterglow of magic. And see? It is."

She handed me the glasses. I had worn them once before, sitting in this exact room. Back then, the only thing that glowed was the video of me destroying the St. Claude Bridge with morning glories, and the poor rosemary plant I had accidentally corrupted with my signature flower. Now, most of the room at least glimmered.

"You're coming into yourself. It's only natural that you would fill and protect your home with magic. Most witches do. But the farther away one is from the wielding, the harder it is to distinguish one

person's magic from another's, even with a pair of these, hard as they are to come by."

Miss Lafleur pulled the glasses from my face and put them back in her bag.

"What does that have to do with saying . . . a person's name?"

"Well, if you've ever invited this person into your home, for example, and this person just happens to be a witch who is as destructive as you're implying, it's possible that person could have left something behind. Something woven into the magic that is already woven into your home. Something that might be triggered every time you mention their name."

My eyes were open so wide it felt like I couldn't blink.

"You think my house is booby-trapped?"

"Oh, yes. It's called name-dropping. It's actually very common, and a day or two after the fact, it would be nearly impossible to trace. Once set, the name-dropper only needs to drink a very simple potion to know if someone has talked about them near the trap and to hear exactly what was said, particularly if it was negative. At that point, the name-dropper usually feels justified wreaking whatever havoc they like in retaliation. The whole thing can be very messy. Which is why I would urge you, out of an abundance of caution, to not mention any names."

Was it just me or did people keep saying that? I'd never heard "abundance" and "caution" put together before that day, but this was the second time today.

"So, what do I do about it? What can I do to get the name-dropping magic out of my house? Is there a spell or something?"

"We're acting in an abundance of caution. There may not be any traps here at all. But even if there were, Hasani, I've seen your magic firsthand. Trust me. You don't need to squeeze it. Spells are fine for some, but for a belle demoiselle, especially one as talented as you are, they're . . ."

"Distasteful?" That sounded like a good Belles Demoiselles word.

"Unnecessary."

"What if the other person is using them?"

Miss Lafleur sighed. "Some swear by spells to free up a space— so-called freedom spells—but personally I don't think they're worth the cost. An ounce of prevention is worth a pound of cure. It's much better to get in the habit of caution than to worry about how to clean things up. Once started, these witch wars have been known to go on for centuries, and every documented case has started with a grievance just as small as this. What's the worst thing that happens? Your first day of school is delayed a bit? I would have thought that you would be excited about a delay to the start of school. What young person doesn't love a little more vacation?"

This young person.

"I'm just—I'm just ready to go back. What can I do to stop . . . 'this person' from ruining my school?"

"You know," Miss Lafleur said, "perhaps an apprenticeship is exactly what you need. In fact, we could start right now. Are you interested?"

CHAPTER FIFTEEN

PROMISES AND

POSSIBILITIES

Y'all, Miss Lafleur said the magic word: "unicorns."

She said a lot of stuff about personal energy and focal points and spending time in Vacherie, too, but the part that stuck was the unicorns. After she said that, my eyebrows spoke for themselves.

Miss Lafleur laughed. "Yes, there is a full blessing of unicorns living on the Belles Demoiselles grounds. I do encourage them toward the stables or the swamp while we have guests, but most of the time they are able to roam free and graze as they please."

Miss Lafleur would have had me right there if I hadn't had my phone in my hand.

Luz was calling me. I ignored it at first, thinking I'd call her back as soon as Miss Lafleur left. But then she called again, and then again.

"I apologize," I said, holding up my phone. "I have to take this. It must be an emergency."

I ran into my room in time to pick up on the third ring.

"Hasani? Check Annie's WeBop."

The way Luz said my name when I answered, I legit thought she was dying. Even when she said "WeBop," I was half expecting to find a severed head. Instead, the first video in my feed was the one Dee recorded of me, Annie, Angelique, and Luz. I'm no expert on WeBop stats. (I'm mainly there for the CatBops.) But the group video we did was looking pretty good. Only day later and it already had 300 slaps and more than 3,000 views.

For a second I panicked.

I was really, really careful not to let any of my magic drip into Annie's video. But had I missed something? Was my fleur-de-lis not working right? The last time that happened, I basically almost ruined Annie's life. Maybe it was all good right now and just getting her a bunch of likes, but maybe it had gone bad somewhere else.

My hands were shaking as I tapped the comments and scrolled through, scanning for awful, hateful words to jump out at me. None did. There was nothing there. All of them were fine. Mostly people from school saying welcome back and stuff. My head was saying *calm down*, but for whatever reason, my heart kept beating like Coach was making us run laps.

"Luz, you scared me, calling back to back like that," I said. "But yeah. The video we did with Annie has so many views. I'm glad she posted it. We should make another one with her. Maybe she'll go viral."

Annie's house. Annie's phone. As long as I didn't touch anything, it was probably safe enough. Then we'd know for sure that the views were all Annie's. I owed Annie at least that much.

"I don't think she needs us," Luz said.

I could hear Angelique in the background. "Did she check Annie's WeBop page?"

"Yeah. I checked it. It's cool, but I have to go. One of the teachers from summer camp is here. She's offering me an internship."

There was a pause.

"If you're cool, I'm cool," Luz said.

I expected more hype in Luz's voice about my internship, but I kind of got it. An internship would just be another thing on my list stopping me from hanging out.

"It's cool," I said.

"It's whatever," Luz said. "Catch you later."

"It's whatever" is definitely not as good as "It's cool," but Luz would understand, especially if I started talking about how good it would look on college applications. We were years away from college, but Luz was all about looking good on college applications.

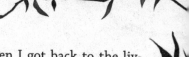

"Everything okay?" my mom asked when I got back to the living room.

"It's fine," I said. "Luz was excited about the views on a WeBop video we were in. It might go viral. Charm," I added for Miss Lafleur. "Only a little. No magic."

Miss Lafleur nodded. "Hasani is a natural influencer. I don't know how much she's told you about her work at Belles Demoiselles, but it was quite extraordinary, particularly for a green witch."

Miss Lafleur and my mom both looked at me to see if it was okay for Miss Lafleur to keep going. I shrugged. I didn't know what Miss Lafleur was going to say, but I wanted to find out. I mean, was this going to be like the time in second grade when Ms. Fitzmorris spent the entire parent-teacher conference telling my mom how much I talked out of turn even though I had straight A's on my report card?

I shouldn't have worried. Miss Lafleur bragged on me so hard, talking about how good I was with all the kittens and how unusual it was to have such a strong command of insect influence, especially since I had never seen anyone do it before, and how she had actually considered teaching me dissuasion, and even though she decided against it, she had literally never considered teaching that to a student before in her entire career. Throw in the bats and butterflies and the heart swans, and by the end,

Miss Lafleur made me sound like some kind of animal guru—but cuter. Not one mention of a petty witch war or accidentally using Miss Lafleur to vouch for me at a witch vending machine. It was literally all good. I was blushing so bad by the time she stopped talking that I could feel my cheeks burning. Part of me wanted to run and check the mirror. Brown girls don't blush enough for it to show that often, and it seemed a shame to miss the chance to see where my blush should naturally fall. But that would have been weird, and the whole thing was already weird, so . . . I just let it be.

My mom's leg was bouncing the way it does when she's trying not to embarrass me by jumping up and hugging me the way she did when I was four. I went over and hugged her instead. That's when the happy tears started flowing. I hadn't influenced her, either. Every time we hugged now, I had to be so careful not to.

"I'm so proud of you, Hasani," my mom said. "I told you you were going to be a good witch."

She did. I don't know why she did, but she did. I didn't say anything, though. I just nodded.

"As talented as you are, Hasani, you yourself must be sure that you are quite ready for the unicorns," Miss Lafleur said. "Unicorns require peace and patience. You're so in demand from your friends and your YouTube channel and your lovely mother. Plus, school will

begin again soon." Not soon enough. "The commitment required for such high-level work may be too much right now on top of your other commitments. Perhaps we should slow down and wait for a more open, peaceful time."

That's when I got it. An open and peaceful time? That was basically the opposite of a petty witch war. Was Miss Lafleur saying she wouldn't teach me if I kept trying to stop LaToya?

"I'd love to work with you again, Miss Lafleur. There's a lot happening, and I could really use your guidance. It might help me . . . find more peace."

My mom gave me a weird look. I didn't blame her, but I couldn't think of a smoother way of working the word "peace" in so Miss Lafleur would know I knew what was up.

Miss Lafleur got my hint. I mean, that hint was big enough to trip over, but that's not the point. "I suppose we could hold off on a full apprenticeship and test the waters a bit here in town. With your mother's permission, of course."

My mom nodded.

Miss Lafleur's phone flipped open like Dee's, but on the inside it looked just like mine. She angled the bottom toward her mouth and said, "I offer the witch in question an unbound position of learning and apprenticeship from now until the end or three days from today's end, whichever is sooner."

"The end? Like, the end–the end?" Did Miss Lafleur think I might die before three days were over?

"It's just a precaution. Without that clause the connection would automatically pass to your nearest connection with or without their consent, and we wouldn't want that, would we?"

"I guess not," I said.

My phone chimed faintly. A thumbprint silhouetted by dragon-flies sat in the middle of the screen. I put my thumb on the drawing and the words *Please record your response* appeared with a countdown below it.

3 . . . 2 . . . 1

"I accept," I said.

There was a click. Miss Lafleur nodded as my phone screen went back to normal.

"Let's get to work."

CHAPTER SIXTEEN

TRAPS AND EXTENSIONS

"**S**ince you're a member of the team now, you should look the part. Here is an official Billiot's uniform," she said, beaming at me like she was handing me an Academy Award. "Get changed. I'll wait here for you."

I think Miss Lafleur was expecting me to just run and get changed in like five minutes. I almost did. Then I heard my mom and Miss Lafleur laughing and talking like they were besties and figured it wouldn't hurt to take my time. The little uniform shirt was cute enough to just throw on, but when I saw myself in the mirror, I thought about how much cuter it would be if I had time to do a full face of neutrals to play against the khaki, with a little butterfly over my right cheek for a pop of color. Actually, the more I thought about it, the more I was itching to record it, and the next thing I knew I was in front of my camera recording a tutorial. Maybe I'd even make it a series. Whimsical Work-Inspired Looks. I mean, most of my audience didn't have jobs or anything, but that's okay. And since so many people had big feelings about my eye shadow videos, I decided to give them an eye shadow video worth getting big mad about.

An hour later, I came out ready for work.

"Your kitten is coming, too, of course. Is he ready as well?"

She didn't need to tell me twice. I always wanted to bring Othello places with me. My mom had just said no so many times that I stopped asking. I ran to grab Othello and his carrier from my room.

When I came out with the kitten in one hand and his carrier in the other, the look on Miss Lafleur's face very clearly said she thought I was the weird one.

"A cage?" she asked. "What about his leash? Do you always keep him so restricted when you go out?"

"Othello's an indoor cat," I said.

The look on Miss Lafleur's face said she maybe didn't believe there was any such thing as an indoor cat, but she kept quiet about it and let me put Othello in his cat carrier instead. Apparently, leaving him at home was not an option.

"Are those rainbow eyebrows?" Miss Lafleur asked as we climbed into the Billiot's Pest Control truck. I don't know which one was more surprising for her: the eyebrows or the cat carrier.

"Full spectrum, but yes." I didn't ask if she liked it because it didn't matter. I did.

I touched the gold INTERN pin on my work shirt just as Othello started yowling to get out of his carrier.

"Is this internship public? I mean, can I talk about it?"

"You mean, can you post about it?"

I nodded.

Miss Lafleur laughed. "Yes, Hasani. As long as you can promise to refer to me as Amy Billiot."

"Oh! Is that your real name?" Most of the teachers at Belles Demoiselles used code names like in spy movies. The other ones all had color code names. LaRose, LeBrun, and Lavande were basically Miss Pink, Miss Brown, and Miss Lavender. Miss Lafleur would be Miss Flower.

"Heavens, no! You already know my real name. I've never seen the need to hide from my own kind. Amy Billiot is a business name. I intend to pass it on to the next owner one day."

"Like the Dread Pirate Roberts?" I asked, hoping Miss Lafleur had seen *The Princess Bride*.

She laughed. "Who knows? It may be you."

I didn't have the heart to tell Miss Lafleur that, no matter how cool she was or how much she taught me, there was no way I was going to be an exterminator when I grew up. So I smiled and changed the subject.

"What are we doing?" I asked.

"We are going to try to solve the problem at your school," Miss Lafleur said. "It appears that your school is sitting on top of an unusual sanlavi."

"A sawla-what?"

"A sanlavi. It's so obvious now that I've walked on campus. I don't know how I missed it. Well, I do know. The last time I was here was more than thirty years ago, and I was probably quite focused on getting to the market nearby. That was a long time ago, of course. Back in the nineties, before Internet delivery services were so efficient. Now I rarely need to step foot out of Vacherie, so I guess that's why I didn't notice it until it was right under my nose. That and the trees. Sanlavi are usually devoid of trees and other complex forms of life, so all the beautiful oak trees distracted me from the possibilities of the land beneath the building itself. This place was a courthouse once."

I nodded.

"Time was, witches sought out places like these to imprison other witches."

"What?"

"Oh, yes. But we've done away with such nonsense. Your school is perfectly safe, though it may feel like something of a prison for you and your friends."

Miss Lafleur chuckled.

It didn't sound like much of a joke to me.

"So it's a trap? A sanlavi is a trap?"

"A sanlavi is a kind of magical dead zone. So yes, it is a trap in a sense."

"I knew it!" I said. Or at least Angelique knew it. "We felt it when we were in the gym earlier. When we met your cat."

Miss Lafleur laughed. I love her laugh. "Lynx and I belong to each other. She's quite intrigued with you, though, I think. She says you have a good vibe."

"When we were in the gym, our magic was . . . trapped. We thought maybe somebody was stoppering it."

"Stoppering?" Miss Lafleur glanced over at me, still grinning. "I see you're picking up a thing or two from that coven of yours. That would be good if their information were correct."

"Somebody was trying to plug up our magic. I felt it," I said. "We all did."

Dag. Angelique and Dee were right. Petty was one thing, but coming from Miss Lafleur, this sanlavi business was sounding seriously above LaToya's pay grade. That didn't stop LaToya from being a grade-A pain, just not old enough to have been around when the courthouse was built hundreds of years ago.

"If you were attempting to use magic in the gym, you would have felt quite stopped up." Miss Lafleur put a little stress on "magic." Not hard, but enough for me to hear. Enough to remind me that what I'm supposed to be using is charm. "On top of a sanlavi, it is nearly impossible for one's magic to flow out. It continues to build inside—it's not stolen or depleted—but releases only happen rarely, and by luck. I thought we had documented all the sanlavi in the region, but I guess we just never looked here. It's unusual to find one so close to the river, especially that close to a bend in the river."

"So how does a witch make a sanlavi? Could someone have done it on purpose? Like, to stopper our magic?" And could it have been LaToya?

"Stoppering magic is a fearmonger's tale. Like telling children about the Rougaroux when you know full well there's been a lycanthropy outbreak. Children and adults alike do much better with real information. I'm not saying that stoppering magic is impossible. After all, magic is the art of the improbable. But what you're talking about is a witch influencing another witch, tapping into her fear and inadequacies so deeply that she's separated from her own life force. I've only ever met one witch powerful enough to do something like that, but I'm sure even that witch doesn't know how to do it on purpose. Quite mysterious. Sanlavi, on the other hand, are well-known, documented phenomena. Even if this one is a bit unusual, all the signs are there. Perhaps there was a sanlavi here before the courthouse was built. Witches slowly sapped it of its strength through use and abandoned it when it no longer suited their purposes. The area recovered. Trees grew. But unbeknownst to us, there was still a pocket of that lifeless magic that managed to seep out. Judging by the depth and height, it's been here at least thirty years. That's long before the incident at your orientation. The termites were just unfortunate enough to get trapped in it."

"Well, since magic is the art of the improbable, you're not saying it's impossible for someone to have made this sanlavi, you're just saying it's statistically unlikely."

"Ah! I forgot that I'm talking to a mathematician. What's the name of the club you were pretending to check on yesterday? The Mathelon?"

"The Mathletes," I said, trying to soothe Othello through the holes in the carrier.

"Well, Mathlete, do you know why witches flourish in hot climates?"

Topic jump! Besides, who was flourishing in hot climates? Not me. I hated the heat. But I played along.

"I don't know."

"Flowers," Miss Lafleur said. "Witches are everywhere, but we do best where things grow easily. Flowers are an excellent cover for the flowers of our magic, but they're also an excellent tell."

We rounded the bend where St. Charles Avenue turned into Carrollton. The bead trees in front of the school came into view.

Miss Lafleur pulled up right in front of the gates, then turned to look at me. "I see you're skeptical, so allow me to offer evidence. It would take a very experienced, very powerful witch to pull off that kind of magic without so much as a stray bud. If you didn't see your former friend's signature flower in the vicinity, chances are she was not responsible."

"She could have pulled them," I said.

Miss Lafleur pursed her lips for second, then shook her head and smiled. "Have it your way, Hasani. Have you ever used an extender?"

Miss Lafleur pulled out a stick that was somewhere between a pencil and a sonic screwdriver.

"Is that a magic wand?" I asked.

"Magic wands are like the Rougaroux—make-believe. There is no stick you can hold that would give you power you didn't have before. But there are ways to get around sanlavi, and an extender is one. Whoever *is* responsible for drawing the termites here probably used an extender, though they would have had to pour quite a bit of magic into it to pull that off. Foolish, but there are few other ways they could have used magic inside a sanlavi. We'll be more careful."

I couldn't exactly see what Miss Lafleur was doing, but after a minute I guessed what it was. She had woven a little tent of intentions around us in the truck. I couldn't see it—not like Angelique's intentions in her car—but I knew it was there, a web of safety surrounding us. I reached my hand out. It brushed against my fingertips. Delicate, invisible tassels on a velvet curtain, but mostly I could feel it when I breathed. Even Othello quieted down.

"The extender works like any charm if you imagine the tool as your fingertip. But careful. Only a drop or two. Once moved out of the body, this power will never return to you, so use only what you must."

She handed me the tool and then took out another one for herself. As soon as I touched the extender, magic rushed to the surface of my skin, pulsing in my stomach and toes. Through the holes in the carrier, Othello tried to rub his cheek against my hand. I unlatched his carrier and let him. It made it easier to let just the tiniest bit of magic flow into the extender, which, on second look, seemed more like an old-fashioned pen. I let my magic soak into the tip, like I was dipping the pen into an inkpot. The second it touched, my magic dove in, lighting the whole device from end to end, tiny morning glories floating through it like glitter in water.

"Cooool," I said.

Okay. Maybe not the most articulate thing I could have come up with, but that was the best I could do. I mean, how do you describe the feeling of seeing your own magic out in the open? Flowers and curtains and rainbows aren't the same. They're all things that happen because of magic. Even seeing your linked sister's magic isn't the same. It's something you can never really touch, like light on waves. My magic in the extender was different. It was like life in a tube. With sparkles.

Miss Lafleur smiled again. The mom smile. I liked that smile. "I'm glad you like it. People's magic appears in different ways, but the glass portion of this extender allows you to see exactly how much magic you've put in, how much magic you've used, and how much you have left."

I looked closer. What I thought were delicate gold decorations were more like the measuring lines on a graduated cylinder. I glanced over at Miss Lafleur's extender, hoping to catch a glimpse of her magic, but from where I sat it just looked like a navy-blue glitter pen.

"Sweet."

"And handy. Even inside a sanlavi, the magic you've stored in an extender is available for use. The extender is not alive, you see, so the sanlavi has no power over it."

"Wait a minute," I said, suddenly getting the picture. "Am I supposed to be drawing influence with this? By hand?"

"Yes!" Miss Lafleur said brightly. "We were preparing the property to let the problem naturally resolve, but that would take weeks. The influence that brought the termites here would wear off in a few days, but it's not their fault that the building they were drawn to is so old and tasty. By the time the magic wears off they might not want to leave. But since you're so determined to have school begin as soon as possible, new trails of influence are the next best thing. Something very similar to the heart swan shapes will do—with a few modifications."

I swallowed. The heart swan shapes were complicated. I thought I remembered them, but that nauseous feeling was creeping in.

"For a million termites?"

That sounded about as much fun as copying the dictionary.

"It's excellent practice." Great. "I'll show you my method, but then it's up to you. You won't be able to refill the extender on top of the sanlavi, but you can come back to the truck if you need to. The intentions I've woven in the truck stave off the effect of the sanlavi even if it suddenly begins to spread. I'm not saying it will. I'm just acting out of—"

"—an abundance of caution," I finished.

"Yes. Normally, trees mark the end of sanlavi, but this one seems to stretch all the way to the fence. I don't know if it will continue to spread, but the truck will be safe regardless."

"Miss Lafleur?" I said. My stomach was officially one giant knot. I wanted to say, "What if I can't?" but I couldn't even get that much out.

The nerves must have been painted right on my face, though, because Miss Lafleur patted my hand and said, "We'll cross that bridge when we come to it. If we come to it. Bring your kitten."

I nodded, held Othello close to me, and followed Miss Lafleur out of the truck, letting the invisible tassels of the intentions brush my face as I did. I think my body was trying to feel just a touch more magic before I stepped onto school grounds.

Like it or not, my life was steeped in magic. I didn't know it before this summer, but magic was everywhere. In the flowers. In the air. In my mother. In me. I couldn't escape it even if I wanted to. Riverbend Middle was the one place I could go to get a break from it. The one place left in my life where magic didn't belong. I was looking forward to that as much as I was looking forward to Mathletes. Which is why it was so weird that when I was finally standing under the bead trees feeling almost no magic, I didn't feel relieved. It actually felt strange and wrong, like something was missing. Maybe it's because I was still holding Othello that I noticed it, but Miss Lafleur was right. My magic was there in me and in Othello, but it was so

far away, trapped inside, that it may as well have been gone. Like trying to eat a Ring Pop without noticing the wrapper was still on. I'd stood under those trees a million times. How had I never noticed how empty it felt?

Miss Lafleur led me to where the azaleas grew wild. Lynx was waiting for us there. The cat circled Miss Lafleur as she pulled out the rose-colored glasses. But instead of putting them on herself, Miss Lafleur handed them to me. A bunch of the workers came out of the building and stood watching us.

I tried to play it off, like I was just trying the glasses on for fashion, but as soon as I put them on, Miss Lafleur moved, drawing magic in the air like a ribbon dancer. She didn't seem to care that her crew was watching, and after a few seconds, I forgot they were there. Magic flowed from Miss Lafleur's extender, colors dripping into each other, moving back and forth in tight lines like rainbow-tinted thread. The strands were so fine that I could barely see them even with the glasses. It was amazing, like watching a spider weave her web. I couldn't look away. Neither could Othello. I'd never seen him greedy for someone else's magic like that. If I hadn't been holding him, I'm sure he would have leapt into the air to reach it. I rubbed under his chin, knowing it wasn't quite as good as usual since no magic dripped through, but that was enough to stop him from jumping in. There was nothing stopping me, though. I leaned in as close as I could. It was beautiful.

I just wanted to see it, but when I got so close that I might have messed it up with my nose, that's when I could see that it wasn't solid. There were thousands of tiny drops glistening in the air. Points on a line that showed you where the line should be, but no line at all.

"It's beautiful," I said, realizing that I had never seen Miss Lafleur's magic before, either. Definitely #goalz.

"It can be," Miss Lafleur said. "Remember to use the power in your extender sparingly. The spiderweb shape is intentional. It should help guide the termites to a central point where we can collect them."

"And exterminate them?"

Miss Lafleur looked shocked.

"The termites have done nothing more than be termites. As much as they are a nuisance in our human spaces, they have done nothing wrong. Even if they came of their own volition, they wouldn't have earned death. But especially in this case, where they were drawn against their nature by a burst of magical energy, it would be beyond cruel to exterminate them."

"But aren't you an exterminator?"

"Pest control," Miss Lafleur corrected. "Why do you think I made sure to take on this case? We only activate the Vacherie crew in the most delicate circumstances."

Duh. That made way more sense. Of course Miss Lafleur wouldn't be out here killing stuff for fun, even if it was just termites.

Something else clicked for me, too. "Wait a minute. Is your whole crew witches?"

"And kismets," Miss Lafleur added.

"My bad," I said.

Miss Lafleur put a hand on my shoulder. "No, Hasani. You're actually very good. That's why I'm giving you this opportunity. Whatever happened here has been complicated by the sanlavi." Miss Lafleur gestured at the workers, who had formed a circle around us. "The Vacherie crew's strength is working as a collective, but the only safe way to work inside the sanlavi is to use individual power through an extender. You see the dilemma."

Once I really started looking, I realized that the workers standing around us weren't just witches and kismets, they were witches and kismets I sort of knew. I had seen most of them before in Vacherie. They were part of Grandmé Annette's coven, a coven I had technically been invited to join. I still wore the dolphin charm every day. The Vacherie coven was basically the opposite of Belles Demoiselles. If you were from Vacherie, you were welcome, no matter how much or how little magic you had or how distant a cousin you were. Under the moonlight in Vacherie I saw magic with my own eyes for the first time—not through rose-colored glasses or on a screen. It was dope. Even the smallest flows of magic were beautiful there, but I could see how if you didn't have that much magic in the first place, maybe you wouldn't want to put it in a contraption where you could never get it back. Especially not over some termites.

"Take a look around you," Miss Lafleur said.

I did. The yard didn't look very different through rose-colored glasses. The chain-link fence was so covered in trees and leaves and shrubbery that it was easy to forget it was there. But just past the fence, there was another one that shimmered, like an aurora borealis, except sprinkled with sparks of lightning.

"We just walked through that?" I asked. It did not look safe.

"The burst of magic that influenced the termites has mingled with the sanlavi's natural barrier. The influence is trapped inside. Normally, magical influence would dissipate in three days at most. But this influence is entangled. I don't know how long it will take to disentangle, but longer than three days, I suspect, if at all. We're prepared to stay and monitor the situation for several weeks—"

"Weeks?" My eyes just about popped out of my head.

Miss Lafleur kept going like I had never interrupted her.

"—or months."

"But Ms. Reid said school would be closed two weeks!"

"Well, if we hadn't said that, your school might have hired another termite company, one that is less humane. And it certainly isn't the termites' fault that they're trapped here."

"But wait. Just to be clear, are you saying the termites might never leave?"

Miss Lafleur sighed. "All magic fades eventually, so as you would say, it is statistically unlikely—but yes. That is a possibility."

As nervous as I was to use magic, I knew I couldn't let that stop me. Honestly, I was tired. Fine. LaToya probably hadn't made the sanlavi, but all that influence messing with the termites had LaToya's name written all over it. No one else thought she could possibly be involved, but it was too much of a coincidence. The worst bullies always look innocent when other people are watching. I didn't start this petty witch war, but I wanted it to be over, and I wanted to be the one who ended it. She wasn't even in the building a whole day. If it weren't for her, the sanlavi might have actually been a good thing. All it was doing was keeping Riverbend magic-free, and LaToya had to go and ruin it. And just like the thing with Annie, she knew she was hurting people and she wasn't doing anything to fix it. At that point it wasn't even about getting back to Mathletes or the straight doom of possibly being forced to spend more time with my dad and Sandy. It was the principle of the thing. I was a witch, too. LaToya could only mess my life up if I let her, and I had no intention of letting her.

I held up the extender, aka, the world's dopest glitter pen.

"How much magic did I put in it?"

"This extender can only hold a very small amount. Luckily, termites are small creatures that thrive on hierarchy. So if they can be moved, it shouldn't take much power to influence them. It's more a matter of pulling the right lever," Miss Lafleur said.

"So I can't use too much?"

"If you're worried about burning out, I wouldn't. Not from this. You're young and privileged. For you, the extender represents a tiny drop in a very large bucket. But it's your drop. Your bucket. It is entirely up to you."

Miss Lafleur didn't get it. Every time I had ever gotten in trouble at Belles Demoiselles, it was for using too much magic. Since I literally couldn't use more magic than I'd put in it, this extender was about to be my new best friend.

Even in the middle of the afternoon, it was strange how standing outside the main door of the school felt like the one time I had been with the Vacherie witches under the moonlight. Vacherie coven 2.0. Except this time, instead of all of us looking at each other and trying to help each other, everyone was looking at me.

The way they looked at me was strange, but it was familiar, too. That's when it clicked. They were looking at me the same way Jenny looked at me at orientation. Not like I was a person, like I was a YouTuber. Like they saw something bigger in me.

That kind of made it easier. It wasn't even a decision. No matter how bad I might screw up, I knew what I had to do.

Unfortunately, I had to do what I had to do without the help of the rose-colored glasses.

"You won't be needing these," Miss Lafleur said, slipping the glasses right off my face and tucking them into her pocket in one smooth motion. "You have Othello. Trust him," Miss Lafleur said. "He'll help you."

I kind of wished I could have both, but okay. All eyes were on me. I turned to go inside, head held high, when one of the Vacherie crew stopped me.

I thought she was going to tell me not to go in. Or maybe the opposite? Give me sage advice like they do in the movies? Instead she held out a long rectangle of khaki cloth the same color as my uniform shirt.

"You remember me?"

No?

"Yes," I lied.

The woman laughed. "You don't remember me, but I remember you. I'm your cousin Cynthia."

Was I supposed to say "Pleased to meet you"? "Nice to see you again"? Belles Demoiselles didn't have a class on how to greet family members you were already supposed to know.

"All that hair, kuzin?" she said. "You probably want this."

CHAPTER SEVENTEEN

PAWS AND PERIMETERS

Walking into your school when it's totally empty is creepy as anything, even if you've been going there since kindergarten. Holding the extender out in front of me helped. It made me feel like a real witch. A witch who could do battle, not just open a flower shop.

I don't know why Cousin Cynthia thought I needed to tie my hair up, but it was cute, so I went with it. Othello made more sense. Miss Lafleur was right. Having him with me did help. At first I was afraid to put him down. I thought he wouldn't follow. That he'd get separated from me the way Lynx got separated from Miss Lafleur.

When I put Othello down, though, he never went more than ten steps away. Once he did he'd run back, rub his head against my ankle, and run out again. It was truly adorable, especially when he stopped right in front of the four lockers we picked and started rolling on the ground like it was a tiny patch of catnip. I knew what was happening. I couldn't see it, but there must have been magic on the ground. How in the world did it get there? I paused and focused, trying to pull my magic to the surface. No matter how hard I tried, it stayed stuck behind the candy wrapper. In the meantime, Othello finished rolling and ran off, presumably to look for more magic. I shook my head and went after him. That's why Miss Lafleur had me bring Othello. Yes, Othello's cuteness did soften the creepy of an empty school, but greedy magic-gobbler that he was, he'd probably lead me to every stray bit of magic around the building, including the termites.

I'm not gonna lie. After a few minutes, following Othello with the extender was kind of fun. He was like a tiny tiger on a hunt, running circles around the Ben Franklin and Oretha Castle Haley statues, pouncing on more than one candy wrapper in a corner, and scrambling up and down stairs like a pro. He even stopped in front of Ms. Coulon's room, where I took the opportunity to tell him that that's where the Mathletes list would be posted once we were done. I didn't know which of his stops were magic and which were kitten exploration, so I followed him down hallways, past new lockers and old lockers, through the cafeteria, back out to the gym, and over to the fence, leaving tiny drops of magic from the extender everywhere he paused. Eventually, there'd be enough dots to make a channel of influence that could lead the termites out. Miss Lafleur and Lynx watched us the whole time. I didn't notice them at first, but once I did it was hard not to, what with Lynx being huge and Miss Lafleur staring at me through the rose-colored glasses. It felt like I was back at Belles Demoiselles and she was scoring my every move, except this time I knew what I was doing. The extender was even easier to use than a pen. The more you squeezed it, the more magic came out. It didn't take long to figure out how to pulse it just enough for Othello to look, but not enough for Othello to pounce. From there, using it was so smooth and free that I wished I could give a shout-out to extenders on my channel. Technically, there was no rule against it, but as tempting as the idea of being sponsored by whoever made this extender was, I was not planning to out myself on my YouTube channel, especially not when my bestie still didn't know. Not even for a free product I could get behind.

We must have zigzagged through the building and the yard thirty times. Othello kept going back to Ms. Coulon's room, which was annoying because it was all the way up on the third floor, but then I realized he was after the third-floor trash, not kittening out pockets of magic. As cute as the idea was of him making a little kitten ball pit out of the empty cups and juice bottles leftover from whatever teacher had tried to buy kids off at orientation, I didn't have time for the thrill of the candy wrapper hunt. No problem. I went old-school, kissing my teeth and snapping my fingers to get him to move on. He always did, especially when he realized I was going to lead us outside. That's because, even though the other Vacherie witches seemed to have gone home, whenever we went back outside, Miss Lafleur was waiting for us. With Lynx.

Othello LOVED Lynx.

He ran to Lynx like she was home base, dashing through her legs just like he did with the statues inside. Lynx could have flattened Othello with half a paw, but she stood still and let him do it.

Miss Lafleur beamed.

"What is it y'all say?" she asked, adjusting the glasses on her nose. "Game recognizes game?"

Nobody says that. I didn't have the heart to tell her, though. So I just shrugged.

"They get along beautifully. I suppose Lynx sees her past and Othello sees his future. It's very charming. As is the shape you're constructing. It's less web, more cone. Is that correct?"

I nodded and tried to play it cool to go with my battle-witch look, but I couldn't help smiling. With the extender, I didn't have to worry about being extra, and I guess that freed up my mind for strategy? Othello had done his part. Now it was up to me to connect the dots. Literally. And I had a plan. Instead of making a web that would trap all the termites in the middle, which is sort of what Miss Lafleur did, I was making a trail that would lead them up and over the fence, past the weird magic force field, so they could just fly away and go back to wherever they came from.

"I think it's more of a wormhole," I said. Or a waterslide tube, but wormhole sounded cooler.

"Intriguing," Miss Lafleur said. "I'd love to hear more of your thought process when you're done."

I thought about asking her for the rose-colored glasses again. It would have made it easier for me to check my work, but since Miss Lafleur seemed to be doing a Mr. Miyagi thing, I kept working blind.

Actually, I don't really know if it counted as working blind. To be fair, I hardly ever saw my own magic. It was more of a feeling thing. That and watching how Othello picked up what I was putting down. So once I got out of my feelings about Miss Lafleur keeping her glasses, it actually worked fine. Othello soaked up like a hundred drops of magic off the ground before I thought, *Duh. Termites can fly,* and started putting them right down the center of the hallway, too high for Othello to reach.

I am a hundred percent certain that I didn't look like a magic ribbon dancer while I was putting tiny drops of magic all over the school, but I caught the rhythm of it. An hour later I had drawn most of an invisible path that basically led outside of the building. The hard part was figuring out a path through and—dare to dream—beyond the weird barrier of magic at the edge of campus.

Getting the tunnel thingy all the way to the barrier wasn't easy. I went out to the truck to refill the extender four times. Lynx sat perfectly still, but it seemed like Othello and every other creature in creation kept popping up to lap up my stuff. Birds, gnats, grasshoppers. Basically everything EXCEPT the termites. Miss Lafleur furrowed her brow so many times that I was sure her forehead would be one giant wrinkle by the time I was done. She didn't stop me, though, so I kept going, stretching the spaces between drops as far as I could until the tip of the cone stretched out beyond the fence, past the barrier of the sanlavi and LaToya's aromatics. Eventually, it stuck. I know because I had to literally chase Othello outside the gate to stop him from trying to lap up what was hovering over the sidewalk.

Miss Lafleur smiled and gave a little nod.

I felt that nod in my soul. Before then, I kind of suspected that I had done a little something. But when Miss Lafleur smiled at me, I knew. If my hair hadn't been tied up, I definitely would have been flipping it over my shoulder. Too bad the Vacherie coven had left. Since practically everybody in Vacherie was my cousin, they wouldn't have even needed the rose-colored glasses to see my li'l termite wormhole.

"Where did everybody go?" I asked.

"I sent them to safety," Miss Lafleur said.

Safety?

But I didn't even get to ask the question, because the next thing I knew, the termites were on their way. You would think I would have been prepared. You know. What with being the person who made the wormhole and everything. But I stood there watching them like I was watching a dramatic WeBop, but instead of the horrifying mass of bugs flying out the door for a few seconds before the video looped and played again, these bugs kept coming, and I could not tap the screen to make them stop.

Before I knew it, the termites were coming through my waterslide so fast that it was too late for me to get out of their way. Unfortunately, I was still on the sanlavi and couldn't use charm to keep the bugs off me, but I still had a little magic left in the extender. I drew a path around me and Othello as the termites flew. The only thing that kept me going was the thought that at least they weren't getting in my wrapped hair. The rest of me was not doing so well.

It probably lasted less than two seconds before my protective circle kicked in, but it felt like a year. For obvious reasons I didn't want to uncover my face. When I did it was to sweep my hands over my face and arms and legs and everything to knock off any bugs left on me. I didn't feel any, but I was doing my crazy swiping dance just in time to see my wormhole working—right up to the fence. A few termites crossed it, but most of them stopped at the barrier, hovering. Like a gross, pulsing, swarming, living fence. I thought for a second that they might push past it, like a mass of zombies knocking down a wall, but no. They were just there. Pulsing.

"Well done, Hasani!" Miss Lafleur said.

Excuse me?

"Did I free them?"

"Heavens, no!" Miss Lafleur chuckled. "But you've made a truly valiant effort. Considering it's your first time and under such extreme conditions, I couldn't have hoped for more. The fact that they're even approaching the barrier is quite extraordinary."

"Now what?"

"Now we wait."

"For what?"

"For them to settle back into the building. If we can't get them out into a more natural habitat, inside the building is the safest place for them. Take it as a learning opportunity. After all, we can learn even more from our failures than we do from our successes."

Back inside? After I had done all that work? No way. I had the sudden image of termites shooting back like the world's worst confetti drop, covering the sides of the building as they crawled back inside. No. No way. Not on my watch. I made a dash for the gate. There had to be something I could do.

"Hasani! It's a waste!"

She didn't shout "waste of magic," but I knew that's what she meant. Tiny drops of magic were no match for whatever was happening with that barrier. The extender was only half full, but on the other side of the barrier I'd be able to use a bunch more.

I don't think I even checked for streetcars as I ran out onto the neutral ground. The Belles Demoiselles charm was warm, but the dolphin charm was the one tingling against my skin. The magic was poised, waiting for the moment it could be released, like Othello waiting to pounce, and as soon as I crossed the streetcar tracks, there was no holding it back. *The Legend of Korra?* Nah. The Legend of Hasani. I was smoother than the last Airbender. Magic passed from the fleur-de-lis to the dolphin and I didn't even need to think. It just flowed. The next thing I knew, the whole mass of termites was crossing the gate and heading for me. Again. I don't know why standing in the middle of the neutral ground made me forget that.

Luckily, my body remembered. There are always mosquitoes in New Orleans. Always. I was so used to holding them off that once I got away from school and I could actually use my magic again, my personal bug barrier snapped back into place. The termites swarmed around me, but none of them got any closer than four inches away, even when I moved my hands around.

Honestly, that was as far as my plan went. And my skills. I probably looked like some kind of swarm monster to the people passing on the street, or at least I would have if Miss Lafleur hadn't been two steps ahead of me. Literally. I don't know how she made it to the neutral ground before I did, but I was glad she was there. Supposedly, curtains of intentions were not her specialty, but you never would have known it the way she whipped one into place around us. The next thing I knew, the look and sounds of the street around us were practically gone. All I could hear was insect wings.

"Be very still," Miss Lafleur said. "We can't see them, but the streetcar tracks are still there. We wouldn't want you to get hit by a stray trolley. I'll have you out in a moment."

The termites at my head started flying away from me. Miss Lafleur was doing something, moving her hands back and forth. The more she did, the more termites rolled away, unwrapped in a spiral like Miss Lafleur was peeling an orange. It looked like they were flying straight out of existence, but the way Miss Lafleur was about animals, I knew that couldn't be true. That and the buzzing. The buzzing was as loud as ever. Maybe louder.

"There." Miss Lafleur did a little twisting motion with her hand. The buzzing got quieter. "That was unexpected, but I've learned to expect the unexpected when you're around, Hasani."

I looked down at the buzzing spot of nothing on the ground.

"Oh, yes! I'm not a skilled weaver, but one can weave a sack of intentions just as easily as a curtain. I didn't start the day thinking

I'd be doing magic on the streets of New Orleans, but I suppose that is always a possibility when one takes on an apprentice. That was quite a burst of power."

It felt kind of cocky to say "Yes. Yes, it was. Thank you." I actually didn't even use that much. I just amplified it with my dolphin charm, so I did a thing I'd learned from Miss LaRose. I deflected.

"How long can they live in the sack?"

"Oh, not long. A few hours at most."

"We can't just let them go? Won't they go back where they came from?" I hoped where they came from was not Audubon Park. Too close.

"Seeking shelter is a normal behavior. At this time of year they'd be deep in their nests, but with their nests nowhere near, they'd seek new shelter."

"And go right back into the school," I said.

"Perhaps. Or worse." There was worse? "This neighborhood has quite a few old homes, and not everyone can afford repairs or has the luxury of magical reinforcement."

Oh. Right. I didn't think of that.

"What if we just nudge them to where they're supposed to be?"

"They're confused enough already. With more influence, they may never come to themselves again. The best thing we can do for them now is to escort them to a place they can rest undisturbed."

Miss Lafleur extended her hand and wiped the area around us. All of a sudden, the world came into view.

"There," she said. "You can keep the extender. It is my gift to you. I should have warned you earlier that all use of that extender is being recorded."

Me. Eyebrows.

"Not with video. I collect data on almost everything I do, and that includes working with interns. The flow of magic in and out of the device is documented so that we can examine your growth and efficiency, then file it anonymously. In my notes your data will be filed under 'Intern X.'"

"Ooh. Like Intern Unknown," I said. Very cool.

"More like the intern after Intern W, but you can think of it that way if you like. Does this mean you'd like to continue your education?"

If it meant keeping the extender? "Yes!" I said.

Miss Lafleur nodded. I stuck the extender into my shirt pocket.

"Now, let's get these poor little ones back to Vacherie."

Apparently the Vacherie crew had been hanging out at the Vietnamese restaurant across the street. They came out together, like they had just finished their lunch break, and joined us between the streetcar track. Half of them were talking to me and half of them were talking about me.

Ti nétwal!

All right na', City Girl.

Good job, Hasani.

I told you that girl was good.

I couldn't stop smiling, not even when it took all of us to drag the invisible bag of termites across the street and onto the back of Miss Lafleur's truck just in time for a group of kids I knew to come out of Louisiana Pizza Kitchen. They were heading right for us. I mean, we were standing in the middle of the sidewalk, but still. It was the bunch of kids who usually ate lunch right by the azaleas. That included Jenny, who was walking front and center. I started to duck away. I didn't want a repeat of her being weird about me having a YouTube channel, or to have to explain why I was dressed like an exterminator, but then I saw LaToya bringing up the rear. She wasn't wearing the faux locks anymore, but it was definitely LaToya.

Seriously? Why. Was. She. Here?

And not just here. Dressed in her private school uniform—again—walking with Jenny and 'em like she really knew them.

"You're an exterminator now, Hasani?"

I glared at LaToya before I realized it was Jenny talking. Jenny didn't look like she was being mean or anything. And, I mean, fair question. I *was* wearing a uniform.

"Pest control," I said, striking a pose. "I landed an internship."

"Cool," Jenny said. "That wrap is mad cute. It's a look."

I smiled and did everything but stick my tongue out at LaToya as they walked past. I mean, I might have, but Miss Lafleur was watching, and I already knew how she felt about petty witch wars.

LaToya couldn't even look me in my face. She knew what she did, and seeing me with Miss Lafleur, she knew I was taking care of it. Enough said.

"Jenny!" LaToya shouted, running past me like she didn't even see me. She lowered her voice when she caught up to Jenny at the front. "We're right by my aunt's office. She's a dentist." As if we care. "And she loves this juice place that's right in the next block. We should go. My treat."

Of course they were all saying yeah. I mean, who doesn't like juice? I tried not to roll my eyes at LaToya attempting to buy herself a new friend group. I don't know what happened to her old group. On Instagram it looked like the cool kids from Belles Demoiselles were still rolling strong. But whatever. I took a deep breath and remembered who I was. By the time I exhaled, I was looking on the bright side. At least she wasn't hanging out with Annie. Jenny had friends. She could handle herself.

"Are we ready?" Miss Lafleur asked, opening the passenger door of the truck. Lynx hopped in. The way Othello had been all up under

her, I thought he would follow. Nope. He ran right back through the gate and into the open front door of Riverbend Middle.

Othello's legs were tiny, but he moved fast. By the time I caught up to him he was racing up the steps.

"We don't have time for you to play in the trash," I called after him. "I'll give you some magic in the truck."

He was not going to make it all the way up to the third floor on his own before I could catch him. But he was scrambling so hard and he just looked so determined that I scooped him up and carried him to the stupid trash can.

What? I'm not heartless. Besides, Othello gleefully frolicking in what was basically a sea of recycling would be perfect for the How to Train Your Kitten playlist on my channel. So I pulled out my phone and plopped him down on an empty bottle of apple juice, waiting for adorable gold, but there was no jumping, no diving, no frolicking at all. Just a juicy glint in his eyes. I knew that look. It was the look he had whenever he found a puddle of magic I had "accidentally" dropped for him, only in this case he was staring at a water bottle that most certainly wasn't mine. It looked just like the bottle LaToya had been chugging during the Mathletes tryout. I didn't need glasses to know it was dripping with magic.

I grabbed Othello and the bottle and ran back downstairs.

Angelique and Dee had already agreed to help me, but I knew their hearts weren't really in it. Once they saw this, they'd really get it, though, and they would have to stop cutting LaToya so much slack. She didn't deserve it, and now I had proof. If the bottle matched Angelique's air sample, they'd be on my side. Then we could take stupid LaToya down and end her stupid pranks-gone-wild scheme together.

CHAPTER EIGHTEEN

HAZARDS AND DUTY

I'm not a tattletale. When my kindergarten teacher was trying to get us to understand the difference between "tattling" and "telling," I caught it in the first round. For real. I was the only kid in the class Ms. Cates officially named as one of the three in her "Ask Three Before Me" rule. That's how much I got it.

But as I burst out of the school's front door holding LaToya's stupid water bottle, I finally understood the tattlers. The whole Vacherie crew was standing there waiting for me. I wanted to hold that bottle up and put LaToya on blast to every witch in range, especially Miss Lafleur. I know LaToya. As annoying as she is, she loves when teachers love her. That's why it bothered her so much when only one teacher offered to let her be their protégé. Technically, Miss Lafleur wasn't LaToya's teacher anymore, but once a teacher, always a teacher, right? LaToya would not want to look bad in front of her. And the juice place she was heading to was only a few blocks away.

But that thought only lasted for like a second. When I came through the front door, I froze. The Vacherie crew wasn't just standing there waiting for me. They were still congratulating me—some of them actually started clapping. It was weird and embarrassing, but a little bit cool at the same time. I didn't know what to think, so I smiled and nodded and said thank you as I walked through the crowd of witches and kismets, but I couldn't enjoy any of the congratulations they were pouring on me because my phone was buzzing like crazy and I had to work really hard to keep Othello off that bottle. He was practically crawling up my arm to get to it. Who knew what kind of crazy magic was on it? All I knew was I didn't want anybody soaking up any of LaToya's foolishness, especially not Othello.

I managed to make it back outside the gate without shouting about my proof of how LaToya was just going around trying to mess with people and school property. It kinda helped that the Vacherie witches were still looking at me like a YouTuber. Not the way Jenny did it—like I was some kind of celebrity/alien she had never met before instead of a girl she had gone to school with since kindergarten. The Vacherie witches barely knew me, but they were bucking me up anyway, and it was cool. Miss Lafleur's bragging on me must've

had something to it. Some of the Vacherie witches could actually see my magic—so maybe I *was* a pretty good witch. Considering.

Well, when everybody is looking at you like you're the golden child, you don't ruin it by complaining. I was belle demoiselle enough to know that, at least. So instead of waving the bottle around, I slowed my walk to an Angelique pace and dripped a little magic to Othello the moment we got past the barrier so that he would look golden, too. I kind of wished LaToya could see us. LaToya's kitten could never, you hear me? Never.

But as soon as Othello and I made it to Miss Lafleur's truck, instead of jumping into the front to be next to Lynx, Othello made another dive for the bottle.

No bueno.

I got him away and into his cat carrier before any damage could be done, but that's when it occurred to me: Maybe damage had already been done.

"Miss Lafleur?" I said, raising my eyebrows high so she would know it was serious. "There's traces of magic all over the building. Influence."

She nodded.

"That's why Othello ran back inside. There was a bunch left in a trash can upstairs and who knows where else. It's probably everywhere."

Miss Lafleur nodded again and walked around to the driver's side of the truck. "That is why I held on to my glasses while you worked. I wanted to continue assessing the influence in addition to assessing your work. There's no point in poking one's nose in deeper than need be, especially where other witches are concerned. Marie? Marie?"

I thought Miss Lafleur was calling the same person twice, but apparently two people on the Vacherie crew were named Marie. I shouldn't have been surprised. There are beaucoup Maries in Vacherie. Technically, I'm a Marie, too. My middle name, but still.

"Can you two stay to oversee the takedown and do the final walk-through? I've already informed the head of school, but it really is imperative that I head back immediately."

"Byin sur," said the shorter Marie.

"Of course," said the one with the braids. "With a little luck, we'll have it down before you make it back to Vacherie."

"No luck," Miss Lafleur said sternly. "Take the slow route."

"But it might take us days."

"I've arranged accommodation," Miss Lafleur said. "This sanlavi is unexpected and unstudied. I have no idea what effect it will have on any of us. We've done quite enough here as it is. Best not to mess with luck, okay? Hasani informs me that there are drips of influence throughout the building. Take the necessary precautions, and once the walk-through is complete, everyone should avoid the interior. And please inform the crew that I've activated the hazardous-duty pay scale."

Hazardous duty? I was just in there. A lot.

Both Maries nodded. The one with pink braids switched to in-charge mode. "No one in the building. Team W is on the dismantle. Team K is on the trucks. This is a big job. Let's not take chances, people."

"But Miss Lafleur," I said as the rest of the crew got to business. "Who's going to make sure that building is . . ." I suddenly noticed a dude within earshot on the corner. He was probably walking to Walgreens, but still. ". . . clear?" I finished.

"No one," she said.

"No one?"

I raised my eyebrows even higher.

"But there's . . . stuff in there. Stuff that might influence people."

"That 'stuff' is none of our concern. What is our concern is getting these innocent lives to safety before they are beyond recovery."

"Termite lives? But . . . what about the people? My school has like six hundred kids. Plus the teachers. Will the influence be gone before school starts?"

"Well, that does depend on when school starts, but I wouldn't worry about it. Even if it takes weeks or months, the lingering effects wouldn't have any impact on you. I believe you know from our previous lessons that talented young ladies are immune to such influence. You and your friends will be quite safe."

Define safe.

In my book, me, Dee, and Angelique against an entire school of kids being influenced by LaToya's magic was not safe. In fact, it was the exact opposite of safe.

Miss Lafleur got in the truck and shut the door, so I did, too, dripping Othello a little something-something so he would stop trying to get to the water bottle. I hated seeing him trapped in his carrier trying to get out, so in the end, I put the water bottle in his carrier instead of him. That kept him off it.

"Miss Lafleur. Please. There must be something that can clear it out. Whoever did this is obviously up to no good, and if they are strong enough to use their magic on the sanlavi, who knows what they're capable of. People might get hurt."

"The influence in the building was likely poured out of the bottle in that cage. I sympathize with your concern, but what's done is done. I said before that there's no point in poking one's nose in deeper than need be, especially where other witches are concerned. That's what I was talking about. People can and do recover from small influences like this all the time."

"This is small?" It almost shut down my whole school!

"Oh, yes. Quite localized. The sanlavi is quite effectively keeping all the influence within the school grounds, so unless the person spends extended time at the school itself, they should see no effects at all."

"Extended time? Does seven hours a day five days a week count as extended time?"

Miss Lafleur nodded.

"So you're basically saying it'll be fine for people walking to the streetcar stop, but anybody who goes to *school* at the *school* would be toast?"

"For those who do spend extended time inside, I can't imagine it would take longer than six months or so for their second brains to completely rebound."

"Second brain" is what Miss Lafleur called gut bacteria in humans. Apparently all the microscopic creatures that were supposed to just be hanging out in our intestines and helping us digest our food actually had a lot to do with our personalities and preferences. What we liked and disliked. Maybe even who we hung out with.

"Well, six months after the influence dissipates, of course. While it is still trapped inside, less talented people would continue to be influenced."

I had a sudden image of Luz taking a deep breath in the gym. Or by our lockers. Or basically ANYWHERE.

"Not all my friends are witches," I said. "And even if they were, it's not fair for everyone else to be influenced like that. There has to be something I can do."

"Clearing out another person's work is inadvisable at best, but the sanlavi makes it even more complicated. Although I'm sure a freedom spell would do the trick if it were strong enough."

A freedom spell—just like me and my coven had talked about before. *Could I do it with the extender?* I wondered.

Miss Lafleur must have seen the light in my eyes.

"I am not advising you to squeeze your magic in any way. Spells, particularly, can be a dangerous business. I don't know where or how you may have stumbled across a freedom spell of any kind, but in case you have, I feel it is my duty to caution you against it in the strongest way possible. Spells are quite specialized. Different users generate different effects. That's why even witches who dabble in such things are careful to keep their recipes to themselves."

"But what if I found one?" I asked. "Like . . . on the Internet or something."

"Go ahead and try it," she said.

"Really?"

"Really. I feel quite confident that anything you find on the Internet won't brew much more than a strong tea. Miss Villere spends the off-season making certain of that."

"Well, what if I found one, like, in a book or something?"

Miss Lafleur sighed and turned to look me right in the eye. "Hasani, dabbling with another witch's spellbook is downright stupid. For the sake of this conversation and my sanity, let's assume that this witch let you look at her spellbook willingly. Now ask yourself, why? Why would any witch knowingly pass a spell along to another? The outcome is never the same, even between identical twins. So either the witch in question is ignorant, silly, and foolish"—no shade, but she was basically just describing Sandy—"or there is something else you need to look out for. Perhaps the witch is trying to waste your time. Or perhaps she's well aware of the consequences and is using you just to see what will happen."

"Like an experiment? On me?"

"Precisely."

Okay. I'm not gon' lie. That freaked me out. I mean, Sandy is annoying and everything, and she has terrible boundaries, and it's so weird that she's attracted to my dad. I mean, from what I can see, my dad really needs to be taking some time to work on himself, but whatever. That doesn't give Sandy the I'm-the-kind-of-person-who-

MARTI DUMAS

would-experiment-on-someone vibe. But honestly, I didn't get that vibe from LaToya, either, and LaToya definitely had me doing a hair-growth spell before I even knew what squeezing magic was. Still, with Sandy I was leaning toward ignorant and silly. No offense.

My phone was buzzing again. Actually, it had never stopped. It was just getting harder to ignore. I wanted to keep picking Miss Lafleur's brain about spells. I knew she knew more than she was telling me. But apparently my notifications could not wait.

As soon as I tapped my screen and the notification previews popped up, I wished I had ignored them. Two texts and a missed call from Sandy, but that wasn't the worst thing. No. That honor belonged to WeBop. There were 1,100 notifications of likes from the WeBop Annie had posted with all of us, but that was nothing compared to her latest post. A post I was somehow tagged in without being in. That one was practically going viral, and from the thumbnail, there was nothing cool about it.

"Miss Lafleur," I said, moving to get out of the truck. "I can't go to Vacherie right now. My friend needs me."

Right after I said it, I realized something. Annie was my friend. I mean, we went to the same school. She was cool. I liked her art. And I didn't want her to get hurt. But you can think all that about somebody and not have them be your friend. Friend is something more. I don't exactly know how to explain it, but whatever it is meant

222

it was on me to look out for Annie, even if that meant missing a chance to see the unicorns. What? I know we were going to help the termites, but Miss Lafleur said when there were no students around, she let the unicorns roam free. No way was I going to forget that.

Miss Lafleur nodded. "Put your seat belt on. I'll drive you."

"But the termites?" They may have been invisible, but I could still hear them buzzing.

"Your house is right by the levee. I'll turn on River Road and you'll be home before you know it."

"Thanks," I said, trying to look back at my phone, but Miss Lafleur kind of didn't let me.

"Hasani, take a deep breath and remember who you are. You're more powerful than you realize. A belle demoiselle is free to do as she pleases, but for me, please, before you decide what to do, consider the crafter."

"The crafter?"

"The person who crafted the freedom spell you have so obviously found and are itching to use. Influence like yours is not without consequence."

I wanted to shout *I know! Don't you think I know?* But I just let my face fall flat and went into full Belles Demoiselles mode. And, for the record, I was *not* itching to use that spell. I was not itching to use anything of Sandy's.

But what I said was, “Yes, miss.”

“You’re impatient. I understand. I was young once, too. Spells can be very inviting. But if you must go that route, at the very least, let the crafter cast the spell. It doesn’t have to be you, Hasani.”

Miss Lafleur didn’t know what she was saying.

Missing unicorns was one thing. Asking Sandy for help was on a whole ’nother level.

CHAPTER NINETEEN

SOUND AND FURY

Miss Lafleur dropped me off at my house, but all I did was go in and ask my mom to bring me to Angelique's. Angelique said she and Dee would explain everything when I got there, and that way we wouldn't have to worry about accidentally activating a booby trap LaToya may or may not have set in my house, or talking in code around Luz. And, believe me, there was a LOT to talk about.

My mom didn't care that I had Othello riding on top of his cage instead of in it, or that I was scrolling through my phone on the way over. Thank goodness. I needed to check Annie's page. See what was really happening.

Annie's WeBop account wasn't old. Two weeks maybe. She started it the day of my dad's wedding. But she had a lot more videos than I thought. All of them had at least 50 slaps on them. I scrolled all the way to the bottom and started scanning from there. I do that on YouTube channels and IG accounts, too. There's something cool about starting from the posts that only have one or two likes on them and watching the person's posts get more and more popular over time. They almost always do. But this time I kind of knew I was just scrolling to watch Annie get the props she deserved. I was avoiding the first one, the one at the top left. Like, if I started from the bottom, when I made it back to the top, it wouldn't be there. The title wouldn't be there. The thumbnail wouldn't be there. And LaToya's stupid face wouldn't be there, pretending to be friends with a girl she had refused to help.

#Besties

I wanted to vomit.

The gall. The ridiculous gall. I wouldn't have thought that even LaToya would sink that low. She knew how much Annie had been bullied. She knew how bad things had been for her, but there LaToya was, pretending to be Annie's friend the same way she had pretended to be mine. How could LaToya use her like that?

I tapped and let the WeBop play for a second. "Dips and Dives." Basically the worst song on WeBop. Of course LaToya would choose that song.

"Hasani?"

My mom was calling my name.

"I see it," I said. And the fact that it was already over 600 slaps after just a few hours. The whole school was watching, and who knew who else. Probably LaToya squeezing her magic. That would only make it worse for Annie when LaToya decided to turn on her.

"Hasani!" my mom repeated. "I said we're here."

"Oh. My bad. Thanks, Mom."

"Are you sure you're okay, baby?"

I kissed her on the cheek. Fast, so I wouldn't accidentally change her mind about anything. "Everything's fine," I said, jumping out of the car without looking to see if I was convincing.

Everything was definitely not fine.

Once I got to Angelique's room, though, the rest of my coven just wanted to talk about the magic at Riverbend Middle.

"It's a sanlavi? No wonder," Dee said.

"That explains it," Angelique said, turning to her computer. I don't know if it was a MacBook Pro or a MacBook Super-Ultimate or whatever the coolest new computer was, but what I do know is that thing was sleek and pretty. It was giving me serious computer envy. "I didn't think of a sanlavi before because talented people usually sense them right away. Even kismets. And you've been at that school for years. But I wasn't thinking about the fact that you're a . . ."

"Wildseed?" I supplied. Angelique didn't like saying that word. I guess it was "indelicate." But me, I loved it.

227

"I was going to say 'green witch,' but yes. If you never felt your magic before this summer, you also wouldn't feel the sanlavi trapping it, either. So gross. It's like having the life sucked out of you." We all shuddered. "No wonder my mom was so cool with me going to school there. These days she's thriving on making my life difficult."

Dee and I both looked at her like, *Ex-squeeze me?*

"You have a driver," I managed to say.

"My mother has a driver. Ms. Nancy only drives me when my mom's out of town."

Dee and I just blinked at her.

"Seriously. You know how bends in the river boost your magic?"

"I didn't, but go on."

"Oh. Okay. Well, they do. They don't give you more magic—they just kind of amplify the effects of whatever you're doing. It works kind of like the Vacherie charm. Or, I guess, the dolphin charm works kind of like a bend in the river, only portable. Anyway, my old school is right on a bend in the river. My mom was convinced that I was just coasting through, charming all the teachers without hardly learning anything at all."

"Were you?" Dee smiled.

"That's not the point." Angelique lifted her chin. "The point is that when I asked her about switching schools this year, she gave in really easily."

"Didn't you say it took a week of nonstop begging and formal presentations? That's easy?" I asked.

"For my mother, that's easy. I mean, at first she was all, 'RIVER-BEND, Angelique?' And my dad was all, 'Give her a chance, honey,' and I made the pitch about Mathletes and getting to spend more time with y'all and everything, but after she visited, she stopped pushing back. She even told my dad she thought it would be good for me to toughen up a little before I go away next year. I just thought she meant because Riverbend Middle is a public school."

Dee and I looked at each other.

"So what did you think? That public school kids just be fighting every day?"

Angelique shrugged, fast-shaking her head. "I don't know. Do they?"

Dee and I looked at each other again. She sighed, but our eyebrows all agreed to cut Angelique some slack. After all, her only day in public school had been Orientation, and that turned out to be not at all a regular day.

"Never mind," Angelique said. "Thanks to Hasani, I'll find out all about public school on Monday."

My eyebrows switched from she-don't-know-no-better to I-am-confusion. "Monday?" I asked.

"You didn't watch the WeBop?"

"Hashtag besties?" I said, not even trying to keep the disgust out of my voice. "Yeah. I saw it."

"Not that one. The new one."

Angelique moved to open her phone, but I got mine open first and went straight to my tagged list in WeBop and tapped Annie's last video. It was the one I had already seen like nineteen times on the ride to Angelique's. I shook my head. "Yeah. I saw it." I mean, if she was going after Jenny or one of the other girls, that would be different. But Annie? After everything she's been through? LaToya messing with her was the worst thing that could happen.

"Not that one," Angelique repeated, turning her phone around so I could see. "This one."

LaToya's face stared back at me, faux locks back in place. It must have been a wig. I just saw her, and she was definitely rocking her usual slicked-back ponytail.

"You follow LaToya on WeBop?"

"No!" Angelique said. "Well, yes. I do now. But this was in my stream. Annie's tagged in it."

It wasn't in my stream.

I tapped the screen. "Annie's the only one tagged," I said.

The video started to play. Angelique hit the volume button. It was worse with sound. A bounce mix of a Tank and the Bangas song I liked. Watching LaToya fake laughing and fake smiling while she was fake being Annie's friend was ruining the song for me. Who else but LaToya could ruin Tank and the Bangas? Even Othello was upset. I had to scoop him up to stop him from chasing Angelique's cat, Snowball.

The video was just LaToya bopping and pointing to words as they appeared on the screen.

When

you

make

600 friends

in

ONE

day.

Then there was a before-and-after screenshot of her follower count.

Thanks, bestie! See you Monday!

I blinked. Othello scratched me with his little claw, so I dropped him to the floor and kept staring at Angelique's phone.

"What's that supposed to mean?"

"Wild guess?" Dee said. "LaToya's going to Riverbend. I mean, it is tagged #RiverbendOfficial #RiverbendStudent #RiverbendBound, but that's just a guess."

"Official?" I asked.

I looked at Angelique. She nodded. "It's official. We start Monday. We already got a letter from the school. The principal even mentions you."

I opened my phone, ignoring the bajillions of WeBop notifications and trying not to think about how many more there must have been on my YouTube channel, and went straight to my school email. There were a bunch of emails from teachers. Probably reminding us about completing summer assignments. Ms. Coulon loved a summer assignment. I skipped those messages and tapped the last one from Ms. Reid.

Angelique was right. Ms. Reid did mention me by name. My whole name.

. . . Lifelong Riverbend student Hasani Marie Schexnayder-Jones showed her Mudbug pride by joining the team of exterminators who so adeptly handled the pest problem. We are assured that the issue has been fully contained and that school can proceed on schedule without needing to implement the virtual option. The teachers and staff look forward to welcoming you on Monday.
Go Mudbugs!

I opened WeBop again, trying to find the post Angelique showed me, hoping that if I saw the description again, I'd realize that we'd

all read it wrong. That LaToya wasn't talking about Riverbend at all.

Okay. It was a long shot. But the thing was, I couldn't find the post.

"Wait. How did you find it?" I asked Angelique.

She shrugged. "Annie was tagged, but I think somebody might have tagged me in the comments, too."

Angelique held her phone out for me to scroll through. Angelique was tagged in the comments. A girl named Stacey did it. I remembered them talking at Orientation when they found out they were going to be in the same homeroom. But Angelique wasn't the only one who was tagged. Scrolling through the comments, basically the whole school was. Somebody had even tried to tag Dee. It didn't work. It was just literally her name typed with no link, but still. That meant basically the whole school was tagged in the comments. The whole school except me.

"It doesn't mean anything," Angelique said, but I could see by the look on her face that she was trying to figure it out, too.

"LaToya must have put something in the code. I bet you can't even tag me," I said.

"The video hasn't been up that long. You probably just haven't been tagged yet."

"I've known a bunch of those people since kindergarten. Somebody tagged LaToya. It's LaToya's post. She doesn't need to be tagged, yet somebody remembered to tag her anyway, but nobody tagged me? Something is up. Angelique, just try to tag me. Please?"

Angelique slid her thumb across the screen. My phone pinged. LaToya's video appeared on my tagged list.

"Wait," I said. "You have magic. You might be doing something to get around whatever LaToya is doing without even realizing it. Untag me?"

I didn't miss the li'l look between Dee and Angelique, but I ignored it and texted Luz to ask her to do the same thing. A second later, my phone pinged. The WeBop was on my tagged list again.

"That doesn't make any sense," I said. "LaToya doesn't even go to our school!!"

"Apparently she does."

I was scrolling through LaToya's follower count. Every one of them went to Riverbend Middle. She had the whole school following her in less than a day.

"Not if I can help it," I said.

Dee sighed. Loud. "Hasani. Dag. You gotta let that go, man. She don't like you. You don't like her. It's cool. Y'all don't have to be friends. Just let it be. You live your life, she lives hers."

"That's just it. She's not living her life. She's trying to live *mine*. Riverbend Middle? Mathletes? Annie? The termites? She's doing all this to get back at me."

"Miss Lafleur said it's a sanlavi, right?" Dee said. She was look-ing at me with a straight face.

"Yeah."

"Sanlavi are natural. I mean, witches usually avoid them, so it's weird you ended up at a school that's right on top of one. But I don't know. Maybe that's why it took you so long to feel your magic. The point is, there's nothing weird about a sanlavi. So maybe LaToya tried to pull something with some termites to mess with you. I'm not say-ing she did, but let's say she did. So what? She probably didn't know about the sanlavi any more than we did. And the termites are safe now, right? We don't need to go starting a petty witch war over that. It's over. You took care of it."

"But wait," I said. "That sanlavi *is* weird. It has trees in it and Miss Lafleur was saying how strange it was that she never knew a sanlavi was there. Plus the border literally has magic trapped in it. It looks like a force field."

"You saw it?" Angelique asked. She was trying to pull something up on her superfancy computer, but that caught her attention.

"Yeah. A little bit. Miss Lafleur let me wear the rose-colored glasses."

Dee whistled.

Angelique looked genuinely impressed. "Well, aren't you just the chosen one? Even my mom can't get her hands on a pair of those.

They're super rare. Like, only-seven-pairs-in-the-world rare. Belles Demoiselles has six of them, but my mom is always on the lookout for that seventh pair. I'm not supposed to know that, though."

Angelique mimed zipping her mouth shut.

No wonder Miss Lafleur only let me wear them for a minute. I'm surprised she let me wear them at all.

Dee shook her head. "Y'all are missing the point. There are san-lavi all over the world. Miss Lafleur is not even from New Orleans. She's from Edgar, and she only comes to the city when she has to. She probably just didn't notice it. That's not weird, and that's not a reason to go after LaToya. What happened to innocent until proven guilty? The only thing you know for sure that girl has done is switch schools. That's not a crime."

It should have been, at least where LaToya switching to my school was concerned.

I pulled Othello's carrier down from the shelf. He was running after Snowball again. I don't know what Snowball had done, but Othello was heated. His fur was practically standing on end. The second I got the carrier down and it was back in a place he could possibly reach it, he forgot all about Snowball and came for the water bottle instead.

"Othello is usually so well-behaved," Angelique said, scooping Snowball up and giving him the slightest pat before placing him on a pillow on her bed. "What's wrong with him today?"

"This," I said, pulling the water bottle out. Othello could not contain himself. He pounced on that thing like he was starving. It was a little embarrassing, but at least it proved my point.

When Snowball started heading my way, Angelique got nervous. "Put it up," she said.

I stuck the bottle back in Othello's carrier, zipped it closed, and put it on top of the bookshelf again. If we left it up there for long enough, I'm sure both kittens would have figured out a way to get to it, but they were still pretty small, so we had time.

"No wonder Othello's being so wild," Dee said. "What's in that bottle?"

"Probably the same thing that's in there." Angelique pointed to a clear plastic shoebox on a shelf in her closet. The strappy pink sandals that had been in it were sitting on top. What was inside instead was a puffy purple paisley bag.

"The air sample from the gym," I said.

"Snowball was going crazy over it. And you know how hard it was for me to get him to behave in the first place."

I didn't. Snowball seemed pretty chill after the first couple of days we were allowed to bring our kittens anywhere on campus at Belles Demoiselles, but it was good to know that maybe only ninety-nine percent of things came easily to Angelique. It made her feel less doll, more human.

"Whatever is in there is really strong. I let Snowball lap up a ton of extra magic, and he was still going after it."

Technically, you weren't really supposed to give kittens as much magic as I gave Othello. Angelique was so perfect with everything. I'm sure that what she considered "a ton" would have been nothing but a snack for Othello. I didn't say that, though. At least she was on my side. For a second it looked like I was about to be out there by myself.

"You think that bottle is LaToya's?" Dee asked.

Dee clearly wasn't talking to me. She was A, Angelique was B, and even though it irked me that she was acting like she couldn't trust what I said, I needed to C my way out and let Angelique do the talking.

Angelique shrugged. "She was drinking out of one just like it during the Mathletes tryout."

"Yeah." Dee rubbed a hand over her fresh fade. "Come to think about it, she was drinking out of a bottle like that in the auditorium, too."

I decided to jump in. "There's more than one of them," I said. "Othello found that one in a trash can on the third floor, but there was another one in Ms. Coulon's room and who knows where else. Othello was having a field day in there."

Dee shook her head and sucked her teeth. A bad combination. "Dag. That's sad."

"Sad?"

"Yeah. She must be bokou desperate to squeeze her magic that hard. She probably didn't know about the sanlavi and just kept chugging, trying make something happen. Poor thing."

"Poor thing? I think we're forgetting that we're talking about LaToya here. There's nothing poor about her. She's just trying to manipulate people. On purpose."

"That don't stop it from being sad."

"Okay. Fine," I said. "But what about everybody else?"

"You mean the termites?"

"No. The people. LaToya's been out there squeezing her magic to influence people. How else would she have gotten the entire school to follow her on WeBop in less than a day? Her influence is all over that place."

Dee didn't usually talk much, but her eyebrows always spoke volumes. Right then they were saying, *True dat.*

"And Ms. Coulon? I mean, y'all don't know her, but even the softest teacher wouldn't let a kid try out for a team when they don't even go to the school yet, and Ms. Coulon is not soft. What else would explain that besides LaToya messing with influence?"

Dee's eyebrows had to agree.

"If LaToya was drinking a potion, it must have been incredibly powerful to overcome a sanlavi. We're talking world-class. Universe-class."

"Well, then that explains the next part, too. Normally it only takes like three days for influence to wear off, even in a sanlavi. But whatever LaToya did isn't going away. It's trapped in there. Miss Lafleur says she has no idea how long it'll take for all that influence to dissipate."

I just let that sink in. No matter what else they had to say, neither of them wanted to live in a world where every kid and teacher in the building was under LaToya's influence.

"Dag, Hasani. I thought you said Riverbend Middle was gonna be, like, a no-magic zone. Sounds like it's full up. There's more magic there than at Belles Demoiselles, and school hasn't even started yet."

Dee held her stony face for like a second, but then she burst out laughing.

I did, too. It wasn't funny, but it kind of was.

"So I'm guessing you want us to go in there and clear it all out?" Dee asked, still chuckling.

"I mean, yeah," I said.

"None of the professional pest control people could do it, but you want to think we can?"

"It's not that they can't. Miss Lafleur said a freedom spell would probably work if it were strong enough. She's just too much of a belle demoiselle to use it."

"I don't know, bruh. After that vending machine, maybe I am, too."

What? Dee was out?

I turned to Angelique.

"Squeeze my magic? I would never."

"Excuse me? Are the two of you the same people who were so hype about finding Sandy's little spellbook earlier? The freedom spell? Remember? Neither of you were going to help me do it?"

"A real spellbook? That's cool. Doing spells? Nah."

"To be fair," Angelique said, "we weren't going to let you do it, either. We're friends now. Friends don't let friends do stupid stuff."

"So why were we looking for ingredients?"

"For the crafter," they said at the same time.

"The etiquette of requesting a crafter do a spell on your behalf"—of course Angelique knew the etiquette—"is that the requester—that's us—brings the crafter the required ingredients as a gift BEFORE making any request. The crafter can still say no, but the gift of ingredients is just common courtesy."

"Grandmé Annette talks bad about people when they show up with their arms swinging. She usually still helps them, but, like, how you gon' show up asking for help and not even have the decency to bring the ingredients?" Dee shook her head. "No home training."

"So wait a minute. If we're the requesters, who is the crafter?"

They both looked at me.

"Sandy?" No way. "She'll probably say no, anyway."

"She won't say no," Dee said.

She wouldn't say no, but still. No way.

"Sandy giving you a spell is basically an open invitation for mentorship. You bring her the ingredients. You make the request. She helps you. Voilà. Riverbend Middle is magic-free. Now that I know it's not dangerous, this is actually kind of exciting. Going to school on top of an honest-to-goodness sanlavi? It'll be an adventure."

I laughed. Angelique had been watching her mom and whoever else in her family do magic since she was a baby. Of course for her, spending a few hours a day without magic was an adventure.

"Plus," she added, "I've never seen anyone do an actual spell before. So exciting!"

"Never? Not even . . ." I waggled my fingers around her hair. My hair was great, but Angelique's tight spirals were so thick and fluffy and juicy that there was no way magic wasn't involved. "Nothing?"

"I mean, I massage my scalp with Naptural85's hair-oil blend every other night. Does that count?"

That did not count.

"You not gon' get to see a spell unless you get Ms. Nancy to drive us to Vacherie so Grandmé Annette can help us get the ingredients. I'm not going up to a crafter with my arms swinging, and we went to a vending machine earlier. It was a bust."

Angelique turned to me. "Dee never finished telling me what happened with the vending machine," she said.

"It wouldn't let us get anything because we aren't members. It's like Costco." I pulled out my phone and swiped to the screen where the 3Thirteen app was still blinking.

"You got an invitation to 3Thirteen? I'm coming. Let's go right now." I've never seen Angelique have so little chill.

"It's just a vending machine, and we can't use it anyway. Our trial membership expired, not that it did anything."

"3Thirteen is not just a vending machine. The vending machine is for outsiders. Outsiders with an invitation, but still outsiders."

"Isn't that what we are?"

"Nope. See that? The app is blinking. That means you still have an invitation."

"But it said our time was up!"

Angelique shrugged. "Well, it doesn't matter if it's a glitch or kismet or someone else put you on the list because, no matter how it happened, you're still on the list. Now you can go and apply for your own membership and I'll be your plus-one."

"Wow, Hasani," Dee said, rolling her eyes a little. "A spellbook, an apprenticeship, and an invitation to something that's got Angelique hype like this? You really came up today."

Mentioning the extender felt like too much at that point. I'd show them later. Plus I was loving watching Angelique being extra for a change.

"What?" she asked. "I was trying to hack into my mother's library account so we could get on the Interweb and see if there's any information about the sanlavi, but if we can get into 3Thirteen, I can get a library card of my own."

I had no idea why Angelique was so hype about a library when Latter Library was walking distance from her house, but okay. The rest of it was perfect. Or almost perfect. It would have been perfect except . . .

1. Dee and Angelique talking about me asking Sandy for help like it was nothing? It didn't sit right. It just reminded me that, coven or not, they didn't really know me. Luz never would have been so chill about me asking Sandy for a favor.

2. Once I got the ingredients, I'd have to do the spell myself. It's one thing to do dangerous stuff before you know it's dangerous, but once you know it might hurt you, it's harder to do. Like when the roadrunner teaches the coyote about gravity. Chances were, I was going to fall. Except I couldn't let that happen. Luz—and all the kids who weren't witches—needed me.

CHAPTER TWENTY

LEAVES AND GRASS

ngelique insisted we get "dressed" before we went to 3Thirteen. To be fair, I was still wearing my pest control uniform, which was cute, but maybe not shopping cute. Angelique wanted me to wear something from her closet. That probably would have been faster, and Angelique had a lot of really nice clothes, but the day already felt like five Mardi Gras days smooshed into one. I was so tired. I honestly could not muster up the energy to wear somebody else's clothes. So we agreed to ask Ms. Nancy to drop us off at my house, but it was late enough that Ms. Nancy asked if we were planning a sleepover, so we went with it.

Dee came, too. She said she had her sketchbook, so she'd just chill until we got back, and I sent Luz a text asking if she wanted to sleep over. The fake Marie Laveau at the French Market had said something about the Friday Market having cheaper fleur-de-lis charms.

I honestly was not thinking about that when Dee and I were in that vending machine, but now I couldn't get it out of my mind. Well, if they had it in a vending machine, they must have it at 3Thirteen, even if it was only half as cool as Angelique was making it seem. If Angelique was right, I was definitely getting a charm for Luz. A slumber party would be the best place to give it to her. That is, if I survived doing the spell.

I know everybody was trying to stop me from doing the spell, but honestly, the more I thought about it, the more I wasn't worried. LaToya got me to do her chevelure spell before I even knew what a spell was. Worst-case scenario? I feel my magic start going out of control and I drink a chicory potion to get it back in check. So, basically, a café au lait would save the day. I just hoped I had enough money for the spell stuff we needed.

Angelique said we should wait until we got to my house to open the 3Thirteen app.

"There are entrances all over. I think it just gives you the one closest to you."

New Orleans is not that big. How many entrances could there possibly be?

Once we got back to my room, the first thing I did was run to mute my computer. The notifications from my YouTube channel were coming so fast they sounded like wind chimes in a thunderstorm.

"It wouldn't be all that if you had a bitbot," Dee said.

She would not let that go. "I get it, Dee," I said, trying not to sound annoyed, and tapped the 3Thirteen app.

Time to expiration: Unlimited.

Wow. That was new.

The same words appeared on the screen in big white letters.

Would you like directions?

I responded "yes."

Voice or visual?

"Voice," I said.

Angelique looked like she was about to squee. "This is so exciting."

Walking, wheeled assist, biking, or driving?

The app used my Siri's voice, which was set to Australian male as usual.

"Walking." I turned to Angelique. "We can always ask Ms. Nancy to drive us if it's too far, right?"

"Uh . . . no. She'd never take us. My mother does not want me to have a library card yet."

Whose mother doesn't want them to have a library card?

I would have asked, but my Australian dude's voice interrupted.

The nearest walking-accessible entrance is 0.4 miles away.
Continue guidance? If yes, broadcast feature will be disabled.
Headphones or ear contact required.

"No," I said, and ran to get ready. We'd do it again on our way out, which had to be soon, or my mama wouldn't let us leave again. I was in and out of the bathroom in a flash, wearing jeans and an adorable T-shirt despite Angelique's objections. The touch of glitter on the shirt picked up the little purple star I'd stuck at the corner of my eye and the shimmer in my lip gloss. I was feeling it.

I thought Angelique had "gotten ready" at her house, but when I got out of the bathroom, she was sitting on the edge of my bed, casually flipping through the spellbook, with her hair completely redone. Instead of the world's most perfect twistout, she looked like the lady from *Breakfast at Tiffany's,* but with brown skin and better hair. She even had a tiara and fancy shoes.

"We're walking," I said.

"I know," she said. "Should we take a picture of the spell to bring with us?"

That was a good idea, but it didn't work. No matter what angle we took it from, there was always too much glare.

That seemed to make Angelique giddy, too.

"I had no idea," she said, scrolling through a whole grid of pictures that were basically just white. "This is so exciting."

So much for pics. I wrote it down on an index card. Thankfully, one of us had pockets.

Angelique really did know how to walk in those shoes, even carrying her clear shoebox and Othello's cat carrier. I was only holding my phone, but it's a lot harder to hold the phone to your ear for a long time than I thought it would be.

The Australian guy talked us down Carrollton and over Freret to the big wrought-iron gate in front of a big fancy house I had seen a million times before. The Australian guy would not stop talking, though.

100 feet.

100 feet.

"This must not be the right spot," Angelique said.

100 feet.

100 feet.

100 feet

100—

"Fine," I said, and kept walking down Freret just so the Australian guy would say something different. He did.

Arrived.

We were standing on a wobbly brick sidewalk in front of a garage. If this was it, I didn't think Angelique's shoes would make it.

She wasn't afraid, though. She walked right up to that garage like it was hers, and as she did, the rickety-looking garage door flowed up smooth and silent.

"Hi! Welcome," said a voice from inside.

I knew that voice. It was Sandy. I didn't know whether to cringe or cry.

Angelique took over, gliding across loose bricks in heels smoother than I did in my sparkly sneakers.

"Sandy! It's so good to see you!" Angelique sang out.

"Same!" Sandy sang back. "What are you guys doing here? Is exploring random garages what the kids are doing these days? Is that what's hot in the streets? Please, let an old married lady know." Sandy tossed her hair over one shoulder. I tried not to roll my eyes.

"Actually, we have an invitation," Angelique said, waving me forward.

I held my phone out. The map the Australian dude had been talking us through was gone. The whole screen was pixelated purple.

Sandy pulled out a magnifying glass, like she was going to get a closer look at it or something, but the magnifying glass beeped, the garage door slid closed, and the whole room changed.

The utility shelves along the wall flattened out, turning into some fairly dope art. Lights shone on the spaces between the shelves so it kind of looked like stained-glass windows, and the whole back wall disappeared, revealing a glass room filled with plants and flowers and a waterfall right behind it. In less than two seconds, the dingy garage had fully transformed into a cross between the insec-

tarium and one of those art galleries on Julia Street. Dee would have loved it.

"Welcome to 3Thirteen." Sandy smiled.

"You . . . work . . . here?" I managed to eke out.

"It's a co-op," Sandy said brightly. "All members have to work at least a few hours every year. I do more than the minimum. A girl can always use a boost. Will you be a onetime guest or are you interested in membership?"

"Membership," Angelique said before I even caught what Sandy was saying.

"Great! That means we can do my favorite part!"

Sandy walked over to a plush chair in front of the glass wall and gestured for Angelique to sit down.

"Have a seat, please. This won't hurt a bit. No blood is required unless you have grass allergies. Do you?"

Angelique shook her head.

"Good. It's super uncommon in witches, but we have to check. Now, all you have to do is put your hands on the grass. Oh! And buckle in. Safety first!"

Angelique seemed totally unbothered by the talk of blood or allergies or safety. She buckled the lap belt, put her arms on the arm-rests like she had sat in that chair a hundred times before, and said, "I'm ready."

Sandy nodded and tapped an open fashion magazine on a stand that clearly was not a magazine at all. The next thing I knew, there was a *whoosh* and Angelique's chair dropped into a hole in the floor that had definitely not been there before. I could still see the top of her head, though. Her chin was level with the ground, and next to her right cheek, a door slid open. The door was glass and not too much bigger than Angelique's arm. It blended into the glass wall so perfectly that I didn't notice it before it slid open like tiny doors at a grocery store. Angelique reached through the opening to touch the grass. For a second, nothing happened. Then, boom. A sprig of flowers in a perfect shade of indigo grew between Angelique's fingers. It was like a time-lapse video without the time lapse.

"Wonderful!" Sandy looked up from the magazine and literally clapped her hands. "You qualify for membership. Of course that includes a library card with access to the Interweb and unlimited trades and purchases, provided they are within your credit limit."

If I didn't know better, I would have thought Angelique breathed a sigh of relief. But by the time the chair had lifted her to ground level, all I could see was a charming smile and her perfectly straight back.

The wall behind the chair instantly reappeared.

I blinked.

"It's refracted light," Sandy explained. "It does that while the system resets. Are you ready for your turn?"

Where witches were concerned, I did not do well with tests, and this was clearly a test. Still, I wasn't about to let Sandy know that, so I sat down in the chair and did my best to channel my inner Lizzo. Beyoncé. Katherine Johnson. Toni Morrison. Any diva would do.

I buckled up, the chair dropped, and I was faced with an empty patch of grass. There was no sign of Angelique's Louisiana phlox anywhere. I knew Angelique and Sandy were both looking at me, but all I could see was a sea of grass and bushes and trees. I couldn't see the waterfall, but I could hear it. It was soothing, like one of those study sound channels, but with a nature theme. It made putting my hand on the grass less scary. So I didn't let myself think about it. I just closed my eyes, took a deep breath, and did it.

After what felt like a really long time, the chair lifted me back to ground level. The room was so quiet, I kind of didn't want to open my eyes. When I did, Angelique looked normal, but Sandy did not. She was smiling, but she looked more nervous than happy. And whatever was happening on that magazine required a lot of tapping. Finally she turned to me.

"I don't know what to say," she said, rushing toward me with her arms out. "That was extraordinary, Hasani!"

By the time I realized Sandy was about to hug me, it was too late to stop it from happening. The grin plastered on my face was definitely more wince than smile.

"So, I qualified for membership?"

"Qualify? You're in the Talented Tenth. You've earned a black card!"

Sandy hugged me again. I think there might have been tears in her eyes.

"Black card? Is that what I need to use the library?"

"Oh my goodness, no. I mean, yes. That membership level does let you to use the library and have unlimited access to the Interweb, but Hasani, it's so much more. You could even shop on the tenth level! This is so exciting! If I weren't on duty I'd show you around. Actually, can you wait? You should really have someone go with you. Oh! And my circle of friends has been dying to meet you! I'm meeting a bunch of them after my shift."

"I'm not alone." I looked at Angelique. Sandy did, too.

"Maybe you need an adult?" she said. "Navigating the credit system can be a little tricky at first."

Well, I must have had at least a little of my mom's kismet luck, because right then the glass garden disappeared, the utility shelves popped back open, the garage door rolled up, and Cousin Cynthia and both the Maries walked in. They were laughing and talking like my mom did when she was with her friends, and as soon as I saw them I wanted to laugh, too.

"That's okay. We're with them," I said.

Cousin Cynthia didn't miss a beat.

"I got you, ti kuzin," she said.

She pulled an orange card from her pocket and waved it over Sandy's magazine. A door slid open.

"Vini avèk mò. Let's go."

CHAPTER TWENTY-ONE

ENTRANCES AND EXITS

"All right, na', ti kuzin-yé. Y'all need to pick up your membership cards or you need guest passes? Lucky for you I still have my two."

We were standing in a hallway in what looked like it should be either a spa or a fancy dentist's office. There were plants and cushy benches everywhere.

"We're supposed to have membership cards?" I asked, trying not to look Angelique's way.

"They supposed to have cards!" Cousin Cynthia looked at the Maries and laughed. "Well, now. What you looking for in 3Thirteen, little miss? If I'm not mistaken, I saw you swimming in the moonlight, didn't I?"

Angelique nodded. Her dolphin charm glinted on cue. "A library membership," she said.

Cousin Cynthia and the Maries laughed again. "They start young Envil. Library or no, my mama didn't let me step foot in this place until I was eighteen."

"Nineteen," the shorter Marie corrected.

"Yeah. You right. Nineteen. And there's an entrance right by my house! So what about you, ti kuzin? How you end up in 3Thirteen?"

She was talking to me. "I got an invitation from a woman named Marie."

"Marie who? Marie Odette? She from Vacherie?"

"No," I shook my head. "The French Market. She was dressed like Marie Laveau. Another lady sent me over to her to get some ingredients, but really I was looking for another charm like this." I touched my fleur-de-lis.

"Dressed like Marie Laveau?"

"Head wrap and everything?"

"Kaitlynn," both the Maries said at once. They also both rolled their eyes. At least one of them sucked their teeth.

Cousin Cynthia managed to keep a straight face. "You looking for ingredients? What do you need?"

I went to pull the paper out of my pocket, but Angelique beat me to it.

"First figs, fresh ginger, and picture jasper."

I remembered the ginger and figs part. It was the adjectives I couldn't remember.

"Ooh. Somebody's crafting up a li'l something," the taller Marie teased, twisting one of her pink braids. "No judgment."

Cousin Cynthia waved her away. "That's easy. You can find that and more at the Rivyèmarché. That's where we're headed. You can come with us. I got plenty credits. Whatever you get there is on me."

"Thank you," Angelique said politely. "Is there a place there where we can get something scanned? I want to find out what's in this." Angelique held up the container with her purple paisley bag inside.

Angelique still wasn't looking at me, but I couldn't tell if it was because she was upset or she was showing off her etiquette for the adults.

My phone buzzed. Another text from Luz. She was probably saying she was heading to my house. That was fine. Dee was there.

"Do they have charms at the Rivyèmarché?"

"You don't have enough charms?" Cousin Cynthia winked. "What, you need a third one to balance the set?"

"It's not for me," I said. "It's for my best friend."

"Is your friend gifted?"

"Or talented?"

Luz was gifted and talented, but I knew what they meant. "She can't do magic," I said.

"Oh!" Cousin Cynthia said. "If you just looking for decoration, we can find that at the Rivyèmarché. Some real charms, too, but you gon' have to use your own credits for that."

"Yeah. Don't go to Kaitlynn for that. Kaitlynn too high," the shorter Marie pouted.

"She does have some nice stuff, though," the taller Marie added.

"How you know?"

"Girl, you think you the only one with access to level five? Please. I'm in and out of level five every time I'm in New Orleans. If I didn't have to make sure all that equipment gets back to Vacherie in the morning, I'd go right now just to show you."

"Girl, hush. I just saw your card, and it's still orange, just like mine."

"You don't know my life! That card don't tell you everything."

"What about this?" I asked, pulling LaToya's water bottle from Othello's carrier.

"Chile, I thought you had a cat in there!" Tall Marie laughed. "I was about to tell you to take that cat out before we get inside. Me, I say live and let live. But most of the folks that hang out in 3Thirteen don't like when people keep animals in cages. Untalented people might get a pass, but you are not untalented."

"No, it's just a bottle," I laughed. Dag. I really did need to get Othello a leash. "Do they sell these at Reeve-Yuh-Mar-Shay?"

"Not that I've seen, but you never know. Let's take a look."

Cousin Cynthia led us down the hall, around a corner, and through a set of sliding glass doors into a giant atrium. It basically looked the same as the testing system, except much, much bigger. There was a waterfall and trees and bushes, but nothing else was alive. The grass was a cool green carpet. The stones and logs were sofas and chairs with cushions. All the other plants were sculptures or lamps or paintings hanging on the wall. If I had Othello with me, it would have been perfect for a photo shoot.

In the middle of the atrium there was a large desk with two people sitting behind it. One had an aqua tapered haircut and black glasses. The other had full rainbow eye shadow, cornrows, and a fluffy ponytail that even put Angelique's hair to shame.

"Stevie." The one with glasses raised their hand.

"Steph," said the one with the eye shadow.

"We know it's confusing," Stevie added with a smile. "But how can we help you anyway?"

"We're all set," Cousin Cynthia said, gesturing between herself and the Maries, "but they need to pick up their cards."

"Ooh! New members!" Stevie said. "We're getting a lot of young people lately. That's good. Step right up, place your hand on the pad, and we'll get your cards right to you."

Angelique and I placed our hands on screens built into the desk.

260

Steph handed Angelique a purple card. "Welcome! All the membership details are in your phone in the 3Thirteen app, but I'll just give you a quick rundown. You can invite up to two guests. Unless you upgrade to merchant, that's lifetime, not annual, so pick your friends wisely. Guests are only permitted on level one, and if the guest doesn't qualify for membership or chooses not to activate their membership, you'll be responsible for all your guest's purchases. The library, spore directory, and net resources are all on level two. Specialty opportunities start at level three, but I won't go into that whole spiel. Most of those are invitation only."

"Uh, Stevie. I think you're going to have to do the level-three spiel," Steph said, her mouth hanging open a little longer than it should. She was holding my black card like it might turn into a peacock or something.

Stevie covered her mouth with both hands. When she lowered them to talk, she literally looked like the shocked emoji. "Oh my days! I have never gotten to orient a member of the Talented Tenth. Trade?"

"No." Steph smiled and pulled herself back together. "I got her."

"What, do y'all work on commission? Leave them alone. They have family here. We'll show them around," Cousin Cynthia said.

"Well, if you change your mind, I'm here until eight! Central!" Steph said. "Or maybe I'll just come find you!"

261

Cousin Cynthia led us under a pecan tree to an arched metal door with a keypad next to it. "This works just like the Paris Metro. You ever been to Paris?"

Angelique said yes at the same time I said no.

Cousin Cynthia nodded. "We'll go. Anyway, scan your card at a door to enter. Then you scan it on your way out when you're ready to leave."

"All right, na', ti kuzin," Tall Marie teased as I tapped my black card next to the keypad. She showed us to a moving walkway and we all stepped on. "You rollin' with the big bucks. With that black card, you ought to be treating us."

I felt myself blush. I tried to look away, but the walls around the moving walkway on the other side of the door were just muddy brown, so I ended up looking at Angelique instead.

"Is there an exchange rate? For U.S. dollars?" Angelique asked, her mouth tight.

"Oh, no, shè. Fiat money is no good in here. Not dollars, not pesos, not Great British pounds. Talented people only deal in credit in 3Thirteen. But you don't have to worry about that." Cousin Cynthia put a reassuring hand on Angelique's shoulder. "I told you. I got you."

Angelique didn't look reassured, but she nodded anyway.

"Now, put those cards away," the shorter Marie chided. "You don't need everybody in there to know what you working with."

Angelique tucked hers in a card slot in her purse. All I had was Othello's cat carrier, so I stuck mine in my front pocket with the extender instead.

"Good. You don't have to pull your card out again at all. Now that we're inside, traders and whatnot can check your account from right where it is."

Cool. I tried to trade looks with Angelique, but all her hype about 3Thirteen was gone and she was staring straight ahead. Yep. Definitely mad. About what? I wasn't sure. I decided to leave her be.

There was a blip in the wall next to me. Kind of like something bumped into it, but from the other side. I jumped, pulling back a little.

"Catfish," Cousin Cynthia said. "You get used to them."

Catfish?

Suddenly the brown walls made sense. So did the fact that they seemed to be flowing.

"Is this an aquarium? There's a tunnel like this at the Aquarium of the Americas. You can see stingrays."

"No, child. We're the ones in the glass box. That's the river."

"The river? The Mississippi River? Are we under it?"

"More like right next to it, but yes. A little under it, too."

"Under it, like underground?"

No lie, being underground sounded more magical than my black card and the extender combined. "But we can't build things underground in New Orleans because we're below sea level and we don't have bedrock and stuff. Isn't that why we don't have a subway?"

Tall Marie chuckled. "Yeah. We do say that, huh?"

"So wait. We do have rocks?"

My mind went back to my "rock" collection when I was four, which was mostly seashells and pebbles from the asphalt and my neighbor's garden path.

"Nope. No rocks at all. Every bit of land for miles was dropped off by that river right there. Maybe they can't build here, but we can and we do and I hope they never figure out how. If they did, we wouldn't be able to find one lick of peace. They'd be hounding us from here to Sunday. So keep this to yourself, Li'l Bit. Not that they'd believe you."

I put my hand on the wall, letting a finger trail across the glass as the walkway moved us along. I don't know. I just kind of wanted to feel the river. On the other side of the glass, a catfish followed the trail of my finger. There were three of them by the time the walkway passed under a catfish sculpture three times bigger than my mom's car. It was painted a bunch of colors and flickered with confetti lights, so I wasn't prepared for the sign hanging underneath it.

WARNING. FEEDING CATFISH CARRIES A HEAVY FINE.

—THE MANAGEMENT

"Girl, stop that." Short Marie shooed my hand off the wall. "Didn't you read the sign?"

"How can I feed them through glass?"

"They like magic just like everything else with whiskers, and just like a cat, they keep coming back. How you think those big ones get that big? Witches need to stop. They gon' get so big they'll never eat enough to satisfy 'em."

I pulled my hand from the wall, but sure enough, those three catfish kept bumping against it, looking for more, just like Othello.

We passed under a bunch more signs.

FAIR TRADE ONLY

TRADE FAIR

ALL TRADES FINAL

PASSPORT-FREE TRAVEL

TRAVEL AT YOUR OWN RISK

Then the walkways started branching off.

LOCAL DESTINATIONS

NORTH AFRICA

WESTERN EURASIA

ICELAND

CARIBBEAN

OCEANIA

"What about South America?" I was really talking to myself. I didn't think anybody heard me, but I guess Tall Marie did.

"Submarines go there, too. You have to get a connection in Havana or Dakar. Same for southern Africa and Asia. You have to connect through Dakar. It's a hub."

We kept going straight. Eventually the walkway stopped splitting off and the entrance to the Rivyèmarché came into view. The letters were thick and golden and showed up perfectly against a background of blue and purple flowers. Mostly Louisiana phlox and irises. I spotted a few morning glories in there, too, but the sign was nothing compared to the place. Even standing on the outside, Rivyèmarché was a hundred times better than the French Market. No offense, but the French Market didn't have ravens and monkeys and scarlet macaws sitting on people's shoulders. That's not even talking about the cats. Some of them were almost as big as Lynx—I'm pretty sure one was an actual white tiger—and not one of them was in a cage or carrier or on a leash.

Cousin Cynthia pulled our group together beneath a golden arch with FUNGIBLE TRADING carved into it in cursive letters. We were standing under another sign. I think it was supposed to be the store hours.

VENDORS OPEN WHEN WE WANT AND CLOSE WHEN WE WANT, BUT USUALLY THERE ARE VENDORS OPERATING AT ALL HOURS REGARD-LESS OF TIME ZONE.

I'm sorry. That was funny. Angelique didn't look at me, but she and I both laughed at the same time, so I know she read it. BE NICE OR LEAVE and CATFISH FEEDING FINES DOUBLED BEYOND THIS POINT would probably have been funnier if I hadn't read that one first.

"Y'all stick close to me. You might mess around and end up half-way to Mozambique before dinner. But look. They have fresh ginger right there."

"Thank you," Angelique said, walking over to a vendor near the entrance. There was a booth in there somewhere, but most of what you could see was grassy stalks so big they looked like bamboo. The counter was filled with piles of ginger that still had the green part attached.

"I'd like some fresh ginger, please," Angelique said, giving the lady her signature smile.

The lady smiled back. "You want fresh, or fresh-fresh?"

"The recipe underlined 'fresh' twice, so I think I should get fresh-fresh."

The lady nodded, then looked straight at Angelique and said, "You only have two credits, baby. That would put you over your limit. You sure?"

Y'all. The horror that crossed Angelique's face. Like the lady had called her out her name.

"Save your credits, kuzin." Cousin Cynthia stepped in. "I told you I got it."

Angelique awkwardly stepped aside. We all watched the lady grow a new hand of ginger in a glass jar on the countertop.

Cousin Cynthia handed it to Angelique with a "quiet word" that wasn't too quiet for me to hear. "Do your hours early, baby. That'll get your credits up to ten. Then you can buy yourself a little something and you won't have to go dipping into favors."

Angelique nodded, but I could tell she was embarrassed. Everybody could. I think that's why Cousin Cynthia and the Maries started walking ahead, talking and laughing among themselves again. That's when Angelique finally decided to talk to me.

"You're not checking your texts," she said quietly. "All my messages are on unread."

Had she really been texting me that whole time? Twenty-three messages. Dag. She was good.

A coven is one thing, but we're co-captains now. Communication is everything.

Co-captains?

Then my brain clicked, and I saw a flash of all the emails I skipped when I went looking for Ms. Reid's announcement. Some of those emails were from Ms. Coulon.

"Tell me now." I was trying to be chill, but my hands were shaking as I scrolled through my unread messages and tapped the one from Ms. Coulon with "Unusual Announcement" in the subject line.

"You're getting Luz a charm?"

"I told you that," I said. Or maybe I didn't.

Greetings, Lucky Recipient of This Golden Message:

Ms. Coulon always played off Willy Wonka in the welcome message. Usually it was cute.

After an unusual end to the summer, our school year will be starting right on time. As usual, the Mathletes will gather for our first practice session on the first day of school. I want everyone sharp and in place, so rather than notifying you by physical mail as is customary, I have chosen to notify you electronically. A physical list will be posted on my door to welcome you back and share your accomplishment with the world.

Angelique Hebert: Captain

Hasani Schexnayder-Jones: Co-Captain

That's where I stopped reading.

Because, seriously? Co-captain? *CO-captain?*

So Angelique was the real captain and I was just along for the ride? Wow.

I'm not gonna sit here and lie and say I didn't feel some type of way about that.

Having Angelique on the Mathletes team was a win-win scenario. She was my friend, and she was really good at math. We were going to dominate. But wanting Angelique on the team was not wanting her to be captain. Inside, I could not deal. Not right then. But I was cool. Well, as cool as I could be. Magic flowed to smooth out my face and lift up my smile. I know Angelique could see what I was doing. She was in my coven. But that was better than saying what I really wanted.

"You didn't know about Mathletes," Angelique said. "I thought you saw. Are you okay?"

"Everything's fine," I said. I just needed to see something good. I had a bunch of texts from Luz. At least one of them had to be a kitten in a martini glass or something. But I am not a kismet. I had no such luck.

I didn't look at all the texts. The last one was enough.

When you get done hanging out with the charmed girls, call me.

I shook my head. Angelique was talking, and I tried to hear what she was saying.

"All I was saying was since we're co-captains . . ." *We're not co-captains. You're captain. I'm co.* ". . . we should practice deciding things together. Kind of like a marriage. My parents make lots of decisions on their own, but if one of them thinks something is a bad idea, the other one really stops to listen."

The charmed girls? Why was Luz calling us the charmed girls? That was more like something LaToya would say. Luz was never so salty.

"All I'm saying is that if you want to get Luz a charm, don't get it here. We could still get her one from Mignon Faget. Like Sandy's. It had all of us fooled."

Ugh. Why was I being so stupid? Of course Luz was salty. She wasn't just feeling left out. I was actually leaving her out. Me. Her best friend. Leaving her out.

"Hasani, you're not listening."

I turned my phone so she could see Luz's last text.

"Okay." Angelique took a deep breath. "New plan. Let's just scan the bottle and the air, then get the rest of the ingredients and head to your house so you can talk to Luz and clear this up."

I stared at her.

"Actually, you're right. Maybe we should skip the ingredients and scanning and just head back. My mom always says we shouldn't buy little things on credit, anyway. The cost is too high."

Maybe for you. I have a black card.

I shook my head. "No. Luz takes care of me. She takes care of everybody. I'm not talking to her empty-handed." You want to be co-captains. Fine. Let's be co-captains. "Divide and conquer. You get the ingredients and do the scans, I'll get the charm."

I wasn't mad at Angelique. Really I wasn't. I just needed her to be on my side.

"Hasani, as your friend and co-captain, please trust me on this. Giving Luz a charm isn't going to change anything. First off, a charm from a witch is probably actually charmed. Who knows what that would do to Luz. But even if it doesn't do anything, it still won't *do* anything. Luz needs the truth, not a trinket."

I tried not to shake my head, but she really didn't get it. Luz was my best friend, and if she was hurt, it was my fault. It was up to me to fix it. If anybody was getting Luz a charm, it was me.

"Okay. A lot has happened today. Maybe we should take a little time to let things settle down. How about we forget everything and leave right now? We can always come back tomorrow. Or, if you really want to, we could come back tonight. They open when they want and they close when they want, remember? We can come back

whenever. We're members now," Angelique said, showing me her phone screen.

I think Angelique meant to show me the 3Thirteen app that was now on her phone, but that's not what I saw. What I saw was a notification of her being tagged in a picture. The thumbnail made me want to throw up.

"Let me see your phone," I said, but I didn't wait for her to hand it to me. I took it and tapped the screen before the notification disappeared. The tagged pic filled the screen. It was Angelique and Annie with LaToya, but that wasn't the worst part. Luz was there, too, and so was another one of those stupid bottles of water. It was off in a corner, but it was still there. And while I was standing there gaping, the heart count went up by one.

This post has been liked by LucitaDulcita and 89 others.

"Here," I said, grabbing the ginger and plopping Othello's cat carrier and her phone on top of the box Angelique was already carrying.

"Wait," Angelique said. "Come with me to the library. We'll scan the bottle and the air sample. Then we'll have more information and it'll give you a chance to calm down."

"I don't want to calm down."

"Why? Because if you calm down you might find out that LaToya has nothing to do with this?"

All I could do was shake my head.

"Fine. I'll get the ingredients. Do what you want."

I needed that freedom spell more than ever. Not for Riverbend. For Luz.

And if a charm from a witch was gonna actually be charmed, that was even better. Anything to protect my friend.

Cousin Cynthia and the Maries were a few stalls away, pretending not to hear our argument. I didn't look in their direction. I just ran back the way we came. Going the wrong direction on the moving walkway made it twice as long, but I didn't even notice. I ran out from under the pecan tree and straight to Steph's side of the desk.

"Can I get that tour? I'm looking to buy something from the fifth level."

"Oh!" Steph's eyes popped open so wide it was hard to see her eye shadow. "People don't ever come out that door. It's an entrance. But don't worry. The exits are part of the tour."

Hopefully, Kaitlynn would be, too.

CHAPTER TWENTY-TWO

BOTTLES AND BAGS

The first level was cool, but the fifth level was everything. The walls were mud behind glass, but it worked? It was like you could see every layer of silt, but instead of thinking "dirt" you thought "modern art." The chandeliers didn't hurt. You couldn't even tell the flourishes were golden crawfish until you got right up on them.

"I know I'm biased, but Kaitlynn really is the best vendor in 3Thirteen. I swear I would say that even if she didn't pay me," Steph laughed. "Some people turn their noses up at the fifth, saying it's not enough below sea level to be worth anything, but I've been to some of the shops on the eighth, and Kaitlynn is just beyond anything they're doing. She doesn't just have a shop. It's a retail experience.

"Honey, do you need a powder room or anything? There's just a little perspiration on your hairline, and I know you belles demoiselles don't like that."

It was one of those places, hunh? My fingers tingled as I lifted a little breeze to dry my face and neck and smoothed my edges with my fingertips. It actually did feel better, though.

Steph seemed satisfied. "Sorry to call you out like that, but my mom's a belle demoiselle so . . . I know all about it."

Steph seemed cool enough, but she was frontin'. No way was her mom a belle demoiselle and she was talking about it in public to a stranger. I know her mom must have been old, but even adults don't want to be deleted from the Internet. And she's lucky it was just the two of us. Otherwise I would have been mad about her outing me. Uncool.

"I got in," Steph continued as we walked past quilts hanging from the ceiling like tapestries, "but I couldn't go. We had to be in Malaysia that summer. Humanitarian work." She nodded like we were about to bond or I was going to give her points or something. I was not. I smiled, though.

"Anyhow, that's how I got connected with Kaitlynn. She makes the absolute best charms out there. Better than Belles Demoiselles. You're going to want to rip that fleur-de-lis right off. Just kidding." She laughed, touching my shoulder.

Derp. I didn't think she was serious.

"It's such a privilege to get to introduce you to Kaitlynn. She's going to love you. Not just because you're in the Talented Tenth or anything. You just have this vibe, you know. You're shiny. Like, not

many people could pull off a T-shirt and jeans, and you totally do. Kudos. Oh, wait, we're here."

The glass slid open silently and the smell of tea and night-blooming jasmine pulled us in. The room was . . . lush. There were potted banana trees, birds-of-paradise, and giant fiddle-leaf figs everywhere you looked. They were shading silver and glass cases that sparkled with a light of their own. It was like Tiffany & Co. and the Amazon rain forest had a baby. A beautiful, elegant baby.

Kaitlynn swept out of the mist and into view. She wasn't dressed like Marie Laveau this time, but her white linen tunic and pants swished like she was still wearing goddess clothes and a tignon.

"Kaitlynn, this is—"

"The charming young charmed one I met in the French Market. I was hoping you'd come."

"Hasani," I said. Thanks to Miss Lavande and the Introductions class at Belles Demoiselles, I didn't have to say facts about myself out loud anymore for people to know who I was. It was in my chin and my shoulders. Weirdly, that made it easier for people who didn't know me to see me. And I wanted Kaitlynn to see me. "You changed," I added. "I like this outfit better."

Kaitlynn's laugh sounded more like a sigh. "You mean my Marie Laveau act? I don't do it very often anymore. People like Steph here usually fill the role these days."

Steph did a little curtsy.

Kaitlynn beamed at her. "You'll have earned that charm before you know it. Not that you need it."

"Thank you, Kaitlynn." Steph grinned.

"But I can't let Steph and the others be the only ones having fun. So every once in a while I spend a morning or an afternoon, and I'm so glad I do. Otherwise I would never stumble across talented young people like you, Hasani. How have you enjoyed 3Thirteen so far?"

Steph was quietly motioning to three people in tuxedos who had silently set up a full-on tea table behind me. China. Pastries. The whole deal. Apparently the peach ranunculus was not in exactly the right place. Steph inched it over.

"I like it," I said. Understatement, but I couldn't come up with anything better with the perfect pyramid of peach macarons in my peripheral vision.

"But you haven't found what you're looking for. I can see it in your eyes. One moment." She turned to Steph. "That will be all."

Steph nodded, then looked at the tuxedoed people, who turned and followed her back out the sliding glass doors.

"Shall we sit?"

Kaitlynn gestured at the table. The chairs were already pulled out for us.

"And how's the temperature? Let me guess. You'd like it to be a touch less humid. Curly girls always like it a touch less humid. But maybe also a bit more rainbow?"

I nodded.

Kaitlynn turned a crystal water pitcher on the table by maybe half an inch. The next thing I knew, there were delicate flecks of rainbow arcing across the table, dancing between the silverware and plates. The air was drier, too. There was still mist, but it stayed around our feet.

"So, now, tell me: What's missing for a young, talented, charmed girl like you? One of the Talented Tenth, no less. No. Let me guess. You're looking to rise. I don't blame you. If I'd had your strength at your age, I would have done exactly the same thing."

"No," I said. "That's not it." Honestly, I didn't even know what she meant. Rise how? Like levitate or be in charge? Either way, I had a feeling I should turn it down.

"Ambition is nothing to be ashamed of. I know you have it. Steph sent me your profile. Your little YouTube channel is making quite the splash. That sort of thing doesn't happen by accident."

I mean, it did. Sort of.

"I need a charm for my best friend," I said. "Before, I just wanted to get her a fleur-de-lis that looked like mine, but now—"

"Now your success is attracting enemies and you need a charm that is not only beautiful but will also protect her."

My eyebrows shot straight up. "How did you know?"

Kaitlynn shrugged. "It's a tale as old as time. Their weakness becomes your weakness. I advise all my people not to befriend the untalented for exactly that reason. But you've had this best friend since . . . ?"

"Second grade," I filled in.

"Second grade! Of course. That's nearly half your life. You couldn't abandon her now."

"Exactly," I said. "She's always been there for me and—"

"—and now you'll be there for her. No matter which witch comes her way. Let me show you what I have to offer. I think you'll find exactly what you need."

Kaitlynn snapped her fingers, the jewels in her nails catching the light. The glass cases rotated, and one moved closer to us like it was on a conveyor belt.

"Let me see. Fleur-de-lis. Platinum or platinum-look? No," Kaitlynn answered her own question. "Platinum. Nothing but the best for your friend, and only platinum will have the proper sheen."

She snapped her fingers again. That case changed place with another. A few of the fleurs-de-lis inside had little crystals or other

embellishments, but most of them were dead ringers for my Belles Demoiselles charm.

"Is there something in particular your friend is in danger of?"

"Influence," I said. "My whole school is, though. There's a girl who keeps squ—"

"Ah-ah-ahhh. The less I know, the better. If you want your friend protected from influence, this is the charm for you."

Kaitlynn drummed her fingers on the table. At that point I was expecting something to happen. But I thought that something was going to be the case flying open or one of the tuxedoed people coming back again. I was not prepared for the monkey.

He was tiny and white and jumped up on Kaitlynn's shoulder for a scratch before leaping to the glass case. Kaitlynn tapped twice and then once and the monkey set to work first opening the case, then taking out the first fleur-de-lis in the second row, then sliding it into a Tiffany-blue jewelry box before closing the lid. Kaitlynn placed a walnut on the table. The monkey leapt over to it, gently setting down the jewelry box before picking up his prize.

"Good job, Jasper," she said, rubbing his head with two fingers. "Jasper is a one-trick pony. Aren't you, Jasper? But his one trick is so important. That charm will bond with and protect the next human that touches it. Jasper is dexterous, but he isn't human. Are you, Jasper?"

I blinked. The whole monkey thing was unexpected. Cool, but unexpected.

Jasper finished eating his walnut, then ran up a tree made of aluminum bottles near one of the fiddle-leaf figs. I blinked again. The bottles had blended in with the surrounding foliage, but I still have no idea how I could have missed them. They were the exact bottles LaToya had been using to ruin my life.

"What are those?" I asked, pointing. I was smooth on the outside, but my heart beat two times faster.

"Those? They're water from the exact point of the sharpest river bend on the Mississippi. Filtered, of course, and with a few proprietary herbs of my own. Quite powerful, I must say—for some at least. The witches who need a boost find them invaluable, but others think of them as just something refreshing to drink after barre class."

"Are they for sale?"

I couldn't take my eyes off them.

"I wouldn't sell them. That would be unethical. The river belongs to all of us. Think of this as more of a gift with purchase. Are you ready to make a trade?"

Was I?

Answer: Yes. Yes, I was.

Mathletes wasn't just about being mathematically excellent. We were—Ms. Coulon made sure of that. But she also made sure we knew how to win. For whatever reason, the schools we matched against in tournaments always underestimated us. Maybe because we were a public school. Maybe because we didn't have matching uniforms. Who knows. The point is that Ms. Coulon always told us, "Let them. It'll only hurt them, not you."

Kaitlynn calling me "little" and "young" and stuff like that only made her seem like one of the fancy teams we beat at the Mathletes tournaments. She thought she could get one over on me. But my mama had taught me about credit, too. It didn't matter how much credit you got on a black card. The question was, could you pay it back. I had no intention whatsoever of going into debt to Kaitlynn, at least not if I could help it.

"Now, I see you have quite a few credits available, but why don't you hold on to those? I'm sure there are a few ingredients you're look-ing to buy on the first level. How about we consider this trade an exchange of favor?"

"What does that mean?"

"That means you hold on to your credits now and pay me in the future instead."

"But I have credits," I said. "Wouldn't it be better if I didn't go into debt?"

"You have nineteen credits. That could buy you at least three of anything on the first level, but this is the fifth level. Quite frankly, nineteen credits would not be a fair trade for this charm. But one of the perks of being in the Talented Tenth is that people will trade you for a favor. I'm willing to part with this charm on favor alone. I think five favors should cover it. That is quite a deal."

"What if I had something else to trade?" I asked. This is the part I had been practicing over and over in my head.

Kaitlynn laughed. Jasper did, too. "No offense, little one, but what would a green witch like you have that would be of value to an established person like me?"

My hands went to my charms. I wasn't about to offer my fleur-de-lis or my dolphin to Kaitlynn, but it was instinct. I guess something in me said to cover them up. Like protection or something.

"You don't have to cover your charms, charmed girl. I'm not a monster. I wouldn't take them from you even if I were. Those are bonded to you, which means they're useless to me or anyone else. I'm afraid it's favors or nothing."

"What about a spellbook?" I asked.

That got Kaitlynn's attention. She looked me up and down.

The way Dee and Angelique were going on about it, it had to be worth something. And I know I didn't want it. I'd do the freedom spell and be done with it. Giving that thing away to get a gift for Luz was basically the definition of win-win.

"Ordinarily I'd say no, but recently I came across one that turned out more valuable than I expected. I tell you what, I'll take a look at it."

"Okay," I said, standing up. Kaitlynn did, too. "I just have to run home and get it. I only live a few blocks from here. Steph can show me the exit, right? I'll be back so fast. I just need to grab some ingredients and do one spell from it. Then it's all yours."

"Absolutely not," Kaitlynn said. "You're wasting my time. Favor or not?"

"Do you guarantee it?" I asked.

Kaitlynn cocked her head.

"The charm," I explained. "Do you guarantee it? I mean, would it work better than, like, a freedom spell?"

"Ah." Kaitlynn smiled. "I would never compare them. Spells are unpredictable. My charms are predictable as rain and guaranteed to work until the end of their wearer's days."

"So that's a guarantee? What happens if it doesn't work?"

"Then I will have reneged on a contract. If I reneged on contracts, I would never have made it to the fifth level. It will work."

I reached into my pocket. Honestly, I was second-guessing it even as I put the extender on the table. Without it, I wouldn't be able to do the freedom spell at Riverbend. The extender was my only way around the sanlavi. But Sandy's stupid spell wasn't guaranteed. This was. Protecting the whole school from LaToya's influence was one thing, but if it came down to maybe saving everybody or definitely saving Luz, I was definitely saving Luz.

"I have an extender," I said, placing it on the table in front of me.

"An extender?" Kaitlynn began, exasperated, but then she saw the way Jasper was looking at it, the glint in his eyes.

"Well," she continued. "I like you. I want to help. Favors would honestly be your best bet, but since it's your first day and you came at my invitation, I'll let you have the charm in exchange for this extender as is, plus nineteen credits and one favor."

"The extender and sixteen credits. No favors."

She tried to play it off, but I could see what she was thinking. My extender was more valuable than she expected. Maybe I could convince Miss Lafleur to give me another one.

"The extender, sixteen credits, and your word that you'll come visit me again. Do we have a deal?"

"Yes, but—" I don't remember the rest of what I was going to say. I couldn't hear myself think over Sandy shrieking.

"Hasani! Don't!"

CHAPTER TWENTY-THREE

PARENTS AND PASSES

The doors opening were silent. Sandy was not. She ran into the room yelling and waving a magazine around like a weapon, as if Kaitlynn were trying to fight me, not sell me something after tea and cookies.

Sandy grabbed me by the shoulders and looked me up and down. "Are you hurt?"

I stepped back. "What are you doing here?" I pulled my chin and shoulders back into place and just stared at her. I wasn't tall enough to look down on her, but I may as well have been. The effect was the same.

Sandy pulled herself together. I couldn't see her magic, but I imagined her calling up the perma-breeze that made her hair look so effortless. I could do that, too.

Steph burst in three seconds later.

"I'm sorry, Kaitlynn. I couldn't stop her. Her pass worked. Then she threatened to get physical and blocked the riverside elevator. I had to go on the lakeside and then run around."

"That's quite all right, Steph. I think we're done here. Jasper?"

Jasper jumped onto the table, picked up the jewelry box, then leapt to where I was sitting. I reached out to take it. I thought he was going to hand it to me. But as Jasper leaned over, the jewelry box disappeared, and so did his arm. It took me a second to catch on. There was a bag in front of me woven of intentions. I put my hand out, and sure enough, I could feel it. Slippery smooth. Somewhere between velvet and silk. I felt for the opening and dipped my hand inside. It disappeared.

"Cool," I said. It was. All the closed parts of the bag were invisible, but I could still see into the opening at the top. The jewelry box was in there, and so was a bottle. The gift with "purchase." I smiled and pulled my hand out, at which point Jasper went back to work. He looked like a tiny mime. A tiny mime with a long tail closing a backpack and then holding it up so somebody could slip their arms in. I did. I could feel it on me, but the only sign it was there were little wrinkles by my shoulders.

"Hasani." Sandy's voice was weird. "Whatever this is, you don't need it. Give it back."

"Why?" I said. "It's not even for me. It's for Luz."

"What's for Luz?"

"A fleur-de-lis charm."

I don't even know why I answered her. I think I was momentarily dazzled by the mom sounds in her voice. What I bought was none of Sandy's business.

Sandy took a deep breath and rounded on Kaitlynn.

"Kaitlynn, she doesn't know how all this works. YOU know she doesn't know how all this works. You're taking advantage of her. Just do the right thing and undo whatever you did."

"I believe you're looking for the fungible section. That's the level just above the mushrooms. This is level five. From here on down there are only non-fungible trades. Perhaps you'd be more comfortable on level one?"

"It's not right," Sandy said. She was really sounding heated. I wished she would stop.

"You know that it's not possible to make an unfair trade in 3Thirteen. Check your ledger. Our trade was fair and binding or it never would have happened."

"Just because it was recorded on the blockchain doesn't make it right. Hasani doesn't even know how credits work. Or favors."

"How do you know?" I asked.

Sandy shook her head, standing between me and Kaitlynn like she was my mama or something. "You're taking advantage of her.

Hasani, this is how she operates. Looking for people who might be strong but don't know any better yet. Usually it's tourists. I never thought she'd stoop this low."

"I prefer to cater to a certain clientele, but my rates are actually quite reasonable. They get something. I get something. That's how fair trade works."

"Fine. Do another trade. I'll trade you a hundred credits to return whatever you took of hers, including the favors."

"You think a hundred credits from you would cover even one favor from a member of the Talented Tenth? A member with a long, long life ahead of her? You're funny." Kaitlynn actually laughed. "How did you even get in here to interrupt us with a trade in progress? The management will be informed of this security breach."

"A parent pass," Sandy said defiantly, putting her hand on my shoulder.

My whole body went cold. "You are not my mother." The words came out way harsher than I thought, but I meant them.

"Stepmother," Sandy said. "I represent the interests of her father."

"Your stepdaughter is sharper than you think. I am running a business. Part of running a business is going for the highest-value trade possible. But Hasani has a mathematical mind. She saw it right away and refused to play ball. Check your ledger. You'll see."

Sandy flipped the magazine open, tapping and scrolling like she was on a phone. She spread her fingers on a page, then looked up at me with her brow furrowed.

"You have an extender? Where did you get an extender?"

"You don't know me. You don't know my life," I said.

Sandy ignored me, though. "Where is it?" she asked.

Jasper had scooped up the extender. He was holding it in the bottle tree, tilting it this way and that to watch the few tiny flowers left inside swish back and forth.

Sandy slammed the magazine shut.

"Two hundred credits," Sandy said.

Kaitlynn smirked.

"Three hundred," Sandy said.

"You don't have three hundred," Kaitlynn said.

"Fine. I'll owe you favors."

"I only accept favors if they are appreciating. Yours are on the decline."

"Okay. Ingredients."

"I can get the ingredients I need right here at 3Thirteen."

"Sure. But how much are you trading for them? I heard you were looking for dragon scale."

"You don't have dragon scale."

"No, but someone in my circle of friends does."

"Hmm," Kaitlynn said. "Maybe if you had the dragon scale with you so I could inspect it. But . . . your credit history at 3Thirteen is more established than Hasani's . . . I tell you what. You can owe me. One future ingredient produced by you within twenty-four hours of my request, and in exchange, I will return Hasani's extender to you when the trade is complete."

"You'll return Hasani's extender unused," Sandy added.

"Unused."

"Done."

Something moved on Sandy's magazine. She glanced at it, but mostly she kept her eyes locked on Kaitlynn.

Kaitlynn looked down at the crystal pitcher. I think both of them were checking the blockchain, whatever that was.

"Fine," Sandy said. "Let's go, Hasani."

I just stared at her.

"Steph was gonna show me the exit."

"No. I will," Sandy said. "Let's go."

"One moment," Kaitlynn said. "A fun thing about the world is that it is constantly moving forward."

Sandy and I both looked at her. I had a pretty good idea where this was going.

"The future is now," Kaitlynn smiled. "A tuft of unicorn hair. You have twenty-four hours. So I guess I'll see you again tomorrow. Until then, the extender goes in S-Crow."

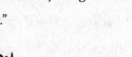

"**C**rud," Sandy said.

We were in the elevator. She was talking to me, but I was most definitely not talking to her.

"My account is frozen. A friend of a friend has a unicorn connection in Madagascar, but they're offline. If I could get there in person, I might be able to find them, but I forgot that future agreements bind your account for collateral. How am I supposed to get to Madagascar on such short notice with no credits?"

I'm not gonna lie. The phrase "That's goodie for ya" came to mind. I didn't need Sandy's help. She was forever jumping in and messing things up. At least this time it was her life, not mine.

"I don't actually have a parent pass," she said. "We'd have to register together. I just didn't want Kaitlynn to think there wasn't anybody looking out for you. I'm still on duty. I used an override."

Silence from me.

"Hasani, you're very talented. I knew that before I knew you were a witch. Your dad was forever talking about you and how amazing you are, so I knew you were special. It took him a while before he was willing to share stuff like your YouTube channel with me. But, Hasani, when I saw you on-screen, three seconds in, I just knew. You shine. But the thing is, when you're shiny, people are always going to be attracted to your shine. That's a good thing, but not everybody has good intentions. You have to let the people who care for you watch out for you. You know. Have your back."

That was too much.

"You care about me?"

"Yes, Hasani. Of course. I care about you very much."

The elevator opened on the first level. The Rivyèmarché was noisy, but even if it had been quiet, I don't think that would have stopped me from getting loud.

"You can't care for me. You don't even know me. What you know about me is whatever my dad told you, and he doesn't know me, either." My fingers were buzzing. My eyes stung. I wasn't trying to hold back tears, but they never came. It just felt like they would. "I don't need your help. In fact, you didn't even help. All you did was get your account frozen over something that wasn't even your business."

"Hasani, all this stuff is new for you. You traded something very valuable for something we could have gotten anywhere. I would have given you mine if I had known."

"I traded MY extender that MY teacher gave to me so I could get something for MY best friend."

"I understand that. I just really wish you had come to me first. Trading an extender is . . . complicated."

"Well, I only traded it because she didn't want your stupid spellbook. At least the extender was useful."

Sandy didn't say anything, but she didn't have to. I knew she was hurt. I could feel it. It was all over her face. But I was hurting, too, and I didn't stop.

"Witches like me don't squeeze our magic. That's for witches like you. And my mom not being a witch doesn't mean you can take her place. You can't just jump in and give me fancy things and think you can buy me just because you're married to my dad now. I can't be bought, Sandy."

People were looking at us. I didn't care.

"I wasn't trying to buy you. I thought the book would be helpful. I thought . . . never mind. You're right. Let me take you home. All iPhone tracking stops working three hundred feet from every 3Thirteen entrance, so to your mom it looks like you dropped off the map. I told her I'd find you and look out for you. She's worried. Ms. Nancy is looking for Angelique, too. Same deal, though I think Ms. Nancy already figured out where Angelique went. I'll take you both home."

"No thanks," I said. "I'll find my way from here."

CHAPTER TWENTY-FOUR

DOWN AND DOWN

I spotted Angelique in the food court, not too far from the elevators. Or, rather, she was watching me, and that level of disappointment on anyone's face stands out in a crowd. Clearly she saw what had just gone down between me and Sandy.

When I made it over to the table, it was all set for two people. Not only that, she had fresh ginger, figs on a branch that looked like it was still growing leaves, and a little river silt–looking stone that must have been picture jasper. I felt bad. I owed Angelique an apology.

"I'm sorry for being so weird about Mathletes," I said. I used "sorry" on purpose because, that time, I really was. "I shouldn't have let myself get in my feelings about you being captain. You're a great mathematician. Congratulations."

I still didn't think Angelique should have been captain. But

Angelique and I were friends. I should have at least congratulated her on making the team. That was my bad.

I expected her to try to bounce the compliment back at me or cover it up by complimenting me, too. She didn't. All she said was, "Thank you. That means a lot coming from you." She looked down at the tea service. "I heard you yelling at Sandy."

"I know."

"A lot of people did."

"I know. Honestly, it's fine. She can go cry to my dad about losing her credits or whatever. I don't even feel bad." That wasn't exactly true. I did feel bad. Just not bad enough to pretend like everything was cool when it wasn't.

"What did she do?"

"Just regular Sandy stuff. Jumping in where she doesn't belong. Do you know she actually told Kaitlynn that she was my mom? Well, stepmom, but still."

"Isn't she your stepmom?"

"Technically, but that's not the point. The point is that I didn't ask her to jump in and quote *help me*, but she did it anyway. I don't know who she thinks she's showing out for, but it's not going to work. And if she got all her credits frozen, that's her problem. Good luck finding a tuft of unicorn hair before tomorrow. Maybe my dad can help her," I laughed.

"Or maybe you could," she said. Angelique was clearly in a #Team-Sandy kind of mood. She didn't laugh with me.

"The way Kaitlynn's eyes glinted over that unicorn hair, it must be worth like a billion credits."

"I thought your black card gave you like a bajillion credits. You can afford it, can't you?"

"Only nineteen. I'm not going into debt over Sandy."

"Sandy's not so bad."

I took a deep breath. I was really not in the mood for Angelique to be taking somebody else's side over mine. Again. I mean, if this was a preview of Mathletes, maybe I needed to sit this last year out.

"She's nice," Angelique said. "Exuberant, but nice. She's only trying to help. I know you weren't thrilled about her and your dad getting married, but I thought you were okay with it."

"I was okay with it. I am okay with it. That doesn't mean that I want to have Sandy in my face every five seconds. If she wants to be with my dad, fine. Be with my dad. They can both leave me out of it."

"Hasani, that's not how this works."

I took a deep breath and tried to keep my voice down, but at that moment, I needed to say what I needed to say.

"How would you know? Your parents are still married. To each other."

"Well, I know blood isn't what makes family. And I saw back there, Sandy is trying to make you her family. But whatever. Your call, Hasani."

I took a deep breath. The conversation was a little more heated than I had meant it to be. I changed the subject.

"Did you make it to the library to get those scanned?" I asked, nodding toward the shoebox and cat carrier at her feet.

"No," she said.

I sensed an awkward silence coming on, so I jumped back in.

"Maybe we don't have to," I said. "I know where LaToya got that water bottle."

"I do, too," Angelique said. She was sitting tall, hands in her lap, looking straight at me.

All I could do was blink.

"How?"

"She told me."

"You talked to her?" "

"Yes, Hasani. I talked to her."

"When?"

"Just now. She caught me on my way down to the library and suggested we have tea."

I looked down. The table was set for two, but the cup in front of me had already been used. I rolled my eyes. Glad I didn't drink out of it.

"LaToya was just here? Just now?"

"Yes."

"And you were talking to her?" I shook my head. I could not believe it. "Why?"

"Hasani, listen. LaToya kind of needs a friend right now. She's got a lot going on, and it seems like maybe she doesn't have many."

"Yeah," I said. "That's what happens when you keep messing people over."

"That's not what I mean. LaToya was trying to help herself. The thing in the gym with the termites? It was her."

"Tell me something I didn't know."

"She added some stuff into the bend water. She wanted to influence Ms. Coulon to get into Mathletes, but it wasn't working. She knew she couldn't fake a paper-and-pencil test, so she kept chugging her potion, hoping it would kick in. That backfired, obviously. She did try to fix it, though. That's why she made that WeBop taking some of the credit for getting rid of the termites."

What?

"But honestly, she really didn't know you got rid of the termites. She felt bad when she found out. But that was like three minutes ago. What could she have done since then?"

"Not been a jerk?" I offered. "Actually help us find Annie when we needed her?"

"She thought you were trying to get back at her for not inviting you into her coven. She didn't think Annie was in danger. She thought you were making it up. Then when everything came out, LaToya tried to find Annie herself, but she was having trouble. That's how she got mixed up with Kaitlynn. I guess LaToya owes Kaitlynn a bunch of favors now. She did find Annie, though. And she told Annie she was a witch and gave her a bunch of those bottles of bend water. LaToya thinks they're a confidence booster for everybody. I don't know about all of that, but she says they're really friends. She likes her."

I could not believe what I was hearing.

"And you believe her? LaToya is a liar. She'll literally say anything to get people on her side. Of course she told you she and Annie are friends. She knows that's what you want to hear."

Angelique shook her head. "I should have been more clear. LaToya did say she and Annie are friends, but I was actually talking about Annie. I called her while LaToya was sitting here."

"Annie needs to stay away. When LaToya turns on her, she won't be able to handle it." My hands were trembling. "I can't believe that you just sat here and had tea with LaToya and now you're still sitting here defending her."

"Hasani, they're friends. You don't have to be friends with LaToya, but can't you just let it go? Annie is happy being friends with her."

"Are you?"

"Excuse me?"

"Are you happy being friends with LaToya?"

"I wouldn't say LaToya and I are exactly friends. I mean—"

"Fine," I said. "Unfriend her."

Angelique stared.

"You're not friends with her, right? You've seen all the videos you need to see? Unfriend her."

Angelique went into her purse, pulled out her phone, and quietly laid it on the table.

"Here. You do it," she said. "I guess Annie and I are in the same boat now. You get to tell us both who we can and can't be friends with, right? So take my phone. Take it like you did earlier. No. Wait. It won't be the way you did earlier because this time I'm actually giving you permission."

I tried to keep my face calm. I really did. But I guess closing my eyes and pressing my lips tight was almost as bad as the eye roll I was trying to hold in.

"Why do y'all keep defending her?" I wasn't shouting, but my voice had a little bite. I couldn't help it.

"Because this wasn't supposed to be about you, Hasani. It was supposed to be about Annie. YOU made it about you. But fine. I'm your friend. If you wanna make it about you, let's talk about what's really bothering you."

What was I supposed to say?

Angelique got up. "I'm going to sleep at my house tonight. You take the ingredients if you want them. Cousin Cynthia got them, and she told me to give you this message, word for word. She said, 'Tell ma ti kuzin I tried to keep her from around Kaitlynn, but now she's gone and gone, that's on her.' And for the record, I was against you getting anything from Kaitlynn, especially not for Luz. We don't know Kaitlynn."

"Wait a minute," I said. "Are you being salty?"

"Excuse me?"

"Is it really bothering you that I got my best friend a stupid charm? One thing you couldn't? I guess being a first daughter of a first daughter in a fancy house, watching your mom and whoever else do magic from the day you were born, doesn't give you enough of a head start over people like me. You get everything, Angelique. You're perfect at everything because you get everything."

Angelique's face stayed calm. But for the first time ever, I saw anger flash through her eyes. "Hasani, sometimes you're so ignorant, it hurts. I don't have time for this. Do what you want with Sandy. It's your life. I'll see you later."

CHAPTER TWENTY-FIVE

PIRATES AND DREAD

*O*nce I had the charm, I had to do the hardest part: Tell Luz. Honestly, if I could have convinced Luz to wear that charm 24/7/365—or at least 7/5/290, while we were at school—I would have definitely gone that route. But Luz is stubborn. And asks a lot of questions. And really likes accessories. Usually those were all good things. Right then, they were backing me into a corner. When I walked into my room, Dee was the only one there.

"Angelique is going to leave the coven," I said. I just dropped it on the floor like I dropped the invisible backpack.

Dee looked up from her drawing.

My channel notifications were pinging on my computer in the background. I tried to tune them out.

"She said that?"

"No! But she might as well have." I flopped down on the bed next to her. The drawing was of Othello jumping out of a giant patch of morning glories.

"That's good," I said.

"Thanks. The perspective is off, but it's all right. I need the practice, especially with ink. You know he stay playing in your YouTube backdrop when you're not here, right? Luz was here," she added. "She left a while ago, though."

"But you stayed?"

"I didn't want to leave you out here by yourself," she said.

"I got her a present," I said. "A real charm. You would think it was Belles Demoiselles if you didn't already know it wasn't."

"You gon' give it to her?"

"Yeah."

"When?"

I needed to change the subject.

"How bad is it when somebody leaves your coven?" I asked. "Is it blood or reverse flowers or what?"

"I don't know, but I don't think you have to worry about that. I talked to Angelique. She said she needed some time to herself, but she didn't say anything about wanting to leave the coven."

"You didn't see her. She was really mad."

"Yeah?" Dee was filling in Othello's fur. He's fluffy. There were a lot of hash marks. The sound of them almost blocked out the notifications. Almost.

"I called her rich."

"She is." Dee's pen kept scratching the page.

"I said if she was really friends with me, she would unfriend LaToya. I probably shouldn't have said that, but I kind of think it's true. If the tables were turned, I would automatically unfriend LaToya."

The scratching stopped for a second, but then Dee started up again.

"She told me that, too. I get being salty about Mathletes and all that, but unfriending people? Why, Hasani?"

"LaToya is toxic," I said.

"Because she was scared and made mistakes? Does that mean Angelique should unfriend you, too? That was uncool, man."

"I know," I said. "Maybe she *should* unfriend me."

Dee kept drawing. Othello was looking more and more real on the page.

"What you gonna do?" she asked.

"Apologize, I guess. But doesn't Angelique being so perfect bother you sometimes?"

"Not really," Dee said. "That's her thing. She can't change that any more than you can change being stupid powerful."

I gave Dee a look.

"You are stupid powerful. And you don't know what you're doing."

"Well, that's at least two-thirds right. I am stupid, and I definitely don't know what I'm doing."

Dee put her pen down. "Are you serious right now? You're not. You joshing me, right?"

I shook my head.

"Hasani, really? You don't know how powerful you are? Why do you think Miss Villere had those teachers breaking their necks to scoop you up off the street? Why do you think Belles Demoiselles was swimming in morning glories most of the time you were there? You telling me you never noticed? Nothing ever tipped you off?"

I shrugged, but then I thought about it. "They gave me a black card," I said. Dee raised an eyebrow. "And they said I'm in something called the Talented Tenth."

"What I told you? Stupid powerful."

"So, you knew? This whole time?"

"Not just me. The whole Vacherie circle was like daaaaang. This girl is bad. And that includes Angelique. I think she even said 'dang' one time."

I laughed.

"Seriously, though. Being stupid powerful while not knowing stuff is your thing. We knew that when we signed up."

I laughed again.

"To be fair, no matter how much magic I have, you and Angelique have an advantage. Both of you got to watch your mothers do magic since you were babies."

"You said that to Angelique?"

I nodded.

"Today?"

I nodded again.

"Mmmh," Dee huffed. "No wonder she's mad."

"I'm just saying. It'd probably be better if I had less magic. I'd do less damage."

"I don't know about all that. All I know is, I'm not the one you need to be apologizing and confessing stuff to."

Othello jumped onto my stomach, but I couldn't ignore my channel notifications anymore.

"I thought I muted that," I said, patting Othello's butt so he'd jump off. "Dee, did you unmute?"

"I didn't touch your computer."

"Well, somebody did."

Six thousand and eighty-nine comments. I could not read 6,089 comments. Not right then. But I had ignored them for so long, it had to be really bad. I kind of felt like I deserved to see how awful they'd gotten. My channel, my responsibility.

I scrolled through the first screen of them. I wasn't leaving double heart, double kiss, flower, rainbow, flower like I usually did on the good ones. I was scrolling for the bad ones. The ones I needed to block. But six screens in, there weren't any. Not a single one. I wasn't happy. I wanted to cry. Instead, I rounded on Dee.

"I know you think I'm an extra-strength hot mess, but I asked you not to and you did it anyway."

"I don't know what you're talking about."

"Fine. Not you. VacherieNOLAARTTeast. I'm guessing that's the bitbot you set up for me even though I said a thousand times that I didn't want one. Dag, Dee. You're as bad as Sandy."

"Anh-aaanh," Dee sang. The longer she was away from Vacherie, the more she sounded like Grandmé Annette. "Nope. You just mad with yourself, now."

"What?"

"Can't be mad at everybody. You just mad with yourself. It used to aggravate me when Grandmé Annette said that, but now I see what she means. You lying to Luz. You mad at Angelique. You mad at LaToya. You stay mad at Sandy. And now you mad at me? Nah. You just mad with yourself. Something is bothering you, and I promise you that something ain't me. You need to figure out what's going on with you before you start losing friends for real."

"Nothing's going on with me," I said.

Dee shook her head. "You been lyin' pretty easy lately. I guess you may as well lie to yourself, too."

"I don't want to lie. I just can't tell Luz the truth, okay?" I wanted to cry, but the pain was trapped in the pit of my stomach just like my magic was in the sanlavi.

"Why? What are you ashamed of? Being special?"

No wonder people had started calling me fake in the comments. It wasn't that many, but maybe they hurt so much because they weren't wrong. How could I possibly be showing my subscribers the real me when I wasn't even showing it to my friends? Or myself?

"I'm ashamed of hurting people," I said. "Annie. My mom. I keep doing it."

Dee shook her head. "So you're hurting people because you're ashamed of hurting people. What kind of sense does that make? You wanna be real? Be a real friend. Just tell Luz the truth. At least then she'll know why you're always pushing her to the side. Maybe she wants to stay friends, maybe she doesn't, but at least she gets to decide."

That's when I wanted to cry. I mean, I kind of always knew it was a possibility, but to have Dee just outright say out loud that Luz might choose to not be my friend was over the top.

I told Dee I'd be right back, then ran to the bathroom and shut the door. I'd heard my mom in there crying enough to know that closing

the door wasn't going to stop anybody from hearing me, but I needed to close it anyway. I needed to be alone for a minute.

What was I supposed to do? Just call Luz and go, "Hey, bestie. You know that girl LaToya? The one you thought was so aggravating and fake from jump? Yeah, well, the reason you're starting to hang out with her is because she's influencing your second brain. Oh, and by the way, maybe the only reason you've ever been friends with me is because I've maybe been doing the same thing to you"? Yeah. Not good. It didn't help that, influence or not, seeing Luz like LaToya's picture really hurt. Luz knew how awful LaToya was.

Then it hit me. Luz didn't know how awful LaToya was. She knew she was stuck-up. She knew she acted like living in a house without a pool and a tennis court made us less important. But she didn't really know how awful LaToya was. It was up to me to tell her, and I didn't need to say a word about LaToya being a witch to do it. I only needed Annie.

It was already past eight. Not all the way dark yet, but late enough that Luz wouldn't be the one to answer the door.

I texted instead.

Call me? I gotta tell you something.

311

No response.

About Annie and LaToya.

The three dots appeared, dancing on the screen for like thirty seconds. Then nothing.

Oh! I have a present for you. Hint: It's an accessory. :-)

Nothing. So I FaceTimed her. Miguel picked up.

"Are you in the bathroom?" he laughed.

"Are you in a closet?" I smiled back. "Let me talk to Luz."

"She says it's too late for a present and she doesn't want to talk to you. That's why I'm in a closet. So she doesn't know I took her—"

"Miguel!" Luz's voice was muffled.

The closet got way brighter, Miguel said, "Oop," and that was the end of the call. I called back three times. Nothing. That's when I really started to cry.

Somebody knocked on the bathroom door.

"My dad's here," Dee said. "I'ma go."

I flung the door open.

"I wasn't really using it," I said.

"I know. I'ma go anyway. Luz is standing on your neighbor's front lawn, and I think y'all could use some space. To talk," she added.

I grabbed the invisible bag with the charm in it off the floor in my room and raced outside. Sure enough, Luz was on the lawn between our houses with no shoes on. She had her arms crossed and she didn't

come all the way to my door, but at least she was there. I could work with that.

"Bye, y'all." Dee waved at us as she got into her dad's car.

"Bye, Dee." Luz smiled, but when she turned back to me, the smile was gone. "I'm listening," Luz said.

"Do you want to come inside?"

"You said you have something to tell me. I'm listening."

"LaToya is using Annie."

"How would you know? Have you talked to either of them?"

"Well, no, but—"

"Save it, Hasani. I didn't come out here with the mosquitoes for gossip. I came to hear what you have to say to me."

"I needed to warn you about LaToya."

Luz shook her head. "You don't have anything to say about *you*? From you to me?"

I gripped the bag a little harder. This wasn't going like I planned. "Like what?"

"Like, 'sorry'? 'Sorry I was ignoring your texts.' 'Sorry I didn't bother to congratulate you for getting captain of the debate team'? 'Sorry I was having secret sleepovers'? 'Sorry I was sneaking around and pretending to still be your friend while I set up new ones for when I ditched you.' 'Sorry I made LaToya seem like such a jerk because now I'm going to treat you just like I treated her'?"

"Luz, no." I shook my head.

"Yeah. I know about what you did to LaToya at camp. I know about how once your channel started taking off, you thought you were too good for her. I never thought you would feel like that about me, but it looks like I was wrong."

"You didn't hear my side of the story."

"You know why I didn't hear it? You didn't tell me. You told me a whole bunch of stuff, but you didn't tell me that."

Luz turned to walk back across the grass.

"Wait!" I said. I was trembling. "There's something you need to know . . . about LaToya." I don't think I knew what I was saying until I actually said it.

Luz looked back at me.

"What? That she's a witch? I know. She told me at Annie's. She showed me. She showed both of us. That's more than I can say for you."

She knew?

"The only reason she did that was to impress you," I said.

"Yeah, well, at least she tried to impress me. Unlike you, who didn't bother to say anything."

I just stood there holding the bag. The only thing I could think of was if I dropped it I might not find it again. Somebody would literally need to trip over it.

"It hurts, you know," Luz said, her voice shaking a little. "Knowing that the person who's supposed to be your best friend doesn't trust you."

"I do trust you," I said.

"Yeah? Just not enough to tell me you're a witch. You know what's sad and scary? Surprisingly, it's not finding out that you and all your new friends are witches. It's that you think I'm so small that I can't handle you being good at something I can't do."

"That's not how I think of you at all."

"Really? I can't tell. Maybe friends don't tell each other everything, but they definitely tell each other the big things, Hasani. You know the first thing I did when I got that debate team email? Call you. That's not even big compared to magic. MAGIC, Hasani. And I had to go figuring it out from old videos after literally everybody else told me. Why on earth would you keep magic from me, Hasani?"

"I was gonna tell you," I said. "I got you a present."

"Keep it, Hasani. I don't want it."

Luz turned and started cutting back across the lawn.

When I called her name, she didn't look back again. It wasn't until I got inside that I realized that holding an invisible gift meant I looked one hundred percent empty-handed to Luz. It didn't matter if I could feel the bag in my hand when Luz couldn't see anything at all.

I ran straight to my mom's room. I'm not even sure I closed the front door. My mom's an extreme morning person, so she falls asleep by 8 P.M. on the regular, but I woke her up anyway. I needed her.

"Mom, I don't feel well."

She snapped into mom mode, putting the back of her hand to my forehead to check for fever.

"You sick?" she asked. "You're warm."

I shook my head.

"Everyone's mad at me. I don't think I can go to school. Will you take me to Vacherie?"

A full-time apprenticeship was sounding better and better. Maybe being the Dread Pirate Roberts of pest control was a good idea after all.

CHAPTER TWENTY-SIX

RECHARGES AND
REFLECTIONS

Of course my mom didn't just get up and bring me to Vacherie.
I mean, I kind of hoped she would, but I one hundred percent
knew she wouldn't. That's not how mothers work, at least not any
mothers I know. They might humor you for a minute, but really it'll
just be their way of getting information out of you.

My mom didn't even bother to humor me. She did what she does,
which is go get tea, even when I say I don't want any.

"Cranberry cinnamon," she said. "Don't look at me like that.
It's delicious."

It was. I mean, she put a lot of honey in my cup, so it couldn't
have gone too wrong, but it probably still would have been good
without it.

"Now, what has prompted this sudden change in life plan? Is dropping out of middle school to start witching full-time a part of the culture that I don't know about?" Mom said while refilling my cup.

If I weren't so miserable, I would have laughed, but I was, so I shrugged.

"I'm guessing it has something to do with your sleepover at which it seems nobody is sleeping over? But I don't want to have to play twenty questions with my only child when both of us know I should be sleeping. Please don't make me drag it out of you, Hasani. Just talk to me."

"It's not that I don't want to, but if we talk here it might kick off a petty witch war, and I already have enough people mad at me."

"I see," my mom said.

The next thing I knew, we were in my mom's car, Lucy, parked by the river at a place behind the zoo everyone calls the Fly. The A/C was cranked high enough for our hot teas to still feel good. I know my mom did that for me. She actually prefers being hot. She does hot yoga and everything.

"Okay, spill," my mom said. "The story. Not the tea. Although if there's tea in the story . . . Never mind. You get what I'm saying."

I almost laughed. "It's fine, Mom."

"Is it?"

"No."

"Well, nobody said being a witch was easy."

"It's not," I said. "It's hard. But being a witch is not even the problem. The problem is me."

"Hasani, you're too hard on yourself. Why would you say that?"

"Luz," I said. A weird thing happens when your best friend walks away from you, especially when she won't even turn around when you call her name. You stop thinking the problem is everybody else and start thinking maybe it's you. "But I don't know what to do about it."

I told my mom everything. EVERYTHING. Something about being tucked into Lucy's front seat, looking out at the moon on the river, made it come out really easy. Or maybe it was my mom. Or holding the empty mug that was still warm in my hands. Or maybe it was all of it put together.

At first I told her the good stuff. How I rescued the termites. My being part of the Talented Tenth. My mom laughed at the funny parts and stopped like every five seconds to say how proud of me she was. That actually made me more nervous to tell her the other stuff, and not just because my mom didn't know much about WeBop or YouTube or any social media. I was actually kind of glad that she didn't, because having to explain it all made it take longer to get to the parts that hurt, but I got there eventually. I braced myself for my mom to tell me what everyone else had been telling me. That I was being extra. That

I just needed to pretend like LaToya had never hurt me or anybody else and just get over it. It didn't go like that, though.

"LaToya sounds awful, baby. I can't believe you were going through all that and I never realized it."

"You had your own stuff going on, Mom. It's okay."

"It's not okay. I can't change it, but that doesn't make it okay. Especially if you don't have friends in your corner. I can't believe they're siding with that LaToya girl over you. Especially Luz. I don't care how much LaToya influenced them with magic. That's no excuse. Luz is supposed to be your best friend."

A weird thing happens when your mom says "supposed to be" in front of "your best friend," especially when you know in your heart that she is your best friend because of everything she does, not just a feeling you get. You defend her. And when you defend her, you know in your heart just how right she was.

"Luz isn't against me. She has boundaries, and she should. Mom, I crossed a line. I really *was* leaving her out. If she treated me like I've been treating her, she'd want me to show my boundaries, too. That's what best friends do. And the better your best friend knows you, the better they have your back. I should have told Luz I was a witch right away. I took too long, and now I don't know how to fix it."

My mom sighed and looked out over the water.

"I told you," I said. "The problem isn't magic. The problem is me."

"Hasani, magic *is* you. You can't run away from that or hide from that any more than you can hide from loving math or making art or being from New Orleans." My mom always called me doing makeup "making art." It used to annoy me, like she didn't like what I was doing, so she pretended I was doing something else. That time it felt different. Like she knew what I was doing was deeper and more important than I had ever imagined.

"I'm not running from magic."

My mom didn't say anything. She didn't need to. I already knew it wasn't true, even if I wasn't ready to admit it.

"Okay," I said. "I'm not running from it, but I can want a break, can't I?"

"A break from yourself? Hasani, you're a good witch. Everybody says so. What are you afraid of? What do you think will happen if you stop trying to keep it in and let yourself be great?"

Tears stung, welling up in the corners of my eyes. I just went through all that with Dee. It was even harder to say to my mom. She was so proud of me. I wanted her to stay proud of me.

"I hurt people," I said. "I hurt them without meaning to. You. Annie."

I expected my mom to say what she usually said. That I needed to forgive myself. That it wasn't my fault. But my mom is always surprising me.

"And Sandy," she said. "You hurt Sandy, too."

I looked at her, confused.

"You called her a home-wrecker, remember? Stirred up so much trouble she had to shut down her account."

"Her new account has more followers."

I don't know why I said that. I also don't know how I forgot about that whole incident. It felt like years ago, when it had really only been weeks.

"That doesn't mean you didn't hurt her. Any reason she shouldn't be on your list, too?"

I tried not to roll my eyes. I figured it would ruin the moment.

"You think she's tougher? Like being a witch means she doesn't have feelings?"

"Witches have feelings," I said. I honestly could not see where my mom was going with this.

"I thought so," my mom said. "That's why I don't understand why you insist on punishing her."

"I'm not punishing Sandy," I said. "I'm just not being all buddy-buddy with her like you. I don't get how you're doing that. I mean, how can you forgive her so fast?"

"It's easy," my mom said. "There's nothing to forgive. Sandy hasn't done anything wrong."

I had to let that one sink in. I mean, my mom wasn't speaking

Swahili or anything, but she may as well have been. She was saying words, they just didn't have meaning.

"Sandy loves your dad. So she married your dad, something she was free to do. And Sandy forgave you after you hurt her, something she didn't have to do. All those things make her okay in my book. The fact that she keeps reaching out to you after you've been rude and hostile to her on multiple occasions is lagniappe. But that's just the part I'm seeing. Since we're talking, I'm hoping you'll tell me what you see. Is Sandy doing something to hurt you? Because, baby, if she is, please believe that I will move heaven and earth to stop it."

I believed her. The problem was that, even though I really wanted to think of something bad Sandy had done, I couldn't come up with a single thing.

"People make mistakes. All of us do. All of us hurt people. And when we realize it, we do our best to correct it. That's what makes a good person a good person. It's not that good people never get anything wrong. It's that they try not to get the same thing wrong again. People don't have to give you third, fourth, and fifth chances. People don't even have to give second chances, although we often do, especially for the people we love."

"She's just annoying," I said. "I didn't ask her to do anything for me."

"Right. That's the point. You didn't have to ask her. You needed help, so she just jumped right in, even though she probably knew you'd be angry, and it sounds like she's suffering some pretty serious consequences for it."

"Is that supposed to be my fault?"

My mom shook her head. "I'm just trying to understand why it upsets you so much that someone is looking out for you."

"Not someone," I said. "Sandy."

"Fine. Sandy. Do you ever think you're being upset with the wrong person? Maybe you're not angry with Sandy at all. Maybe you're taking it out on Sandy when the person you're really upset with is your dad?"

"Yeah, well, that wouldn't happen if she weren't always . . . there."

Mic drop, but not on my mom. I don't know how I did it, but I dropped the mic on myself.

"She's always there," I repeated. "And she doesn't have to be."

I didn't love Sandy, but honestly, I didn't need to love Sandy. I just needed to not be a jerk about it.

"I'm not saying what happened with Sandy at the witch mall was your fault. You don't need to wallow in guilt over it. That doesn't help anybody, either, especially since you're right. Sandy is an adult who made a decision and will deal with the consequence of it. It's not like you're sitting on a solution to her problem and refusing to help."

I grimaced.

"Actually, I kind of am."

My mom looked at me.

"Maybe. Hold on. I need to send a message."

I didn't have Miss Lafleur's business card with me, but turns out that tapping the image that I saved in my camera roll did the same thing. She answered on the first ring.

"Well begun is half done." Was she quoting Mary Poppins? "I'm afraid that if you want to begin a second task, you must first complete the first."

"Okay?"

"Okay. How soon can you get here?"

I lowered the phone and turned to my mom. "Mom, now can you really take me Vacherie? Miss Lafleur wants me to finish what I started with the termites."

"And you want to?" My mom sounded skeptical.

"Yeah. Actually, I do. They got hit with a lot of influence. I want to see how they come out. So, can you drive me?"

"Not tonight." My mom pointed to Lucy's instrument panel. The battery said twenty-five percent. "I guess we had the A/C cranked a little too high while we were talking. If you want me to drive, you'll have to wait until tomorrow. But you know who might be able to take you tonight?"

One of the perks of having magic that loves tech is that I could have gotten my mom's car battery to recharge pretty easily. But I knew where she was going, so I went with it.

"Sandy?" I asked.

"Yep. Sandy. I bet she's up. She's a night owl."

"Won't it be weird, though? Shouldn't I try to surprise her or something? That way if it doesn't work out, she won't have been stuck driving me for nothing? I mean, I'm basically asking Sandy for a favor to do something that will only *maybe* help her. It's kind of twisted. Is that allowed?"

"Yes, baby." My mom smiled. "Family is like that sometimes. It's complicated."

I shook my head at the family comment, but I didn't contradict her. She wasn't wrong.

CHAPTER TWENTY-SEVEN

COOKIES AND DOUGH

*S*andy suggested meeting us up on the Fly, but after my mom assured her Lucy would survive the five-minute drive back to our house, she agreed to meet us there instead.

I'd be lying if I said she was anything but the same old Sandy. Her hair was swept up and she was wearing yoga stuff instead of beach stuff, but otherwise there was nothing different about her. The one who was different was me.

"Thanks for coming, Sandy," I said. "I appreciate you helping me out on such short notice."

Sandy looked at my mom, who gave her a tiny thumbs-up. I think it was supposed to be subtle. It wasn't, but it was fine. I didn't care, and actually, it was a little bit cute. A *little* bit.

"Thanks for helping, Sandy. I think this trip might be more in your wheelhouse. Emergency Mom Mode has me all keyed up. I think this is a good time to check my social media. The trolls won't know what hit them!"

"Check my social media" was the most awkward thing I'd heard my mom say in a long time, but then I remembered that Sandy was helping my mom get her tea business's Instagram off the ground, and I gave her a pass. I couldn't imagine how many trolls there could possibly be on the page for a tea business that wasn't even open yet, but if there were any, apparently they weren't going to know what hit them. LOL.

We drove off, and Sandy decided to extend the awkward by saying, "Hasani, just let me say that it is truly an honor for you to have asked me to drive you. I feel . . . honored!" Sandy laughed.

Seriously, what was I supposed to say to that?

I didn't really have to say anything, though. If anybody knows how to fill a car ride with chatter, it's Sandy.

"I know we got off on the wrong foot, and I'm sorry about that."

"It's okay," I said.

"It's my fault, really. I tried to get Bobby to tell you about us so much sooner, but he just kept dragging his feet. I thought it was because he wasn't as serious about me as I was about him, but then he popped the question and I was like, 'Nope! That's not it.'"

TMI, dude. T.M.I.

"But all that's probably boring to you. Let's talk about something else."

"Boring" was not the right word, but changing the topic was a good idea.

"So . . ." she began. "When did you first blossom?"

Record scratch.

Sandy glanced over at me. *Excuse me?* was written all over my face.

"It just means when is the first time you accidentally spilled magic somewhere. You know. Because of the flowers that bloom? Blooming? Blossom? Get it? You've never heard that before? Witches say it all the time. I'm surprised the other kids weren't saying it at Belles Demoiselles. It's kind of a standard get-to-know-you question."

"I missed all the get-to-know-you stuff," I said.

"Oh. That must have been rough."

"It was," I said. "But it's cool. I figured it out."

Sandy was shocked that my blossoming was on the St. Claude Bridge. "That made the news! No wonder Belles Demoiselles grabbed you up. You are destined for greatness, chica."

I didn't say anything, but Sandy kept talking. Eventually I got her whole life story, including where she blossomed. Turned out Sandy was a navy brat.

MARTI DUMAS

"Civitavecchia," she said.

"Is that in Italy?"

"Yep. My mom was always on the hunt for rugs. I guess the navy wives never felt like they had enough rugs at that base. Anyway, my mom was trying to talk another mom out of a kitchen mat, of all things, and it was so embarrassing. Eventually I just had enough. My mom hustled me out of there so fast!"

We both laughed. Sandy talked and talked some more. Beaches. Backpacking in Europe. Trying to find hair products in Portugal when she didn't speak the language.

When finally she left another gap in the chatter, I threw my own question in.

"Why did you give me that spellbook?" I asked.

"It just felt like you were carrying a lot of stuff. You're just a kid. It's not fair. You should be free. And since freedom's my thing, I figured I should share."

"So you thought I'd do the freedom spell on myself?"

"I mean, yeah. How else would you—? Oh, wait. I'm thinking of me, not you."

"I don't get it. What's that supposed to mean?"

"Well, Hasani, not all of us are blessed with a Niagara Falls level of power. Compared to you, the flow of my magic is more like a faucet."

330

"Oh," I said, debating if "that sucks" or silence was more appropriate. "I didn't know."

"How could you? We're not blood relatives and we're not in the same coven, although, BT-dubs, my circle of friends is itching to meet you. Anyway, don't feel bad. I'm working with what I've got, and believe me, at this point I have learned to work it." Sandy snapped after the last two words. I managed to downgrade what should have been a full eye roll to a lid flutter. "You know what the secret is?"

"What?"

"Charm, not magic."

Sandy looked super pleased with herself. I think she thought she invented that.

"No, seriously. You'd be surprised how powerful you feel when you direct your magic back into yourself instead of constantly trying to work on other people. Other people will just drain you until there is nothing left, but if you do the same thing as a charm? Boom. Works like a charm, even if you're not working with much, if you know what I mean."

"Wait a minute. Is charm just magic you do on yourself?"

"Yeah," Sandy said. "They didn't teach you that at Belles Demoiselles?"

No.

No, they did not.

Or maybe I was too busy cleaning up morning glories to remember.

Nope. That wasn't it. They just never said that. To say my mind was blown would be like saying the sun is a little far away.

It took me a minute for that to sink in, but once it did, I just had more questions. Maybe Sandy could answer some stuff after all.

"Okay, but what about spells?" I asked. "Isn't it dangerous to do spells that come from other people?"

"Only if you were planning to do it without help from the crafter. What? Were you planning on not inviting me to my own spell?" Sandy giggled.

Kind of?

Sandy's laugh turned into a nervous cough when she realized I wasn't laughing with her. "That's okay. My spells are easy breezy. You could do them anywhere. Even in a sanlavi. A witch like you could probably do them even without the crafter . . . if you didn't want the crafter around or whatever."

We pulled up to a creole cottage next to a cane field. There was more than one creole cottage and more than one sugarcane field in Vacherie, but Miss Lafleur was standing out front, so I knew we'd found the right one.

"Welcome, Hasani and guest!"

"Miss Lafleur, this is my stepmother, Sandy."

Sandy was extra, but she really wasn't that bad. I figured I'd throw her a bone. When I saw her grin, I was glad I did.

"Hi! It's so good to meet you. We didn't get a chance to talk at Hasani's completion ceremony. The campus is amazing."

"Thank you," Miss Lafleur said. "It's been built over centuries. We're quite proud of it."

"I know that I'm not allowed on campus right now, but do you happen to know if there's anywhere closer than this that I can get on the Interweb?"

Sandy held out her phone for Miss Lafleur to see.

"To my knowledge, that is the closest entrance to 3Thirteen. It's about a mile from here. But if you don't need access to all the library resources, feel free to stay right here. Our guesthouse has a strong Interweb connection."

"Thank you. And just to be sure we're on the same page, I'm talking about the Interweb, not the Internet."

"There's a difference?" I blurted.

"Oh, yes," Miss Lafleur said. "The Internet is a good copy of the Interweb, but its limitations make it unsuitable for witches. If we relied on the Internet we'd have to worry about things like hacking and bandwidth and planetary power outages."

Sandy smiled. "I'm trying to track down some ingredients in Madagascar, and I'm on a little bit of a tight timeline. Is it okay if I use it?"

"Of course. I was just tending to the mushroom this morning. Some new spores germinated."

"Perfect! Thank you so much. Hasani?" Sandy turned to me. My phone dinged. "I'm gonna stay here, but now you can track me wherever I am. Just in case."

Sandy could code? "Witchy." I grinned.

"Oh! No. That's just an iPhone thing. Text me when you're done!"

Sandy went into the house, but I followed Miss Lafleur through a cut in the cane that disappeared as soon as I passed through it. Well, it didn't exactly disappear. It filled in with sugarcane, not intentions. I couldn't have walked back if I wanted to, but I definitely didn't want to. Whatever was at the end of the path seemed too lush to miss, even in the moonlight.

"Your extender has been sacrificed to a higher purpose, I see."

Miss Lafleur was pushing the growth at the end of the path out of our way. Giant leaves and bunches of mostly ripe bananas started where the sugarcane ended.

When she said that, I froze. Lynx jumped through a gap that should have been way too small for her and nuzzled her furry head against my shoulder.

"Are you mad?" I finally asked.

"Lynx is disappointed that you didn't bring Othello, but neither of us is angry with you. Why would you think that?"

"I don't know. Most people get mad when you give away something they gave you."

Miss Lafleur laughed. I loved her laugh. "Well, I guess that's more proof that I am not most people," she said. "I told you it was yours. In my book, once something is yours, you can and should do with it as you wish. If you want to exchange it, so be it. I was actually quite happy to see you give it away."

"Really?" I asked.

"Really. After talking to your mother, I was afraid you would use it as a crutch. Like training wheels on a bike."

"I had training wheels on my bike."

"Did you? Well, I can assure you that you didn't learn to ride until the training wheels came off. Delaying the inevitable is not always a bad thing. Sometimes the person needs those wheels to build strength and stamina in their legs or lose their natural fear of falling, but that does not change the fact that the actual learning doesn't begin until those crutches are gone."

"So, trading the present you gave me was a good thing?"

"Exactly," Miss Lafleur said. "There. Things should look a bit more familiar from here."

The walk leading up to the Belles Demoiselles house was overgrown. The paths were covered with fallen petals and leaves. The rainbows were gone, and the swans paddled aimlessly in the moonlight.

"This is what it's like when school's over?"

The air was thick and warm and smelled like rain, but it still felt good. Less sauna, more bubble bath.

"We let things rest as much as we can. Nothing can be perfect for too long. Are you disappointed?"

I looked past the swan lake to the house in the distance, overgrown willow tree branches dancing in the breeze.

"I don't think I've ever seen anything more beautiful," I said.

Miss Lafleur smiled. "Then let me show you to the termites."

We got in a boat and paddled to a muddier, swampier side of the lake that I had never been to before.

"Technically, these termites are an invasive species. No more than we humans are, though. All the more reason to take care of them. The more support they receive, the less they need to lean into the side of their nature that we humans consider destructive. Of course, what we call destructive, the termites merely call living."

Miss Lafleur tied up the boat in a place where the ground was just as squelchy as it looked. She didn't have to waggle her fingers to get the fireflies to light the way up a path of planks, but I knew it was her doing. The fireflies released as soon as we passed them, like the extra-dope version of motion-detecting floodlights. Smooth. Real smooth.

The planks led to something that was too big to be a Scooby-Doo van but way too small to be a house. But it was obviously a house. Why else would a van be surrounded by a million potted plants and have a front porch attached?

"Is that where you live?"

"Sometimes. I vary the location, but yes. Lucinda and I have been together for about as long as I've known Lynx."

"Lucinda? My mom's car is Lucy."

Maybe naming cars was a magic thing.

"How lovely," Miss Lafleur said. "Well, I hope your mother and Lucy get along as nicely as Lucinda and I do."

Miss Lafleur turned off the plank path toward a bunch of piles of dry-looking mud.

Miss Lafleur swept her arms wide, like she was doing a big reveal. "The termite recovery zone," she said.

"Is that dirt?" I asked. Was that what I was supposed to be seeing?

"Yes! Termite excrement, chewed wood, and soil. Isn't it wonderful? Excrement and chewed wood means they're eating, and building is an excellent sign of recovery. The termites are coming back to themselves, and that's always a good thing. Now, are you glad you came?"

"I guess?"

"Try sounding a little less skeptical, Hasani." Miss Lafleur laughed. "No. On second thought, don't. Your candor is one of the most refreshing things about you. Elegance is a good tool to have, but it's not the only one."

"Tell that to Miss LaRose," I mumbled. Dee's mom had basically kept me trapped in etiquette boot camp the whole summer.

"If the only tool you have is a hammer, everything begins to look like a nail. One of the many reasons I am happy you accepted my mentorship offer. I think I'd find myself checking up on you even if you were never my protégé."

"Me? Why?"

"That's what protégé means. It means you were under my protection. During the program, that relationship was automatic, but it was also temporary, meant to last just long enough to get you ready for the world."

"I am NOT ready for the world," I said. "Maybe that means you're not finished yet."

"I'm still looking out for you. A mentorship is nothing to scoff at, even if it's only a few days."

"Yeah. I mess stuff up a lot. You probably shouldn't stick with me for too long."

I was trying to be funny, but Miss Lafleur got serious.

"I wouldn't be a very good protector if I let you enter such a permanent relationship while you're so young. There's so much of the world to explore, and believe me, the world is wide open to you, Hasani. When you're ready."

"I don't know when that'll be. You were right about the extender. I almost didn't give it up. I wanted to keep it for exactly the reason you said. I was going to use it to do a freedom spell to get LaToya's magic out of my school."

Miss Lafleur did not seem excited when I said LaToya's name, but she didn't stop me. "Why didn't you do that?"

"I'd rather protect my friend, not that she's talking to me," I said. Miss Lafleur didn't jump in, so I kept going. "I probably couldn't have done it, anyway. I probably would have exploded the extender or something. I'm dangerous."

"I agree," Miss Lafleur said. Her voice was a little too chipper for my taste.

"You agree?"

"Yes. Wholeheartedly. But in my estimation, the problem is not your strength or your inexperience. What's making you dangerous is fear, not magic."

"My mom was saying the same thing. Like, I'm scared of being great or something."

"What do you think?"

"I don't know."

"That's understandable. Having so much influence is frightening."

I shrugged. "I guess that's why the termite thing was cool. It was nice to see my influence doing something good for a change."

"Influence does good things all the time. And bad. That's how the world works. That doesn't mean we can shy away from it. Take the queen, for example."

"Of England?

"No, dear. This queen." Miss Lafleur pointed to a giant grub-looking thing.

Seriously?

Seriously.

Miss Lafleur held out a pair of glasses.

"Those aren't rose-colored," I said.

"No. They're black glass, an enhanced infrared custom-made by a boutique glassmaker in New Orleans. I use them for occasions such as this, when even the smallest amount of light would disturb. You

can lean in close, but don't touch the ground. The disturbance may be more disturbing than you'd intend."

The lenses looked like charcoal. I didn't think I'd be able to see anything through them, but when I aimed my head toward the pile of termite dirt Miss Lafleur had pointed me toward, I saw something I instantly wished I could *UNsee.*

It looked like an ant trying to squeeze its way out the back end of a flesh-colored caterpillar. Gross.

"That is the termite queen. She reminds me a lot of you."

"Wow," I said.

Miss Lafleur kept going like she had no idea exactly how offensive that was. "Oh, yes. Obviously she's lovely, but she's suffering the most from the influence. I suspect it's because, under ordinary circumstances, she would be wielding influence, not having influence levied against her."

I could get with a lot of stuff. Calling that thing "lovely" was not one of them, but Miss Lafleur had caught my attention.

"All of us have influence, Hasani. We may manifest it differently, but we each wield it. Witches like us who are gifted in influence are really no different than this queen. Through no fault of her own, she was given a power that affects multitudes."

"Multitudes?"

"Oh, yes. As long as she lives, there will never be another queen.

Her mere presence stops any other termite from ever being capable of laying eggs. Whether she's tired or not, she must soldier on for the good of the colony. As soon as she dies, her influence lifts, and three or four potential queens develop. I'd hazard to say that, if she could, she'd change places with either of us in a moment. For her, the top position is a certainty, but unlike us, she has no choice."

"I don't really have a choice, either. You just said so."

"Oh, you always have a choice, Hasani. For us, being queen and controlling every little thing that happens is not the only way to protect the colony. There are other tools in our toolbelts. Other tools that are better suited to this particular problem."

"Like what?" I asked, but my mind was already turning. I think I got it. I wish Miss Lafleur hadn't made me look at that termite queen, but I got it.

"I'm certainly not going to tell you. The lessons handed to you are the ones that stick the least. Instead, I will offer you this: Did you know that the only creatures more difficult to influence than humans are cats?"

Huh? "I influence Othello all the time."

"No, you don't. You only think you do. Sure, you can try to get them to do what you want them to do, but that's not influence. No matter what you do, you can only ever get cats to do what they wanted to do anyway. The trick is to know what the cat wants and do that,

which technically means that the cat is influencing you, not the other way around. The influence is with cuteness, not magic, but the result is the same."

"Ohhh!!!" I said.

"Looks like something may be getting through, which means"— Miss Lafleur clapped her hands—"well begun is now done."

"That's it?" I asked. "That's the whole lesson?"

"You're welcome to stay until the queen either fully recovers or dies, if you like. I'm sure the process will be fascinating. Lynx and I will be happy to have you."

I shivered. No offense, but the termite queen was not my thing. "That's all right," I said. "I really came to ask you a favor. For Sandy."

"The tuft of unicorn hair!" Even in the dark, Miss Lafleur's eyes twinkled.

"How did you know?"

"I told you! The extenders are monitored. Audio only, of course." Of course. "But that was enough to catch the gist. My answer to that is a resounding yes. Apprenticeship does have its privileges. If you're willing to promise not to mention that the tuft came from this herd— they're protected—and you promise not to turn this into a routine commercial venture, and you're willing to collect them yourself, I say take as many as you need. The full baker's dozen!"

"Okay! Where are the unicorns?"

I thought Miss Lafleur and I were going to head over to some fancy stables. Maybe not My Little Pony level, but something close. Instead she pointed to a lumpy, tannish pile of mud on the ground a few feet away.

I looked at her, confused.

"Oh, 'tuft' is a misnomer. Like 'panda bear.' If you tried to cut a tuft of a unicorn's hair, you wouldn't live to tell the tale. The hairs are collected by hand where they naturally fall, then bundled into what we call a tuft. There is usually a hair or two left behind on the unicorn's droppings if you're willing to sift through them."

"Are you telling me that I have to look through unicorn dung?"

"Yes," Miss Lafleur said cheerfully. "Let's give the fireflies a rest. I'll get you a lantern. And a ruler. Hairs in a tuft are always at least three inches long. Best you measure to decide which ones to keep."

You know when you dream it's your birthday but then you wake up and you really just have three tests and a pile of chores to do at home? Yeah. This was worse. It doesn't even matter that it smells like cookie dough. Poop is poop.

I did catch a glimpse of a unicorn, though. If Miss Lafleur hadn't pointed him out I would have missed him. His head was poking out of a stand of night-blooming jasmine and, y'all, I died. Dead. He blended in perfectly. Even his horn. It looked like a clump of branches. And when he saw us looking and ran to hide behind some azalea bushes, he blended in there, too.

I don't want to talk about how long it took, but let's just say breakfast should have been served. And lunch. I didn't stop to eat, though. I didn't want to cut it too close for Sandy to make her deadline. When I had finally found enough, Miss Lafleur helped me wash, dry, and bind them together in Lucinda, which somehow had a fancy full-sized kitchen and a laundry room. Miss Lafleur promised to give me a full tour the next time I came.

"Now that that's settled, I'd hurry along if I were you."

I mean, I wanted to catch a little nap or something, but I wasn't going to do it there, no matter how comfy her flower hammock looked. I needed to get back to Sandy so she could get back to Kaitlynn before I had spent the night digging through unicorn poop for nothing. I figured I'd crash in the car on the way back to New Orleans, but the way Miss Lafleur was talking was making me nervous.

"What am I missing?" I asked.

"Well, if Sandy doesn't make her deadline, I think you'll find YOU are still in quite the pickle."

CHAPTER TWENTY-EIGHT

BOTS AND BOUNDARIES

"**W**hy didn't you say so?" I wasn't exactly yelling at Sandy. I was too sleepy for that. But there was a certain amount of shriekage in my voice.

Turns out, if you're ever going to trade a used extender with a witch in a market, you should check to make sure the extender is COMPLETELY empty first. The extender I traded to Kaitlynn? Yeah. It still had some of my magic in it. According to Miss Lafleur, having an extender with someone's magic in it was even better than being able to forge their signature, but way more dangerous, because MAGIC.

Apparently, every agreement between witches is secured on a giant public database called the blockchain. According to Miss Lafleur, we should all be grateful that the blockchain is digital now, because that means it no longer involves titanium blocks or chains of any kind, which was "obviously tough on everyone back then."

Not every promise you make to a witch gets put on the block-chain. If you just say something like "See you at lunch" or "Sure, you can borrow my shoes," it doesn't count. Unless you say it in 3Thirteen. Then it totally counts. But if you're out in the world, there are two ways to sign a witching contract:

1. **New-school, using your phone.**
2. **Your witching signature, which is—you guessed it—just a drop of your magic.**

I basically gave Kaitlynn a glitter pen with at least a hundred of my witch signatures in it. I don't know Kaitlynn like that. Who knows what she would do?

"I didn't want to freak you out. It was too late, anyway. The trade was already recorded, and I didn't want you to trade a bunch of favors trying to get it back. That would have been just as bad. Maybe worse."

"Sandy, you really didn't need to do that," I said. "Thank you. I appreciate it."

Sandy let out what seemed like a sigh of relief. "I know you think I'm trying to buy you off or something. Maybe to get points with your dad? But I promise you, Hasani. I'm not. I just want to get to know you."

Extra only feels extra when the person is only ever extra in their own favor. My mom was right. Sandy was cool.

"If I had a few more hours, I think I could have pulled it off, but do you have any idea how many favors you saved me? I think I might have called in every favor I had and *still* not gotten it in time. Thank you, thank you, thank you for convincing your teacher to give me a tuft from her private store. All those trips to Madagascar? She's making me wish *I* were a zoologist. I'm a hundred percent going to pay her back."

"She said she's fine." I yawned. "She's not, like, a money person."

"Maybe a gift then? A photo shoot? Is your teacher on Instagram? I know my followers would give her page a boost, especially if she and I did a photo shoot in Madagascar."

I'm sure Sandy kept talking, but I really could not keep my eyes open one second longer. The next thing I knew, we were pulling up in front of my house.

"Wait," I said. "Are you going to 3Thirteen?"

Sandy nodded. "Yes, oh sleepy one."

"I'm coming," I said.

"You most certainly are not. You are going to bed."

"But I have to go with you." I was kind of sleep mumbling, but Sandy caught my drift. Sort of.

"I will give Kaitlynn this tuft of unicorn hair. That will complete our transaction. The extender isn't mine, so I can't collect it for you. It will stay locked in an S-Crow account where you can pick it up at your convenience, which will most certainly be after you have had many, many hours of sleep."

"That's good, but I wasn't talking about the extender. I was talking about going with you. I want to go back with you."

"We're both members. It's like a twenty-four-hour Costco. We can go anytime you want. What do you want me to help you look for?"

"Nothing," I said. "You said we'd have to go together to do the parent pass thing."

Sandy froze.

By the time I blinked, she was talking again, but my sleepy brain couldn't make out what she was saying. The words weren't clear until she was hugging me, saying, "Yes! Yes! Let's see how your mom feels about it, but if she says yes, then I'm a double yes!"

My mom came out a minute later. By then, Sandy was full-on ugly crying.

"I thought I heard y'all. Wait," my mom said, rushing to Sandy's door. "What's going on with Sandy? Sandy, are you okay? Hasani, is she okay?"

"I asked if she'd be my guardian at the witch mall," I said. "Do you mind?"

My mom smiled and let out a breath like that explained everything. "Of course I don't mind," she said, and then proceeded to try to talk Sandy into coming inside for a cup of tea before going on her errand. How my mom caught the word "errand" in all that blubbering I'll never know.

"Dee's in there," my mom said as I slipped past her and Sandy.

Now ordinarily, if every single one of your friends is mad at you and you can't even blame them because you were the one being a jerk, when the one friend who is still talking to you shows up at your house, you're grateful. Even if that one friend is not the one you would consider your *best* friend. Well, I did feel grateful, but after having been up all night sifting through unicorn feces, not only was it unlikely that I would ever eat cookie dough again, but it was also true that, on this, the rarest of occasions, I would rather have been sleeping than hanging out with Dee.

Luckily, Dee hadn't come to hang out. She had come to show me something on her laptop.

"Check this out."

Dee hit CTRL+U to reveal the code on the "Strictly Stripes" video that auto-posted that morning on MakeuponthCheapCheap.

"See that?"

"Yes?" I said. Code still mostly looked like gibberish to me, but Dee had taught me a little something-something. I could usually at least tell where it started and ended. What I could see this time was that the code Dee was showing me had a slight magic glow on it, like maybe she or Angelique had done something to it a few days ago.

"Wait a minute. That video just went up this morning," I said.

"Exactly," Dee said.

"But when you and Angelique do stuff, it's usually brighter."

"Exactly."

"That doesn't make sense. I mean, who else's magic can I see without rose-colored glasses?"

"What were you saying about not having a mama who can do magic?" Dee said it chill, but she knew she was dropping a bomb. "It looks like your mama can do magic just fine."

"Mo-om!" I shouted. "Who is VacherieNOLAARTTeast?"

"Vacherie NOLA Artiste? Oh!" She poked her head into my room. "That's me! Sandy was telling me I should start a YouTube for my tea, so I made that account. But I'm not going to do it. It's just too much work. I've just been using it to make comments on videos sometimes."

"When was the last time you used it?"

"Well, I logged in yesterday after you left with Sandy. Before that it was a couple days ago. I was going to help you sift through the comments, but then I had to leave that alone. I don't know how you do it, Hasani. Some of those comments are downright nasty. Your father and I already decided we're going to pay for you to have a virtual assistant to go through those. Nobody should have to read all that when they're not at least getting paid for it."

"Thanks, Mom," I said.

"What? You're not gonna argue with me about it?"

"Nope," I said.

"Well, let me get out of here before you change your mind." My mom chuckled and ducked back out.

"You know that's a bitbot, right?"

"I figured. Do you seriously think my mom LUCKED a bitbot into being?"

Dee shrugged.

"I mean, it's kind of wobbly, but yeah. It works. You want me to leave it up?"

"No," I said.

Dee sighed.

"If it's wobbly, let's take it down. Not today, though. Let it run until we have something better. I'd rather have one you help me build from scratch. That is, if you're willing to."

"I'ma do you one better. I'll build it for you. No virtual assistant will ever compare to the bitbot I'm about to construct for your chan-

nel. Especially not if you throw a little sauce on it at the end. Prepare to be amazed."

"Thanks, Dee!" I said. But I didn't have to prepare. I already was amazed. Dee was amazing.

After that, I fell asleep hard, but not before saying "Mommy, don't delete your channel" two or three times. I remember saying that exactly zero times, but my mom and Dee laughed about it forever, so I guess it happened. I was glad my mom didn't delete her channel, though, because when I woke up I finally understood what Miss Lafleur was talking about with the termite queen and cats and everything. It was a two-parter, and part one involved using my mom's account. I was about to boost LaToya.

I know, I know. Hear me out. It didn't make sense to me at first, either, but the more I thought about it, the more I realized that it was the right thing to do.

I figured Miss Lafleur was trying to get me on board with the idea that I could use my influence to make something good happen, but it just wasn't clicking what that had to do with LaToya. Then I remembered one of the few things my mom's mom used to say around me.

Do good as quietly as you do bad.

I hadn't thought of it in years, but once I did, it made everything make sense.

The truth is, whether I meant to or not, I did hurt LaToya. Maybe she was really trying to be friends with me from the beginning. Maybe she wasn't. It kind of didn't matter. Everything Luz said LaToya told her about me was true. I did go sneaking off without telling her. And I did come back with a magical charm and just try to play it off instead of telling her what I could about it. No matter what my reasons were, maybe those reasons gave LaToya real reasons not to trust me. Angelique was right. There was probably more going on with LaToya than I realized. I didn't need to know what it was to know that it wasn't even about me going high when other people go low. It was about being a good person. Good people make mistakes, but once they see they caused harm, they do everything they can not to make that mistake again. And if they hurt a person, they do whatever they can to try to make it better.

LaToya obviously wanted friends and followers. I didn't know if I was ready to be her friend, but followers I could do. That's where my mom's account and my grandmother's advice came in. If I boosted LaToya's account from my channel or something, she'd just come back with some haterade response. Petty witch war in full effect. I didn't need that, and neither did she. But pushing stuff through my mom's account would give the boost just enough cover to not have it look like it was coming from me. That way it would be a love bomb, not a straight-up bomb. And nobody would be able to

accuse me of helping LaToya just to make myself look good on the Internet—not even me.

The only person I told was my mom because, well, she's my mom and I was going to use her account. Between her luck and my influence, it'd be hard to trace it back to us, but LaToya was smart. Anything was possible.

My mom was shocked at first, but good shocked. Not bad shocked. She agreed, and after I set little spawns of her kismet-made bitbot in motion, I only checked LaToya's account once, just to see if they were working. Those bitbots probably wouldn't run forever, but at least they'd give LaToya a start.

Part two of my realization was a little harder to admit, but easier to change. Angelique was right. It didn't matter if I was using magic on my friends or not. The effect was basically the same. I was trying to tell her and everybody else who they could be friends with. Instead of being a kitten trying to control people with cute, I was trying to control them with friendship. As gross as it was, I was being more like the termite queen than I realized. The termite queen only had two choices: Be alive and have everybody do what she forced them to do, or die and have her influence disappear. As long as I was trying to force people to be on "my side," I was as limited as the termite queen.

I was acting like friendship was a light switch—on or off. Either people picked me or they picked LaToya. My influence was going to die at some point if I went that route. Luckily, I didn't need to. I was an influencer, but I wasn't a termite queen. My influence wasn't like a switch, it was more like a touch screen, and I was the one who chose whether I moved it up, down, or sideways, or shut it off completely.

But before I put part two of my plan into effect, I needed to talk to Luz.

I did not expect Luz to listen to anything I had to say. Not after the way I treated her.

So I sat down in front of my backdrop and clicked record.

"This video is me apologizing. I understand if you delete it without watching the rest, and if you do I promise I won't get mad. I get it. I hurt you. And like my mom says, nobody owes you second and third chances . . ."

I started from the beginning—me and my dad on the bridge—and ended with her walking away from me on the lawn. I told her the whole thing with me and LaToya, not just the parts where I was hurt. I used fake names to avoid the possible name-drop trap, but I told her I was doing that, and I told her why, too. I told her about being the monster who messed up the algorithm, tanked Annie's channel, and sent all those horrible comments her way. I told her

about hurting my mom. I told her about being afraid to hug her, because I didn't want to accidentally influence her again. I told her how I was afraid that my dad only came around because I had influenced him, too, and even more afraid that I had been influencing Luz this whole time without knowing it, and otherwise she might never have been my friend.

The video ended up being almost an hour long. I'm sure I could have said more. But I exported it and sent it with a trigger warning right up front.

I know I shouldn't have, but I literally sat on my bed with Othello on my lap and my phone plugged in. I kept tapping the screen to keep it awake. Five minutes later, a message came through.

Why did you send me a video?

I typed back.

I didn't want to force you to see my face in person. I figured it was easier to delete a video or ignore it than if I showed up at your house.

Her response was quick.

That's so stupid.

Then that was it. No more messages.

I sat on my bed, wondering what my life without Luz would be like. Would we pass each other in the halls and pretend not to know each other? Our lockers were right next to each other. There was no way I wouldn't see her unless I changed schools or something. I didn't want to change schools. I didn't want her to change schools. I just wanted everything to go back to normal. I wanted her to give me a pass. No. I wanted to earn one.

> You know I could have outed you with this, right?
>
> I know.
>
> And you sent it anyway?
>
> Yes.

I should have told her all that weeks ago, but I couldn't go back and do the right thing from the beginning. Sending it now was the best I could do.

The next thing I knew, Luz was tapping on my door.

"You so stupid!" she said.

Stupid? Or stoopid? But by the look on her face and the fact that she was in my room at all meant it was at least a little more double O than U.

"I was friends with you first," she said.

"Huh?"

"In second grade. I was the one who saw we were twins. I was the one who talked to you first. I had already decided we were BFFs. If anybody influenced us into being friends, it's me, not you. And since I haven't spontaneously grown any flowers yet, I'm pretty sure it wasn't by magic."

Tears started rolling down my cheeks. The good kind.

"If a video like this got out it could mess up your whole life," she said. "School. Your channel. Everything. You trust me that much?"

I nodded.

"You sure?"

I nodded again. "I should have told you from the beginning."

"You're right." Luz held her phone so I could see, and deleted the video. "So tell me again, from the beginning. No, wait. Start with Othello. Is he seriously magic?"

"Yep. Sort of. I mean, all cats are . . ."

My mom brought us tea. And then snacks. And then more tea. I think she just kept making excuses to come in so she could see us talking together again. I couldn't blame her. I knew the feeling.

"I'm still salty about being the last one to know," Luz said. "But keep talking."

I started talking again, and while I did, Luz pulled up YouTube on my computer. The next thing I knew, she was monetizing my channel. With my permission, but still. A few days before, I never would have agreed to it. I guess monetizing your channel is a whole process, and Luz was right: If YouTube was going to show people ads anyway, I may as well make sure I knew where at least some of the money was going. We decided on an anti-bullying organization to start, but if it grew, maybe we could do more.

"You're not the last to know," I said. "I still haven't told my dad."

"Wow. High bar." I could hear the eye roll in her voice. "But in better news: I'm done. We should get a decision in six to twelve weeks."

"Wow. That is a long time."

"I know," Luz said. "That is why I told you to start a long time ago. You should have listened to me."

"I should have," I said. "My bad."

"Yeah. Your bad," Luz laughed. "I bet you won't make that mistake again."

I sure hoped not. If I did, it wouldn't be for lack of trying.

"You know what else you're wrong about?"

I shook my head. I mean, I was wrong about a lot of stuff, I just didn't know which stuff Luz was talking about.

"La—"

"Shhh!!!" Phew. My heart was beating so fast. That was close. "I'll explain it, but say 'the girl from camp.'"

"There were a lot of girls at your camp, but okay," Luz said. "We were both wrong about that girl from your camp. She's not all bad. Y'all actually have a lot in common."

"Like what?"

"Like, her parents are getting divorced and she's having a really hard time with it. Like, she ran away to her grandma's house when she found out, just like you ran away to my house when you

found out. That's why she was wearing that uniform. Her parents thought she was going to the Academy, but she wanted a clean start. That last part sounds like you, too. Anyway"—Luz turned around from the computer—"about that present. I believe I was promised a charm."

I don't know how I was supposed to feel about LaToya, but I had already told Luz all about the charm, including the fact that it was actually charmed. It was a good distraction. I don't think the fact that it was magic sank in until I pulled out the invisible bag I had been keeping right next to the wall of morning glories.

"Are you serious right now?" Luz asked, eyeing the air suspiciously. "You want me to put my hand? In that? It won't disappear?"

"No," I said. "It's just a bag."

"A really cool bag," Luz said, but she still hesitated before she put her hand in and pulled out the little jewelry box.

"Okay. Hold up," I said. "Before you open it, I just need to make sure you know that once you touch it, it's yours."

"You said that already," she said. "You also said that once it's bonded with me I'll basically be immune from influence, even yours."

"Even mine."

"I don't know why you didn't say that in the first place. The way witches have been coming out of the woodwork, I would have *been* taking it," she laughed. "But seriously. I know I'll be good, but what about everybody else? What are you going to do with the magic the girl from your camp left around the school?"

"Nothing," I said.

"Really? You're just gonna leave it?"

"I'm not a termite queen. If she wants to be an influencer, that's on her."

"So you're just gonna let everybody join . . . ?" She held up her phone, where she had typed out #TeamLaToya on her Notes app.

"Yep. I'm gonna let her do her. I'm having enough trouble just doing me right now. She can handle herself." And any followers she pulled to her side. Having a lot of followers can be a lot of work. I know from experience.

"Ooh! Maybe we should start Self-Care Sunday! But first . . ." Luz did a long, dramatic opening of the jewelry box.

"Aw, it looks cheap." Luz fake pouted, then grinned. "I'm just playing. It's beautiful." She put it on without hesitating.

I let out a huge breath. I didn't even know I was about to cry again until the tears were streaming down my face.

"What's wrong?" Luz hugged me, and for the first time in too long, I didn't have to shake it off.

"I don't have to worry about influencing you by accident anymore," I sobbed.

"That explains why you've been so weird. I thought I must have BO or something and you didn't want to tell me."

"If you had BO, I would tell you. Trust me."

"Good! You had me doubting myself, taking two or three showers a day and everything."

We both laughed.

"I'm glad you took the charm," I said. "I went through, like, a lot to get it. It involved unicorn poop. I didn't tell you the story earlier because I didn't want you to feel pressured about taking it, but now that you have I can tell you the whole thing. In great detail. Trust me, it'll ruin cookie dough for you forever."

"No thanks," Luz said. "I'm good. Do you have anything else in that magic bag, though?"

"No but I was wanting to call a coven meeting, and now that you have that charm I don't have to worry about calling it someplace special. How would you feel about being literally surrounded by witches? Oh! And I was thinking about inviting Sandy. She keeps saying she wants me to meet her circle of friends, so I'm thinking I might tell her she can invite them, too, if she wants."

"But I'm not in your coven," Luz said.

"Neither is Sandy. Neither are her friends. But you don't need to be in my coven," I said. "You're my best friend. That's way better."

CHAPTER TWENTY-NINE

GUESTS AND PASSES

did try to send LaToya a message. After what Luz told me, how could I not? I sent the same one to her IG and her WeBop. I didn't want to make her feel bad about Luz telling me a bunch of personal stuff that LaToya hadn't told me herself, so I just sent a little thing saying I like her uniform. I did. She looked cool in it even when she was wearing fake hair and a fake nose ring. Maybe especially when she was wearing fake hair and a fake nose ring.

No response.

I can't say I was surprised, but over the next few days I let myself get distracted with filming and planning and editing. Luz and Dee helped A LOT, so much that I made sure I shouted them out and gave them crew credits at the end. Once we had the rest of the videos for the back-to-school series on my channel ready to go, it was time to

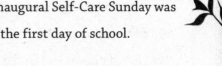

turn my attention to relaxation. The inaugural Self-Care Sunday was to be held at 3Thirteen the day before the first day of school.

*t first my mom said she'd rather spend Self-Care Sunday having the house all to herself, but eventually she decided to come with us. My mom, Luz, Sandy, and I went early in case there was any trouble getting my mom and Luz in. I got to use my first guest pass on Luz, but Sandy and the person at the entrance both insisted my mom get tested. She qualified for membership, although her card was a shifting rainbow reflection, not a solid color.

"It's because kismets can only deal in favors," Sandy explained. "It's every color because, since it's luck, you never know what you're going to get. Don't worry about not being able to trade, though, Nailah. I've met quite a few people who pretty much only trade with kismets. They say it's fun. Like playing the lottery."

We went to get my extender out of hock. Y'all. Why was it S-Crow, not escrow? There were actual crows. I wasn't prepared. I should have been, but I wasn't. My mom and Luz were both less freaked out by the talking crows than I was. Or maybe they were just more in shock. The contract I had to sign was written in corvidae, but Sandy assured me there were no hidden terms. I hope her corvidae was as good as she said because Google Translate was no help.

After that, we went to the office of Major Minor Affairs for Sandy and me to register for the parent pass. Tears were shed, but my mom and Sandy both mostly held it together. Mostly. I did, too.

Once all that was settled, we made our way over to one of the tea shops in the food court. There were at least two dozen of them. Apparently witches like tea. Sandy insisted on ordering a little something from all of them. She was saying stuff about wanting to make sure we had enough food, but I think she was nervous about having us finally meet her friends, or friend, since all but one of them said they couldn't make it.

"I just really hope Beverlyn comes. She has work tomorrow, though, so she wasn't sure," Sandy said. More than once. "She is so cool. Did I tell you she makes glass? Gorgeous stuff. She made this."

Sandy showed us her solar system necklace. Again. It was cool, though. It included Pluto and Eris and used a shadow/reflection trick to give Jupiter, Saturn, Uranus, and Neptune their rings.

I wasn't ordering all the food in creation, but I was nervous that one of my friends wouldn't come, too. My apology to Angelique didn't go over as well as my one to Luz did, and Angelique was nothing like Dee. But talking to her, I realized . . . that was about all I knew about her. Besides both of them being good at coding, Angelique was nothing like Dee. Could I really call myself somebody's friend if all I really knew about them was that they were the opposite of somebody else?

"You never asked," Angelique had said. "You don't know my life. You just looked at me and made a little box for me, just like you did to Annie, and just like you're doing to LaToya. Rich girl, victim, and villain, right? Well, I'm not that small. They aren't, either."

I apologized. I said I'd do better. "I really do think you're cool," I said. "I always have, even when you were being mean to me."

"That's just the charm," she said. She softened a little. "Look, it's not all your fault. Friendship is a two-way street. You could have asked, but I could have offered more, too."

"Well, can I ask you something now?"

She nodded.

"I know I was being a jerk about Sandy, and I was a jerk to you about being rich and stuff, but why did all that make you so upset? I mean, you have a right to your feelings. Don't change them. It's cool. You're cool. And I want to be your friend. I really do. It just feels like I'm missing something, and I think if I don't get the part that's missing I might keep hurting you even when I don't mean to."

Angelique sighed.

"You don't have to answer," I said. "I was just putting it out there."

"My mom adopted me," Angelique said.

This was both news to me and confusing about why it was news.

"That's great!" I said. "I mean, great that you're adopted. Adopted children are special because they're chosen, right?" I think I heard that in a movie once. "Oh! And my mom's second cousin Terrance is adopted. He's cool, too."

Angelique rescued me from the awkward. "My dad's my biological dad. My mom adopted me when they got married. I was still a toddler. Anyway, that's not the point. The point is that I can't see my mom's magic."

"So, your magic coming from your dad's side . . ."

". . . is something I say so people don't bug me about it. There is magic on my dad's side. His grandmother was a belle demoiselle, but she died before I was born. So every time you try to act like just because someone isn't blood, they're not really your family, it hurts. My mom is definitely my family. It hurts almost as much as when you act like I'm good at stuff because I'm rich."

"I'm so sorry, Angelique. I had no idea."

"I know."

"Will you forgive me?"

"I'll think about it, Hasani," she said.

On TV they always hug it out at that point. Unfortunately, we weren't on TV.

I invited her to Self-Care Sunday, but I didn't know if Angelique had decided to come until she walked up to our table. She sat next to me and said, "We're co-captains, so we need to work this out. This morning, Ms. Coulon sent us the tests of everyone who qualified for Mathletes. We're supposed to choose the alternates and send them to her today. I made a spreadsheet of all the question categories, sorted the responses by areas of efficiency and error rate, and compared those to people who've already made the team. Considering those factors and the fact that they may need to replace any member of the team with any specialty, our best choices for alternates are Kasim and LaToya."

Angelique held my gaze. I think she was waiting for me to get upset. I didn't.

"And that is why Ms. Coulon made you captain," I said, smiling. "I like spreadsheets, but I would not have worked that the way you just did. Give me a checklist any day."

"Did you hear what I said?"

"You said you want Kasim and LaToya to be alternates. It sounds like you did a lot of work to figure out who would be best, so I'm happy to follow your lead, captain."

Angelique relaxed a little. "Co-captain," she said.

"No. You're the captain. I'm the co-. Trust me. Ms. Coulon doesn't do typos." I nudged her with my elbow. "Just take it, okay? Congrats."

"Thanks," she said.

The tea was all right, but my mom's was way better. Beverlyn didn't show up, but that didn't stop Sandy from taking Self-Care Sunday seriously. Mani-pedis. Dolphin dips. Deep condition and style. The whole nine yards.

It was cool. So cool that I was thinking maybe Sandy was right about more than I had already given her credit for. I did feel like I was carrying a lot of stuff. Some of it wasn't even mine. I wanted to let go of it. I wanted to be free. Sandy's spell sounded like just the thing— not to do on a whole school for a whole bunch of people who might have been perfectly happy no matter who the queen was. For me. A self-improvement project. And if doing it on myself made it charm, not magic, that was even better.

While everybody was settling back into the food court for an early dinner, I sneaked off and used some of my credits to buy more first figs, fresh ginger, and picture jasper. I had all of that at home, but being at home meant I couldn't "request the crafter" right then, and especially with none of Sandy's friends showing up, I wanted to do something that would make her feel good. Besides, I saw a booth that gift wrapped things in faux peacock feathers. No way was I letting that opportunity pass by.

I didn't know what the rules were about crafters, but I figured if spellbooks were secret, asking people to help you with spells was

something to keep quiet about, too. So I asked Sandy if she was available to help me with a personal improvement project. "Charm," I added. "Not magic."

Sandy squeezed my shoulder. "I'm with you either way. Ooh! Beverlyn! Beverlyn!!"

Sandy jumped up, waving someone down who turned out to be way too familiar.

"Beverlyn!" Sandy hugged her and air-kissed both of her cheeks. "I'm so glad you made it."

"I was here on time, but while I was on the moving walk I got a message that there was a problem at the glassworks in Amite, so I hopped a gondola to go take care of it."

"I thought the one in Amite was just a summer camp."

"It was, but we came across so much talent that we decided to keep the program going year-round. It's all taken care of now, though. Is it too late for me to join y'all for dinner? That is, if Miss Schexnayder-Jones and Miss Hebert don't object, of course."

Seeing teachers outside of school is always weird. Seeing Ms. Coulon in 3Thirteen was just beyond.

I don't know about Angelique, but I barely got it together to nod.

"Good!" Ms. Coulon said. "Then dinner's on me."

She waggled her fingers, and one of the waitstaff came over to the table. "Would you please make sure that this meal and any other charges of theirs are transferred to my account? It's the least I can do for being so tardy."

"Right away, miss. It's always a pleasure to serve one of the Talented Tenth. Would you like the meal to be moved to a private dining room?"

"No. This is perfect."

After the shock wore off, I had to agree with Ms. Coulon, aka Beverlyn. It was perfect. We laughed and talked all the way through dinner. Ms. Coulon was the first to leave. She put her reading glasses on, double-checked the blockchain ledger, and got up to go.

"I hate to arrive late and leave early, but I have a long day tomorrow. You do, too, co-captains."

Co-captains? With an S?

"Practice begins at 3:30, but I expect both my co-captains to be there by 3:17 at the latest."

"Wait. We're both co-captains?" I asked.

"That's what 'co' means. With. By definition, that would be two or more. You and Miss Hebert both had perfect scores. At that point I can pick one of you at my discretion, but since your stepmother and I are such good friends, making you captain on your own seemed unfair, but so did leaving you out entirely since you've been a cornerstone of our team for so long. Do you have a problem sharing the role?"

"No!" I said. "I just—that's not exactly what the email said. And I thought you didn't do typos."

Ms. Coulon tapped her phone screen, scrolled, and said, "Mmph. Apparently, I do. See you tomorrow, Mathletes."

I might have had a lot left to learn about Angelique, but one thing I did know for sure was that, at that moment, she was giving me her I-told-you-so face.

By the time we made it home, the light was fading and it was almost time for bed, but I didn't want the day to end. Dee, Angelique, and Sandy had all gone home, and my mom rushed inside to put some rose hip and sorrel on to brew. Luz and I were still outside, halfway between our two houses.

"Want to see me do something magic?" I asked. "You don't have to if you don't want to."

Luz held up a counting finger. "One. I know I don't have to. Two. Yes, I want to. And three. Took you long enough."

She laughed. That was good. Really good.

CHAPTER THIRTY

WHAT HAPPENS AFTER

A HURRICANE?

*O*n the first day of school, Luz and I sneaked in early.

Well, I said "sneaked," but the gate was wide open. I guess the teachers do get there way before us. And I said "Luz and I," but Dee and Angelique were there, too. They were just waiting outside the gate. Oh! And Sandy was there, too. Sort of. She was on FaceTime.

"The two of you look so cute in your little outfits," Sandy said. "Do y'all dress alike every day?"

"Only for special occasions," Luz said.

"I have to warn you, though," I said. "This is gonna be charm, not magic. It might not look that impressive."

Luz grinned at the screen. "I still want to see."

"Okay," I said. "Magic would be more impressive, so don't say

I didn't warn you. Riverbend is on a sanlavi. We can't do magic here, anyway."

"Hasani," Luz said gently. "You sound nervous. Are you sure you want to do this?"

"Yeah, Hasani," Sandy said from the phone. "Are you sure you wouldn't be more comfortable doing this at home?"

Sandy said that her spell works best in the place you feel most like yourself. I knew the spot right away.

"No, I want to stay right here under the bead trees," I said. Even on the edge of a sanlavi, with Luz right there, the spot under the bead trees was still the place I felt most like me.

Magic sloshed against my skin, but I wasn't worried. The nearby sanlavi would keep it in. It was like the best of both worlds.

"Ready?" Sandy asked.

I nodded. Luz had my checklist ready, but I didn't need it. I ate the biggest fig off its branch, then rubbed the ginger against the picture jasper until ginger juice dripped off the stone. Sandy nodded and I said the incantation. Out loud, so she would know whether or not I said it right.

Mo lib.

To lib.

So lib.

No lib.

With every word, I could feel the lightness building like helium inside a balloon. It weighed less than nothing, but from the pressure of it, I thought I might burst. But I needed to burst. Something needed to relieve the pressure so I could be free.

There was a pop, and the next thing I knew, we were standing in wind like a hurricane. No one else. Just me and Luz and the trees. My phone went flying, but Luz and I just held on to each other until the wind died down. There were beads everywhere. Most of them were plastic, but some of the old-school glass ones had shattered like glitter across the pavement. I didn't know what had happened, but whatever happened, I felt good. I felt free.

"Are you okay?" I asked Luz.

"I'm fine, but if that was charm, I don't think I'm ready for magic."

Dee and Angelique came running toward us.

"Uh . . . bruh. Did you just cure the sanlavi?"

"Oh my god. Hasani," Angelique said, rubbing her fingers together. "I think you did."

"Y'all think this is a sanlavi?" LaToya's little voice squeaked through. She gestured, and a group of kids squeezed closer, Annie among them.

"How many people come to school this early?" Luz mumbled. "It's like seven o'clock in the morning."

"See the trees? See this?" LaToya formed a gladiola in her hand. "Not a sanlavi. This is what happens when fake witches spread fake information just to impress people. That's why the library is our friend, people. So is the Interweb. Who's joining me for coffee at my aunt's coffee shop?" All the hands went up. "Great. We'll discuss it more there."

"Hey, LaToya," Angelique called out. LaToya and her crew turned around en masse. "There's Mathletes practice after school today."

"Thanks, captain." She was talking to Angelique, but she was staring me down.

"Co-captain," Angelique corrected. "You and the other alternate should be there promptly at 3:30."

Angelique's voice was gentle and polite like it always was, but her words were spitting hot fire.

"Don't worry. I won't be an alternate for long."

LaToya may have been staring at me, but I was looking at Angelique. After everything that happened, I didn't know she would still stick up for me, especially not where LaToya was concerned.

"Thanks," I said.

"No need. Next time I'll make sure she calls us both co-captain. That is our title, after all."

"And so it begins," Luz said.

I shook my head. "It doesn't matter who else is here. This place will always belong to us. Maybe not just to us, but still. To us."

"Mudbugs4Life?"

"Mudbugs4Life."

I put a few morning glories in a circle around our spot and on the path up to the building. So what if I wasted a little magic? Apparently, I had magic to spare. Besides, I was beginning to think that maybe my magic *did* belong at Riverbend Middle. Magic was a part of me, and I know I belonged at Riverbend Middle, so by the transitive property, my magic did, too.

I was looking forward to eighth grade the way eighth grade was meant to be: surrounded by old friends and new friends and magic.

Acknowledgments

Love wrote this book. Well, maybe it didn't sit at the keyboard tapping out words and sentences. Maybe it didn't tie all the loose ends and make sure each character got the time they needed, but love was there doing its own kind of work to let this story come to being. Without love, my best friend since seventh grade wouldn't have stayed up through the night reassuring me that I was on the right track. Without love, my children wouldn't have brought me iced coffee and packed their own lunches to make a little more room for Mama's art. And without love, I would never have known what real friendship is. It lifts you up. Makes you better. Lets you see the magic in things.

Thank you to Maggie Lehrman and the whole team at Abrams for believing in Hasani and the importance of the joy and power she

ACKNOWLEDGMENTS

brings to the world. Your skill and support have been invaluable, as have the words of encouragement and notes from teachers and kids. Thank you, coffee, both with and without chicory. And thank you to Candace, Leah, Judy, Ha, and Lanette, whose love always helps me find the magic, no matter where it is hiding.